REVIEWS

In Rescue 12 Responding, Faye Hamilton rips through the curtain that separates the spiritual world from our own. In the same vein as classic Frank Peretti, readers see not only the classic battle of good and evil, but the sliding slope of Greed, Anxiety, Pride, and Compromise personified. As we ride along with EMTs David and Jonathan, the story takes us to places where physical trauma confronts spiritual trauma, blending faith and healing in body and spirit. While I enjoyed the fast-pace of the driving plot, I was most drawn by Hamilton's deft portrayal of a character dealing with his sexual orientation. It is truly a thoughtful, dignified characterization.

-- **Allison Pittman**, *author The Seamstress (Tyndale)*

Rescue 12 Responding is not just a book about the medical care and drama two seasoned paramedics face on their 24 hour shifts. David and Jonathans' lives change when they come face to face with the dark forces of evil.
The author spins a page turning account that you won't want to put down until you find out what happens to David, Jonathan and every character in this novel. You will become immersed in the stories, and unseen forces beyond the natural. Readers will find they relate to the conflicts and victories David and Jonathan face.
As a nurse, I found the medical aspects captivating.
As a Christian and mother, I applauded as I saw tragedy turned to victory through intercessory prayer. My faith was strengthened!
You'll see a collision of good and evil and cheer for Joey and Jonathan!
If you like Frank Perretti, I think you'll enjoy Ms. Hamiltons' novel. This novel will appeal to believers and non-believers alike and both will clap at the ending.

-- **Joan Herr**, *RN, MSN-ED*

ACKNOWLEDGEMENT

25 years ago, when this book was written, I worked as a Paramedic and through that career had the opportunity to work with real heroes; men and women who risked their lives to save lives and make a difference. I want to acknowledge and thank my friends and colleagues in EMS, Fire and Police. Specifically, I want to acknowledge Tom Batchelor and Bobby Jones, two exceptionally fine paramedics who made working on the rescue unit a treasured experience. The engine crew at station 12, Richard, Carl and Dean were fearless, compassionate firemen and were right there supporting me through the process of writing this book. It was a great team. Like so many paramedics who eventually have to leave the streets, I look back and realize the friendship and life we shared can never be fully understood by others nor fully appreciated by ourselves until it is gone.

When I finished the manuscript, my 7-year-old daughter, Tiffany, wanted to read it first. She was an avid reader at that age, and she quickly came back with the typed pages and told me there were grammatical errors. She was right. Grammar is not my strongest ability. So, I reached over and handed her a red pen and asked her to fix it. The light in her eyes filled the house and her pleasure was tangible. At that point, seeing how much she loved this story and loved helping me with it, I had decided that if no one else in the world ever read it, she enjoyed it and that was enough. Matthew, my son, was an adult by the time he read the manuscript and he encouraged me to get it published. Without that push, it may well have remained somewhere in the closet.

A few months ago, when my dear friend, Lissa White, offered to help me polish the book you have today, this story came to life again. Her effort to clean and correct the grammar and push me to more clearly remember what I had seen so long ago when I first penned this book has resulted in this finished product. To say she has changed this book and my life for the better is an understatement. I am so very grateful for all her help.

I am also grateful to Allison Pittman, who helped with the formal editing and Peter with Bespoke who created this awesome book cover.

To the friends and family with whom I have shared the very rough draft of this book: Thank you for your support and words of appreciation for this work. It has given me the hope that others will also be encouraged by the love of God revealed within this novel.

TABLE OF CONTENTS

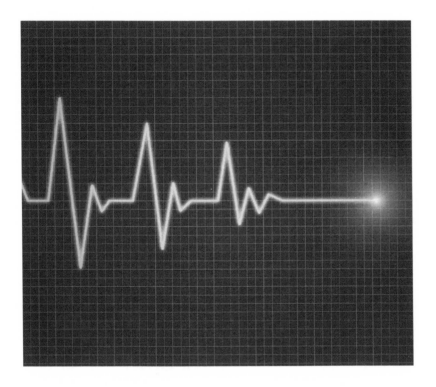

Chapter One

JUST THIS ONCE

Excitement and friendship enveloped Terri like a shroud. This is what she wanted more than anything. She had made the right decision. She had arrived! The girls acted like she was their sister, and the guys were hot! They laughed together. Heather handed Terri a beer, and they all lifted them up as Tommy offered a toast, "To the great and mighty gods of Rome, who have given us victory on the battlefield, as well as in bed. We thank you!" They were seniors in high school, members of the winning football team, the Tampa Gladiators, and friends since grade school. Life could not be better. And tonight, Terri was allowed into their private party.

Laughter erupted into ecstasy as Tommy quickly swallowed his drink and reached over to kiss Terri. Her heart raced, and her hands began to sweat. Tommy was the star quarterback of their high school football team, and he had invited her to this after game party with some of his closest friends. Terri's head spun in pleasure.

Debra walked from the kitchen where the cooler of beers and bags of chips were laid on the counter and held the camera out to take her next selfie. Heather joined her as they smirked and flaunted beautiful breasts pressed firmly against their tight shirts and took pics to share with classmates not lucky enough to be here. Giggles marked the self-satisfaction these pics created. Terri laughed while holding on to her date. Tommy used to date Debra, but apparently, they were cool with new adventures. So, she relaxed a little more and walked over to talk with Debra and look at the selfies. This was her chance for new friends. Not just any friends, the popular kids in school. This was a dream come true.

"Whatcha doing with a loser like Tommy?" Debra jested.

Heather jumped in. "Loser? The hottest guy in school? The best football player ever?" She laughed. "Oh yeah, he is a loser ... He let you get away…" She busted out laughing, and Debra began to laugh too.

"Well, he's not all that good at things that matter," Debra said as she shot Tommy a playful glance. He didn't seem too upset at their play at his expense.

Tommy pulled Terri in a bit closer, "Well, maybe Terri is a better judge of performance than you are." He winked at Debra and reached down to kiss the top of the head of tonight's date. Terri beamed as he kissed her. She didn't understand but definitely enjoyed the attention.

Debra rolled her eyes at the kiss and walked back into the kitchen. "I need another drink. Who wants one?"

After her second beer, Terri was amazed at how good it had begun to taste. She knew she would have to make the decision to stop soon, but not yet. She thought she was still in control. *I can go a little farther*, she said to herself as she sat down by the others, trying to calm the guilty feelings raging within. But, just as the beer had begun to taste better after the second can, so the inner voice of guilt and warning became quieter, almost more distant, until finally, she was left with only the happiness of the moment.

Tommy said that he was going to go into the back and change, and asked Terri to come with him. Terri felt passion flood through her body as Tommy looked at her with desire. She felt a tingling at the base of her spine that ran up and down her entire body, and it felt good. Terri giggled as she agreed to go with him. The giggles were repeated by the other girls, and the redness of her face was hidden in the darkness of the hallway. Terri was embarrassed, but then she thought the girls were only laughing in good-natured fun. She hoped they really had accepted her.

"Oh God, help me stop before I go all the way," she whispered. Then, almost word for word, she repeated the words of the voice that had become so familiar to her. "I can go a little farther. He said I am beautiful. He said he would love me if I would…"

Tommy shut the door behind her as she entered.

The demons of Popularity and Compromise danced in the intoxication of the sacrifice. The god of Immorality was present and was pleased that another virgin was being presented tonight. Any act of immoral sex was to his liking, but the desecration of a virgin was always to be highly rewarded. He longed for the act to be completed, but he knew if he moved too quickly, she would cry out for help and all would be lost.

Tommy moved to her. His body held her captive with desire. Slowly, he laid her on the bed. His hands danced in her hair. Her neck curled back in pleasure. He kissed her, his hand moving up her thigh.

The Spirit of God that dwelt in Terri spoke, "Terri, stop, this is wrong!"

The demons shut their mouths. Terri sat up in bed. Chills replaced the warmth. She was instantly reminded of her promise to God to stop, and her prayer to Him to remind her. This had been her only request in this battle. There was no deceitful voice brave enough to speak to her now. The decision was hers alone.

Tommy felt the coldness on her back. He knew he was close to the "touchdown." This was going to be his big play. Another game won… he knew by experience that he shouldn't wait and needed to move quickly. He knew that most girls fought with their conscience the first time. The first time… He had often noticed that after he had sex with a virgin, he seemed to run faster, and play harder. Whatever the reason, he knew he liked the conquest and the reward. He would win again. The guys of the team had laughed together, saluting their Roman soldier god, their mighty school spirit, that gave them the victories that young men sell their souls for. He would have his Win.

The voice of Conquest, so familiar to Tommy, was silenced in the presence of the voice of God. Suddenly, Tommy called a time out. He didn't know why, but he had to get out of that room.

"Terri, I really want this to be special. Hey, let's stop and party with the gang. They are probably already starting without us. Let's go. I promised you a really good time. Come on." Tommy spoke with an urgency that surprised himself.

Terri rose and began to follow him out of the bedroom. She knew she should leave this house, as well. She felt the presence of God warning her to leave. She turned and walked toward the front door, but then turned and walked past it, toward the dining room. Suddenly, her mind quieted from the thoughts of warning. She had decided to stay. There was no leaving now. The decision was made, and it was hers, but the consequences would be beyond her control.

The evil voices breathed deeply, then laughed.

Tommy pulled a small white bag from his jacket as he walked to the dining room table, and carefully poured the powder from the bag onto the table's edge then cut ten thin lines. He was the first to bend over and inhale the cocaine. Terri watched as a few of the others quickly inhaled their line of coke.

Debra rolled her eyes at her friends. "Come on Tommy! You said you were going to stop using this crap! Heather come on! You don't need this stuff." Darien laughed at her and turned his back on her and bent down to the table.

'Come on Debra don't be a prude. This is nothing. A quick 30-minute thrill ride. Come on! Stop acting like you don't like it." Heather begged her friend to join them, "Really, what is wrong with you?"

Debra rolled her eyes at her friends and turned to Terri. "Really, you come here tonight with Tommy and you are just going to go along with these idiots!" She turned to her friends, "Really? Fine! Then I am going to the store for some cigarettes. I am not going to just watch you make fools out of yourself." Debra spun away from them and stomped off. She wouldn't be run off by her friends, but she wasn't going to stop them either. "You guys are idiots!"

Tommy walked over to Terri and pulled her tight against his strong chest. "Come on! Don't pay attention to her. She can be fun, but she only wants things her way! Ya wanna be with me, ya gotta party with me." He kissed Terri as Compromise came and wrapped his arms around her.

Compromise spoke to her, "Just this once."

His voice was familiar and comforting. "Just this once," she repeated, as she lowered her head and bowed before the table. The rolled $10-dollar bill laid beside the white stripes. Before she could change her mind, she took it and inhaled the coke through the bill. Sharp pain filled her nose and throat. Her eyes watered and she coughed. The others laughed at the inexperience of their new friend.

Tonight, the cocaine these teenagers inhaled had not been cut enough and was almost completely pure and laced with Fentanyl. The gods danced in the dark, as the teenagers bowed at the table of sacrifice. One choice resulting in one outcome, their deaths.

Laughter filled the house, as the rush of cocaine flooded their minds and bodies. The rush of drugs brought them to their feet, and they danced to the music. None seemed to notice the others as each was aware only of their own racing heart, and the growing need to sleep. Terri sat on the couch, as Heather and Darien curled up on the floor. Heather seemed to quickly fall asleep, but Darien spasmed before he lay still.

The Voice of Conquest brought Tommy to his feet. It possessed him. Tommy had been unable to resist the Voice of the Good One when he had not taken her earlier. There was no longer time for slow victory. Tommy, because of the poison of coke and alcohol, was captive enough to the darkness to accept the Voice of Rape.

Tommy laughed with pleasure as he approached his date, feeling the strength of control and conquest flowing through his veins. He sat beside Terri on the sofa. Forcibly, he began to touch her, pressing her. Instantly, she knew that this embrace was different. It was as if his hands had thorns, and these thorns cut deeply into her heart. She suddenly knew she was wrong to be here, that she had made the wrong decision. She no longer wanted him to touch her, and she began to fight him, trying to push him off. Tommy's voice changed to reveal the hideous laughter of the evil within.

The Voice of Cocaine had hoped to weaken her with fear, by the weight of the chains of drugs and alcohol that bound her. Instead, the small amount of cocaine she inhaled began to reveal the hideous forms and the dark voices of the demons that worked around her. She began to tremble in fear as she became aware of a world that she had only heard of before. She could hear the screams of horror and of evil laughter. The demon stood before her mockingly, until from her lips, he heard his defeat. Terri cried out for God, "God, help me..." And God heard.

Death pushed back the impotent demon of Rape, "I'll take this male captive – Now! You lost your virgin prize. I'll not wait any longer." Rape had no choice but to turn in his defeat and release Tommy. One stronger than he required his prize. Conquest kicked Tommy in his frustrated impotence. Tommy released his attack against Terri and fell quickly from the sofa and onto the floor. His body spasmed and shook. His eyes rolled backward, and his mouth filled with white foam. Suddenly, he stopped shaking as his body jerked forward. It looked as though someone unseen had kicked him in the back. Terri watched as he lay perfectly still. Tommy's eyes were wide open. His pupils were fully dilated as if he were in a dark, dark place. Forever dilated, forever dark, forever dead.

Cocaine squeezed his hands around his last unclaimed captive. Terri's heart began to race, exceeding 200 beats per minute. It beat so fast she was sure it was about to burst in her chest. She rubbed her sweating face with her trembling hands and noticed the white powder that had remained under her nose. Fear gripped her as the reality of Death cleared her mind of the effects of the Cocaine and numbed her to the knowledge that the others were probably dead, and she too, would die soon.

So, she prayed: "Oh God: I'm so sorry. I am afraid. I know you warned me. I knew I shouldn't have come, I knew, but I did it anyway. Please forgive me." She opened her eyes, feeling her heart racing and her head spinning. She gasped, trying to think and all she could see was her mom and the pain that would come. Tears ran down her face, "Please, tell Mom I love her. I am so sorry." In that last breath, fear released, and peace settled. Terri closed her eyes and submitted to the darkness of impending death, held firmly in the arms of Peace. "Mom, I love you...

Instantly, Terri sensed that she was somehow walking within the darkness that surrounded her. The farther she walked, the more she became aware of her own senses. The drugs and alcohol lost their hold on her with each step she took. Suddenly, eternal light broke the darkness of death. Terri looked around and saw a Great Light before her, and she began to walk a little quicker. A few steps farther, and she began to hear angels rejoicing. She was not alone. Peace who had held her as she transitioned into death, could now be seen. Terri smiled as she looked at Him who silently walked with her.

Terri stopped and paused to look around at all that was before her. She breathed deeply of the revelation that the acceptance, for which she was so willing to compromise, was surrounding her freely. Her heart rejoiced as she walked deeper into the Light.

Mrs. Blake, Terri's mom, had the worst day she could ever remember. She arrived home at 8:00 pm, tired and stressed from the pressure of putting together proposals for the school board funding. The tight finances and emotional involvement of all the people kept her mind bouncing from line items to available funding. Her mind was trying to resolve the struggle. She was looking for a moment to rest. She was so tired. As she entered the kitchen of her home, she saw a note. Before she could get it off the table, a deep fear for Terri's safety jumped into her heart. The note said that Terri had left on her date and that she would be home late.

She sighed deeply and rubbed her eyes as she momentarily tried to understand why she suddenly feared for Terri. *Maybe it's just because I'm so tired?*

Mrs. Blake went to the refrigerator and made a quick ham and cheese sandwich, and then walked into the family room and turned on the TV. She knew she shouldn't have let Terri go, she knew she should be praying for her, she knew. "Pray, pray, pray," cried the Spirit of God unto her. She reasoned to herself, she would pray when she went to bed, as was her custom. She thought she had time. But she didn't. She fell asleep.

"Mom, I love you…"

Terri's mom awoke from a dark dream. She had heard Terri's voice from within her spirit. She knew something had happened.

She fell to the floor and prayed. Maybe, she wasn't too late. Her prayers were more like groans, not words, and not her own. The Spirit of God was interceding through her. Images came to her imagination and wisdom in how to pray flowed to her. Spiritual power surged through this mother's prayer.

Debra returned within the hour to her friend's home. The music was playing loudly as she opened the door. "Hey, guys, where are you?" she asked as she walked in. Suddenly she froze and screamed as she looked around the house and saw her friends all lying still and unmoving. She grabbed the phone and dialed 911, then fell to her knees and began to cry.

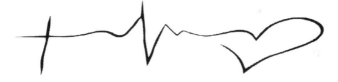

Just west of Interstate 75 on Gibsonton Drive sits a small firehouse in a small rural community, just south of Tampa, Florida. There are three firemen and two paramedics that wait there. The two paramedics ride together on an Advanced Life Support rescue ambulance known as Rescue 12. They had been partners for years. David, the senior paramedic, had just laid down at midnight to sleep, and Jonathan was trying to finish up some paperwork when the loud alarm went off.

"Rescue 12, respond to 'Unknown,'" the 911 dispatcher declared. Simultaneously, the fire engine crew was dispatched to the same location to provide manpower for the call. All five men raced into the dark and towards the 'unknown.'

Arriving at the scene together, the five men walked up to the ranch-style red brick home to enter through the carport door. Jonathan was first in, his arms full of emergency medical equipment. The dining room was immediately inside and offered the only light. For a moment, he froze at the door, and the other men behind him stopped to look at the horror that covered this veteran paramedic's face. Instantly, he sprinted in. His fearful expression helped prepare them as they entered the house. They knew it was bad.

Yet nothing could fully prepare them for the horror they were about to face. Each fireman had to pass by the dining room table that still had a few of the straight white lines of cocaine. Each man raced in and stopped at a different teenager. Cool and lifeless, stiff but flexible, one by one, the teenagers were rolled over onto their backs and were examined for breathing or a pulse. The rescue team were looking for someone that they might be able to save. Each man knew as first responders that they had to contain their emotions so their heads could be clear enough to seek out any that might still be alive.

Jonathan took the Electrocardiogram Machine, the EKG machine, and pulled the large black paddles off, pressing the paddles against the bare chest of each teenager. At each confirmed death, the teenager's expression of horror was sealed upon the heart of this paramedic. He swallowed deeply, trying to remain in control. *Paramedics aren't allowed to stop and cry,* he demanded of his thoughts as he forced his emotions into submission. He pressed on to the next of death's victims. One by one, each heart created nothing but a straight line on the display screen.

David yelled out, "Jonathan, come over here with the EKG machine. This one is still warm, and I think I had a weak pulse! But..." He paused as his hand searched for her carotid and femoral pulse, "I can't find it now!"

Jonathan ran over. Quickly, he placed the black paddles against the bare chest of a blonde sixteen-year-old girl. The EKG machine display panel revealed a heart rhythm of chaos – Ventricular Fibrillation. Jonathan held his breath as he shouted, "Stand Clear!"

The firemen ran to that call. They knew that command meant that one might survive. Instantly, Jonathan pressed the red button on the EKG machine, and the young girl jumped from the electrical current that shot through her body.

"The EKG shows a supraventricular tachycardia. Do you have a pulse?" Jonathan was not looking at his partner for the answer. His eyes were fixed on the EKG machine.

"Yes, yes I do. We have a pulse, but, it's weak," David responded in guarded pleasure. They watched as the young patient took a deep breath.

The paramedics looked carefully at the patient. Jonathan responded in a monotone voice, "Her heart rate is 240 beats per minute."

A firefighter grabbed her left arm and took a blood pressure reading. "Blood pressure is sixty over zero."

Without much speaking, the two paramedics established an IV line into her arm and silently administered medications that might keep her heart from returning to the chaotic rhythm. Her breathing remained steady and supplemental oxygen was given to her through a mask.

"Her heart won't take much more of this. She will probably return to V. Fib soon," David whispered to the others. His voice was low for fear of breaking. Any minute, they knew her heart would begin to spasm and contract in chaos, shaking, no longer pumping blood, and would stay that way. An overdose of cocaine has that effect on the heart. They suspected that drugs were the cause of the death of the other teenagers. Their hands were tied. There wasn't anything they could do that would reverse the effects of the cocaine overdose, but they worked to do all they could until the end.

Outside the house, police were arriving and immediately began the process of determining what had happened. Debra sat quietly in the back of the police car, crying and waiting for her mom to come and get her. The neighbors had gathered outside the house and tears flowed freely between them,

The paramedics began the emergency transport to the hospital. Jonathan drove the ambulance while David watched and waited with his patient in the back of the unit. But there was a Physician in that ambulance that they could not see. One whose hands were free, and in whose hands was healing.

Terri awoke in the back of the ambulance. Her heart rate spontaneously dropped to 140 beats per minute. She whispered something. The paramedic bent down to hear her. She said it again and again. "Holy, Holy, Holy is the Lord God Almighty, who sits on the throne." Then she fell asleep.

David checked the pupils of her eyes for a response. They were responsive but were constricted, as if seeing a great light. "What happened?" he asked, as he awakened her again. Her vital signs were all within a normal range. Now it was his heart that was beating fast. He knew she should not even be alive. Quickly she answered each of his questions with such clarity that he was baffled. She should have been more confused, but she was not. Her eyes were now focused and full of life. "What happened? How are you feeling?"

She looked at him, "Wow! You're not gonna believe me, but I'll tell you. The party went bad, really bad. But then something amazing happened." She began to think about all that she had just experienced, "I saw a Light, then I saw heaven." Her words gushed from her, "I saw my mom there, too. She was on her knees praying. I saw her prayers surround me. I thought I was going to die. I told God I was sorry and then the darkness disappeared." Terri stopped talking for a moment and looked beyond David to the memory relived.

She continued in whispered amazement, "I kept walking, and in the Light, I could see and hear like I could never ever explain. It was so beautiful. There were angels there too, and they kept saying, 'Holy, Holy, Holy is the Lord God Almighty!'" Terri's voice filled with awe. "I just stood there and felt such love and acceptance. I knew I was home and at peace. Somehow, I knew that 'holy' meant God had everything in control and everything is ok. All of a sudden, I could hear God speak in my heart. He said that if I wanted to I could stay there in heaven, but my mom had asked for me to return. He would let me choose. It was so hard because I was so happy there. It was so wonderful. I knew I should come back and as soon as I thought that, a lamb ran up to me, and I bent down to hug him, and then Jesus came from beside the throne and held me. He told me I was his little lamb and he will watch over me. He said I was forgiven, and my life has purpose. He told me that he would never leave me, that he will always be with me, and then I woke up here with you." She looked up into the eyes of the paramedic and saw tears running down his face. "I can feel Him here now. Can you feel Him here too?"

David spoke in a whisper. "I felt like there was someone in here with us when we left the house. I have felt that presence before, but usually, it was when someone was dying. I assumed you were going to die." David looked into the young girl's eyes.

"I wanna know this God of yours. He must have brought you back to life and, yes, I can tell he is here now."

Terri took his hand. The ambulance continued on the way to the hospital. Life and death were again in the balance in the back of the ambulance. But this time, the patient was bringing healing to the paramedic.

She spoke. "You can receive Him by just asking. Let's pray together. I'll say the words, and you repeat them."

"Dear Father God... I am a sinner... Please forgive me... come live in my heart... be the Lord of all my Life... and all my decisions... Thank you... in Jesus Name I pray... Amen...."

Another battle for life was won for the Kingdom of Light.

Terri let go of the paramedic's hand once the ambulance arrived at the local hospital. She watched as he took the IV bag off the hook and held it. He disconnected the oxygen and EKG wires from the wall. David's partner, Jonathan, came from the driver's seat and opened the back door of the ambulance. He looked at Terri with surprise. She was doing so well! He released the stretcher from the clamp that held it securely in place on the ambulance floor and pulled it out quickly, he could hardly wait to turn Terri over to the ER staff so he could find out what David had done to have made such a difference in her condition.

The report was given to the ER nurse. "The patient was critical, and then she had a remarkable spontaneous recovery." David knew there was more, but he only had to report on the medical physical aspect. He nodded goodbye to Terri, then walked out of the patient's room. The bathroom was the only place in this busy ER that he could be alone. He went there quickly.

David stood at the sink. He pressed the soap in his hands and lathered fully up to his upper arms. His pale face reflected a brightness in his eyes that seemed odd to him. What happened in the ambulance? What had he just seen? What had he just heard?

"Dear father God," these foreign words lingered on his tongue, "What does it mean?" Questions flew in David's mind. He looked in the mirror again, trying to analyze what was different in there. "Please help me. Please teach me." David tried to adjust the outward mask of control that would hide his new inward emotional dilemma, yet also, joy.

"And please show me I'm not crazy!" He laughed at himself as he walked out of the hospital bathroom. He felt cleaner than he had ever remembered feeling before. David decided to follow this newly discovered inward journey and find out.

Terri was in bed 2 in the ER. The monitor was recording all the vital signs and relaying the information to the nursing station. Terri's mother arrived by police escort a few minutes later. Tears flowed down her face as she looked at Terri and rushed to her daughter's side.

"Mom, thank you," Terri's voice broke at the sight of her mother's tears.

"What do you mean by thank you? I just heard they found you at Tommy's house! My God, what happened?" Terri's mother held the bed railing for support.

"Mom, Mom, please listen to me! I don't know how to tell you this, but I... I died," Terri paused and looked into her mother's eyes, "I saw you praying for me. You saved my life." She paused again and took a deep breath, "Thank you." The light that came from Terri's face brought a peace to her mother that strengthened and consoled her. "Mom, I saw Jesus. I will never be the same."

Terri's mother held the railing a little tighter still. The two spoke of things present and things to come. There was peace. In the midst of this storm, there was peace.

David walked into the room. "Terri, may I speak to you before I go?" His voice was soft and barely heard above the beeping of the EKG machine.

Terri held out her hand to David, and then introduced him to her mother. David looked with awe at the woman Terri had seen in her vision.

"Mrs. Blake, your daughter has quite an experience to tell you about. She is an amazing patient. Never had a patient like her before." David's gaze dropped to the floor. "Did she tell you she prayed with me?" His eyes rose from the floor and focused on this powerfully spiritual woman.

Mrs. Blake's voice whispered joy and acceptance, "David, you were right to believe what she said. I'm proud of Terri and happy for you." She paused and considered her words before she continued, "You found God in the back of your ambulance. Learn the first lesson: He is always there! He is always with you. David, He is now in you." Again, she stopped and looked deeply into David's eyes. "Learn to listen for His voice. You will know it when you hear it. There is no voice like His." She smiled, revealing a truth held so precious to her, "David, always follow that voice, and He will always lead and teach you. He often speaks loudest in the language we understand best. To the fisherman, he speaks of fishing. To the farmer, he speaks of planting. To you, as a paramedic, listen and see if he speaks the clearest to you from the ambulance. The lessons can be learned right where you are, all you have to do is listen."

David felt a hunger in him that he had never known before. Something deep inside him cried out for more. He drank the words of Mrs. Blake, and they satisfied him. "Can I call you if I have any questions? I mean, if you don't mind?"

Mrs. Blake took out a worn book that she carried in her purse. She opened the leather cover and wrote her phone number. "This Bible is used, and it has a lot of underlined parts that have meant much to me over the years, but I would like to give it to you. Please call me anytime. David, if you will ask God, He will, Himself, teach you more than I ever could."

He took the Bible and rubbed the cover. "I don't know what to say," he stammered, "but thank you." Two loud tones pierced the quiet. The portable radio interrupted their conversation.

"Rescue 12, respond emergency to 5521 Elm Street. Shooting," declared dispatch.

David nodded in farewell as he left. He knew he was not leaving that room alone. There would be an unseen Physician on board his ambulance. "God… I'm ready, teach me…" David whispered his prayer as he hurried down the Emergency Department corridor to take the next emergency call.

Two demons of distorted form and power stood watching. They had set the trap. All they had to do was watch and wait for the door into the thoughts of a human to open. Tonight, they would take their pawn to a new place of captivity to their evil voices. Their faces smug in the simplicity of their plan. Everything was working according to their schedule. It was just another night on the streets. Tonight, an angry young pusher would be freed to murder.

The human players were in place. It was an exchange of money for drugs delivered. Simple. The wrinkled unwashed addict, aged greater than his years, had begun to tremble with his need. While he didn't have enough money, he still hoped for a miracle. Maybe, he could get the drugs and leave fast. Maybe, Joey wouldn't count all the money right now. Maybe.

"This is so easy," spoke Greed, who stood present, but unseen and unheard by human ears. "The payment required for handling my merchandise tonight is blood. I will have payment now. I will wait no longer. It is time for Death to come."

Anger sneered in agreement, "Humans are just pawns in the war for men's souls." Their eyes returned to their prey.

Slowly, Greed bent forward, whispering, "Joey, count the money."

Anger spoke next into the young pusher's ear, "Make him count it again! He's cheated you! That worthless snake has tried to cheat you! Threaten him again. Make him beg you for his life, and then your anger will be satisfied."

Greed turned on Anger, "Nothing shall ever satisfy me! I will not be filled until I have killed, stolen, or destroyed all! This man has embraced me, and he shall do my bidding. I shall not let him go!"

Anger faced his co-worker. His eyes filled with hatred as he spoke, "He is my pawn to do my bidding. See how his mind allowed my anger to poison his reasoning. I am his lord!" For a moment, their attention was taken off their captive and on to each other. It was only their task at hand that kept them from tearing one another apart. There was no joy in the destruction of a human, only darkness.

Death appeared, his eyes ablaze. "Shall we claim another captive for Hell's fire? Let us then be done with it," Death watched the humans argue, and then continued, "I choose to linger in this human as I take him tonight. So much destruction already fills him. Alcohol and Heroin have eaten his mind and body well. Tonight, I will claim his soul. I will taste his blood as it slowly drains into the ground."

Greed approached the young drug pusher. "Joey, make an example of him! Make him pay! All men will fear you if you take his life in payment for trying to steal from you!"

Anger tightened his grip on the pusher. "He is worthy of death. Feel my anger. Embrace it like a robe about you. Kick him!" Immediately, the pusher smirked tauntingly, as he kicked his captive to the ground. Anger continued speaking into the mind of this pusher, "See how that satisfies you. He is nothing!" Joey pulled out his gun and held it tightly in his hand. Often, he played with it, knowing that one day he would use it. Tonight, he would choose that path. Anger coursed through him, strengthening him with the resolve to go beyond threats and into a new realm of power and control.

His captive cried out one more time. "Please, give me some time. I'll get the money. Please," he cried, "You don't have to do this, please." His cries made the path clearer. The pusher knew what he wanted, and this was the junkie that would get him there. He would have respect.

"So, you think you can trick me! I'm gonna make you an example of what I do to anybody that angers me or steals from me," he said fiercely, "You're a fool if you think I will show you mercy," he taunted. "Nobody's gonna cheat me ever and live to talk about it." The dark creatures watching and whispering, wrapped their words in his mind, as if they were his alone. Joey pulled the trigger, and the bullet struck the junkie's stomach. Horror filled the dying man's eyes. The warmth of his own blood surrounded him as he fell to the ground, groaning. Joey walked over to the dying man and boasted, "I am going to party at Tommy's, and you are going to hell. Die sucker!"

The demons watched as the young man of their bidding ran off. They laughed as they sensed his fear beginning to rise. The gods of this battle were pleased. Another victory, another slave. Fear left with Joey to begin his own evil twist of torture on this young pusher's mind. The other gods would remain to watch and drink in every drop of blood that fell to the earth from this sacrifice.

The ambulance lights spun in syncopated rhythm. Red and white lights fought the darkness of night with a mechanical dance. The sirens screamed the alarm. David and Jonathan mentally prepared for their next battle with death. "Shooting" was their only clue when they had been dispatched to the call from the emergency department. They had no idea what to expect. The address indicated it was just another side street.

"Rescue 12 on scene," Jonathan advised dispatch of their arrival.

"Acknowledged," dispatch responded.

Anger and Greed mocked the ambulance's arrival. "We shall see man's attempt to stop Death. Let us watch and enjoy their sweat!" Death became quiet and stared at the ambulance. He didn't like what he sensed.

David and Jonathan swiftly removed boxes and machines from their unit and approached their patient. The fire engine crew would arrive soon to provide the backup personnel they would need. There was also Another who followed at David's right side, one that men could not see.

Anger, Greed, and Death froze in their places, beginning to fear their defeat. "Look at the size of that warrior! He is truly mighty! What is he doing here? Who are these men that such a great one would be sent to keep them?"

"Hush, you fools! I'm greater than this warrior! This man shall die!" Death declared. Death spoke from experience. The presence of a strong warrior did not mean his defeat. Often the men given these soldiers were unaware or unconcerned that these soldiers were there to aid them in their contract with the Good One. "And, look at the captive;" gloated Death, "his heart is nearly empty of blood. His brain dies now for lack of oxygen. He is mine!"

David felt for a pulse. It was weak and thready. Only the pulse at the side of the patient's neck could be found. David rolled the man over onto his back and rapidly cut off his clothes to find the wound. He saw an entrance wound in the lower left side of the patient's belly. There were no obvious exit wounds and very little blood pooled around him. His belly was firm to David's touch, which David knew meant there was blood freely flowing where it did not belong and could result in this patient's demise.

Jonathan and David glanced at each other and nodded. Their teamwork might save this man... if it wasn't too late. Jonathan immediately attached the EKG monitor to the patient's chest to give a reading of the pulse rate and rhythm. David's hands moved swiftly to the patient's right arm, and he placed a large needle in one of the many scarred veins. IV fluid was then attached to it and poured at a wide-open rate into the patient's blood system. It would hopefully replace enough of the fluid that the body was losing to the pooling of blood in this patient's abdomen.

The patient now took slow, shallow breaths less than ten times per minute. The fire engine arrived on scene, and its team quickly ran to assist in this battle. David spoke to them. "His breathing is getting too slow. We need to secure the patient's airway before he vomits."

Jonathan took a large, firm, football-shaped bag, called an Ambu Bag, and attached it to a mask. He placed it over the patient's mouth and began to force air into the patient's lungs every time he would inhale, as well as an extra ventilation every time there was a long pause between his own breaths.

Death stood next to his captive. He laughed in the emergency crew's face for their vain attempt to stop him. He would take the captive. "Now!" he declared.

"David, check for a pulse. He just went into V. Fib." Jonathan's eyes focused on the EKG monitor.

"He doesn't have one," David's words held the command to begin the code.

Jonathan charged up the electrical paddles on the EKG machine and immediately defibrillated the patient. 200 Joules of electrical energy flowed into the man's chest. His body jumped in response. His heart continued to spasm in chaotic death.

"No change. Stand clear." Jonathan pressed the button to shock the patient again with a higher dose of energy. "No change," he said. A third defibrillation attempt was made, this time at the highest electrical setting. Still, "No change."

David unrolled an orange pouch that contained multiple sized airway tubes and a thin plastic disposable lighted curved tool, nicknamed "the blade," that would help him see the patient's airway. He checked the light at the end of the four-inch curved blade. His left hand gripped the handle as his right hand grabbed the long, narrow ET tube. It was ready to be placed in the patient's throat. He pulled the patient's head back and opened his mouth. The blade slid in beside the tongue and curved around the back of the throat. Its light provided the only help in finding the trachea.

David mumbled as he peered into the small, dark hole, "His trachea is deep in there, I can barely see it. Let me try..." In one swift action, David bent down and inserted the ET tube deep into the patient's mouth. As soon as the tube touched the back of the throat, reflex caused the patient to vomit. David sat up just in time to save himself, "Great, just great!" David saw precious seconds wasted as he cleared the patient's airway of the fluid. The suction machine cleared the mouth, but there was no time to clean the fluid that clung to the patient's face and ran to the ground.

Jonathan again began to ventilate the patient with the Ambu Bag. Now the patient was not breathing at all on his own. Chest compressions were begun by a firefighter on scene to help. David picked up the ET tube again. Slowly he bent down and laid himself at the head of this patient so he could be in a better position to see clearly, yet careful not to rest in the pools of vomit settling around the man's head. Under his breath, he breathed a prayer, "God, please help me this time..."

Death laughed at David's request. The captive was his. The mighty warrior standing beside David watching, suddenly spoke, "The Lord rebuke thee!"

Death stood to this warrior, "Who are you to speak to me? I AM DEATH!"

The warrior pulled out his sword of fire and placed it at the neck of Death. The point pierced his foul skin. "THE LORD REBUKE THEE!"

David found the airway instantly. "Jonathan, I have it in! Check the lung sounds." David quickly attached the Ambu Bag to the end of the tube that now hung from the patient's mouth and pressed air into it. The patient's chest rose and fell with the pressure.

"Lung sounds are good on both sides, and it's quiet over the stomach. You're in!" Jonathan stated with pleasure. He tried to defibrillate the patient once again. "Stand clear," his warning went out to the emergency workers. The patient again jumped as the electrical current flowed through his body. This time the EKG monitor's screen changed from the chaotic course line to a recognizable heart rate of 120 beats per minute. "Check for a pulse. We have something here,"

Immediately, David reached over and touched the man's neck feeling for the carotid pulse. "We have a pulse! Let's get moving to the hospital, now! I'll give him medications while we're en route," David spoke, and the team immediately moved to do just that.

Only a few minutes later, once again David stood at the sink in the emergency department bathroom. This time though he was far more tired and worn. And, once again, the lather covered his arms. Even for a veteran paramedic, this shift was worse than normal, if there is such a thing as a 'normal' shift. David stared into the mirror and spoke to his image, "When will 7 A.M. come? I'm ready for a break!" He groaned again at the few hours that remained on this shift, and then splashed some cold water in his face. That helped a little in awakening him, so he moved to sit at the table in the nurse's lounge to begin his paperwork. As he reached into his pocket to pull out the strips of paper that contained the record of the patient's heart rhythms, his hand felt a rectangular object. Being too tired to remember what it was, he pulled it out.

It was the little Bible that Mrs. Blake had given him an hour ago. "Only one hour. Boy, how time flies when you're having fun!" His tired humor was lost in the empty room of the nurse's lounge.

"Open it and read," spoke a still, soft voice, a thought, within his mind.

David held the book. He thought how often he had tried to read it, but that it never seemed to make sense. His hands thumbed through the thin pages. "I wonder where I'm supposed to begin."

"Open it and read," again the thought whispered.

"Ok, let's see what's in here," David whispered to himself, "Mrs. Blake said that God, Himself would talk to me." David let the book fall open and then focused on a certain passage to see if it would indeed show him anything. "I will instruct you and teach you in the way you should go; I will counsel you with my loving eye on you." David felt the words penetrate his heart and mind, "These words are for me." again he whispered, but this time in awe.

David closed the book and opened it again and read: "Whether you turn to the right or to the left, your ears will hear a voice behind you, saying, "This is the way; walk in it." He flipped through the pages and suddenly was drawn to a passage marked by a yellow highlight. He smiled as he remembered Mrs. Blake and the gift of her well-loved and marked Bible and read "And the prayer offered in faith will make the sick person well; the Lord will raise them up. If they have sinned, they will be forgiven. Therefore, confess your sins to each other and pray for each other so that you may be healed. The prayer of a righteous person is powerful and effective."

David held the book in awe. What had he found today? His tired body was suddenly full of energy. David remembered the quick prayer he said for the last dying man. He had asked for help, and the man should have remained dead, but suddenly responded to their treatment. Adrenaline pumped into his system. Could it have been his prayer that changed this outcome?

Do you think this book is true? Do you think you can believe that what it said is true for you? He wondered as his heart filled with faith. He knew that he felt clean inside, he figured that was what it meant by "sins forgiven." And, then, he decided that if this book revealed the truth of a God that has such power as to heal by a prayer, it must be true.

A smile filled David's eyes and covered his face. He spoke again to this God within. "Dear God: I think I'm going to like you teaching me. I will make a deal with you; I will do what this book teaches, if you'll help me." He paused as he considered his last patient, then continued, "And, thank you for healing that patient. I will always know that it was you."

David completed his paperwork, and expectantly awaited the emergency calls that would give him the opportunity to learn more about God. Mrs. Blake had said he would hear His Voice from the ambulance.

As he closed the Bible, his eyes focused on another highlighted text. These words became sealed upon his heart, "I am the God that heals you..."

The stillness of the night filled the house. The snooze alarm sounded but was quickly silenced by a slap in the dark. She didn't want her husband to wake as she prepared to leave for work. Quietly, she walked into the bedroom of each of her two young children and stood there watching them sleep. The night light from the window cast a blue shadow on the peacefully content children. She walked over to their beds and straightened the blankets around them. Her son wiggled under the blanket and then lay still. Her daughter moaned a few words and then was quiet. Joan blew them a kiss as she closed the door.

Sleep pressed at her, calling her back to bed. She fought the temptation to return to rest a while longer. "I am so tired. I love you," she whispered to her sleeping husband, as she placed a small kiss on his cheek. Quietly, she departed for work.

That morning she left the stillness of her home, the sleeping family who never saw her leave, and her own dreams. Once the car was started, the alarm buzzed to remind her of the seat belt, but she drove off quickly without putting it on. She was only going to work and knew the buzzing would stop soon. Joan pressed her hands back and forth against the steering wheel, trying to awaken, trying to focus on the road, trying to beat sleep.

She was so sleepy…

The 911 alarm sounded. The printer began to spit out the address of the call. The paramedics rose from their sleep. Another call tonight. Sleep ran from them as the adrenaline in their bodies coursed through their systems. When they arrived at the unit, their minds were focused and alert. 911 dispatch advised them of the call, "Rescue 12, respond to a single car accident at Symmes and Highway 301."

"Copied, Symmes and Highway 301," Jonathan replied.

The roads were empty, and the lights of the unit gave a red glow to the streets as they pierced the early morning fog. The overturned car was visible at a distance. Jonathan and David looked at each other.

"It doesn't look like it hit anything," Jonathan remarked as he peered down the road towards the car.

"No, I bet whoever was driving just hit the soft sand beside the road and merely flipped once," David stated as he drove the ambulance toward the overturned car.

"Well, I hope so. If that's all that happened, then we should be back in bed in 5 minutes." Jonathan stretched forward, bent down, and retied his shoe. "I really hope so."

The ambulance pulled up behind the late model Chrysler Sebring. Its engine was still running. Other than being upside down, it appeared to have no damage. Jonathan jumped out of the passenger's side of the ambulance and went rapidly over to the driver's side of the car. He knelt and reached in for the keys to turn off the car. His hand jumped back before he was fully aware of what he had just seen. He looked again for the second time.

"Hey, Jonathan, I can't find the driver out here. Do you think they just walked home?"

Jonathan slowly drew his words. "No, no. I'm afraid they didn't just walk home. Look in here." David recognized Jonathan's tone. He knew what to expect when he knelt to look inside the car.

David's mind focused as he swiftly walked over to the driver's door. The car was without a scratch, the windshield and steering wheel were intact. The car would be able to be driven, when it was flipped back over onto its wheels. He bent down and looked within the car; eyes focused on the victim of this accident who lay still across the ceiling of the car. She appeared to have no broken bones, no bruises, no cuts. His eyes moved up her frame – no movement at her chest, no breathing. His hand stretched inside the car and found her wrist – no pulse.

He grimaced as he continued following her frame with his eyes toward her head. He stopped and closed his eyes, then slowly, they opened and refocused on this woman and the cause of her injury. Without the restraint of her seat belt, her head had found the sun roof, and the car was resting on her head. The soft sand below had allowed for a lot of room, but not quite enough. Her head was both pinned and crushed.

David's mind began to race in thought. What are my options? I could try to save her, but I can't get her out from under the car in a reasonable amount of time. I have no options. Slowly he released his hand from hers and reached for the keys to turn the car off. The early morning was again filled with the stillness of sleep, the sleep of death.

The sheriff's officer arrived within a few minutes. Rescue 12 was released from the scene immediately. There was nothing for them to do but get back in service for the next call. David and Jonathan looked at each other. Their burning red eyes watched each other as each one simply placed his own seat belt on. "Rescue 12, back in service. No transport," Jonathan said quietly.

"Rescue 12, return to your station," the monotone voice of the dispatch replied.

The quietness was broken as Jonathan vented his frustration, "Why is it so hard for people to do the simple things that are right? Why do we hide behind the big things we do to show love and never stop to do the little things? Did you see her key ring? It was one like my ex-wife has – the clear plastic squares with the pictures of her two young kids. How old do you think they are?"

"About my kids' age. The girl looked about seven, and the boy about five," David rubbed his red, burning eyes. As they backed the unit into their station, the heaviness of death rested on the dark streets. "All it would have taken was a seat belt. That's all. She would still be alive, and those little children would still have their mother," David whispered as the stillness of morning began to touch him.

Quietly, they returned to bed. An hour later they were awakened. This time it was for the shift exchange. David slowly rolled out of bed. Sleep had not been so restful this time.

After the report had been given to the oncoming crew, David silently walked out to his car. No one was around. He reached over and pulled his seat belt across his lap. All alone, he spoke out, "I love you." His mind pictured his wife and kids, those that he worked so hard to support, that he had to leave so often in the early morning to go to work, just like the dead woman. The seat belt clicked. David headed home.

David found that this simple thought on love somehow stayed with him. He could hear within himself, for the first time, an awakening to the "rightness" of love. He could hear... and he spoke to the One he knew was there.

"Dear God: Please help me never to forget to do the simple little things. This woman thought she was showing the greatest love by getting up to go to work, but had she stopped for one second, and just put on her seat belt, she could have given her children a greater gift: the gift of her life and of their mother. May I learn to always look for ways to show the greatest love."

He turned on the radio and pulled out onto the highway. The sun was beginning to rise, and the brilliant colors of a beautiful Florida morning began to appear. This would be a very good day to rest from work. He knew it was worth enduring their twenty-four-hour work shift for the forty-eight-hour breaks between shifts. There would be time to rest, and time to think.

Chapter Two

MONDAY:
IN THE TWINKLING OF AN EYE

The off-going crew gave a quick report of their shift. The ambulance was checked out, and all the drugs were accounted for. "What a horrible shift we had last Friday," Jonathan moaned as he saw David come in the door of their office. "I went home and slept all Saturday. Let's hope we don't have a repeat performance today. I don't need any more excitement for a while." They both knew the odds for a slow shift were slim. Their rescue unit usually responded to at least twelve emergency calls a day. Sometimes, much more. Somehow these two paramedics, like all the other first responders who survive the streets, found a way to discipline their bodies and minds to take the stress of the calls as well as the long hours. Nonetheless, twenty-four hours is a long time.

David shrugged his shoulders in agreement then changed the subject. "You know, ever since we transported that girl Terri to the hospital, I've been thinking."

"Uh oh, we're in trouble now!" Jonathan jested. "You really did a great job with that kid. I didn't expect to find her alive by the time we got to the hospital. And she was so awake and alert! What did you do back there anyway?" Jonathan's admiration for David was obvious, as was their genuine friendship.

"I really didn't do anything after we had that IV and oxygen established on the scene. There really wasn't anything else we could do at that point. But there was something…" David paused to consider his next words, then continued, "She apparently had some near-death experience. It was weird. But the strangest thing is that I really believe what she told me." David took his eyes off his friend and looked at the floor. "Maybe I have been doing this job too long, seen too much death and other things I can't explain." He stopped to look at his partner. "Jonathan, you are my friend, and I have trusted you with my life before on the streets. Can I be honest about what happened back there?"

Jonathan leaned forward. "You know you can trust me."

David stared at the floor as he began to tell Jonathan about the vision Terri had and the prayer. "The really weird part is, I feel different. I can't explain it, but I feel clean inside. You know my dad was an alcoholic, and honestly, I have never even been inside a church. I felt like I didn't belong there. But…"

David reached inside his uniform jacket and pulled out Mrs. Blake's Bible. He held the book between both his hands and pressed it together as if he could squeeze out some explanation for what had happened to him. "I don't even know what is in this book, but something in me keeps telling me to find out. Sunday when I was finally awake and mentally ready, I looked at the index and found out that apparently, the Bible is actually a collection of many small books. Did you know that?"

"Yeah..." Jonathan's expression urged David to go on.

"Well, I didn't know where to begin so I noticed that one of the authors had your name: John. So, I figured I would try that one first."

"So, did you read it?" Jonathan asked with a little more reservation.

"No, I've not read all of it yet. But this man Jesus... it is amazing. It seemed like his words just leaped off the page and inside of me. I have never read anything like it. Do you know that in the second or third chapter, he said, 'God loved the world,' that he loved everyone and all you had to do is believe in Him?" David stopped his mind from racing. He needed to focus his thoughts. Slowly he took a deep breath and continued. "When I read it, I almost fell off the bed. Jon, it was like I could hear him say it to me directly." He turned his face to the wall. "I really felt loved. I must be going crazy." He pulled back and got very quiet. He knew he had said too much. He trusted Jonathan to handle the truth and help him.

Jonathan stood up and walked to the kitchen for coffee. "Where is a call when you need one?" he muttered under his breath. He wanted the conversation to change. The unspoken rule at work was to be personal – but not too personal. Because this job was hard on the emotions, Jonathan, as well as David and every other paramedic, was trained in basic stress debriefing. And the first rule of dealing with stress was to give your partner the encouragement to open up and show emotions. But this – this was too close to home. Jonathan's mind raced for an escape. He returned to the office with two cups of coffee.

Jonathan would have preferred a change in conversation, but he knew he had to help his friend. He chose to be honest. "David, I never told you this before, but my Dad and Mom used to take me to church every week when I was a kid," He paused a moment before continuing, "I don't go now that I live on my own. But I do know what you are talking about." He looked deep into David's eyes and spoke each word slowly to accent the truth within. "You are not crazy."

The lights and horn went on at the same time. The printer began recording the information for the first call of the day. "Rescue 12, respond emergency to 8780 Arena Drive – Shortness of breath," dispatch declared.

The men jumped up and ran to their ambulance. Jonathan grabbed the microphone and advised dispatch, "Rescue 12 responding." David reached over and pressed the red switches on the console. Red and white lights flashed against the garage walls as the unit pulled forward.

In the darkness of the evil kingdom gathered the creatures of eternal damnation. Creatures who had been created by God, beautiful and strong, but who eons ago decided they had the right to choose their own destiny. Their leader had convinced them that he could be as God and choose another path. They followed him away from God. They had only known life before. But, to walk away from the Giver of Life was to walk into the darkness of death. Immediately, they loved the darkness for their deeds were evil. So, in the darkness, those who had been angels of Truth, Love, and Life, became twisted and ugly and they took on new names of Deceit, Hate and Death. Their leader who, in times past, had been the chief musician and praise-giver to God, in the darkness had become the Adversary of all that was good. One-third of all the angels had followed him away from God, when he declared to God and to the host of witnesses, "I Will Be as God." Each follower of the Adversary became the demon perversion of what they had been in the light. These were eternal beings with eternal power to speak to men. Yet, they were banished to the dark and condemned to eternal separation from God. For a short season, a vapor of time in eternity, they were free to roam on Earth.

God created another eternal being. This one he created with the right to choose. One that He created to be more like Himself. One He could love. One who could, like God, love. And like a Father desires the love and obedience of his son, so God desires the love and obedience of His children. He created a male and a female, and called them Man. And He loved them… yet from the beginning, Man chose the darkness. The sins of rebellion polluted Man's seed and all his children after him. God, who so greatly loved his Man-being, chose to permit a season of light and darkness, hoping his Man would one day choose the Light and walk out of the darkness. He promised to forgive their sins if they but ask and come into the Light. So great was His love that theirs was the power to choose: his kingdom and light or darkness and death. It was their choice. This was His gift to them. He would let them choose.

"Just this once," spoke the voice of Deceit, "I would like it if there wasn't such a tall wall of protection that surrounded those who blindly walk into the Light."

"Who is it that is adding the strength of their faith to this paramedic's wall?" spoke the Adversary.

From the back of the room, a demon whimpered. He knew his back would be beaten and he would bleed from these stronger demons' response to his knowledge, "It is Mrs. Blake again. She is praying for the Good One's protection and His guidance for this man." The demon's voice was weak and trembling, "She is surrounding him with her faith and prayer."

Hisses rose from the front of the room. They knew that they had all lost to this woman's prayers, and therefore, recognized the size of the battle that they were headed for.

Adversary's voice rose above the fears, "Well, what is war for? We can win. We must win. Our loss can be won back, listen and watch this paramedic. We will find just the right voice to penetrate this new convert's heart. As for Mrs. Blake, get her mind off this man and see if you can get her occupied with telling everyone about her daughter. Pride, you go. Maybe a little spiritual pride can speak to her now. Distract her!" The Adversary spoke with the clarity of a general preparing for war. "We must do it quickly. If she doesn't forget about this paramedic soon, and quit praying for him, our job will just get harder. You know the Good One will be working swiftly to teach and lead this new convert during this time that our voices are quieted."

The warriors of darkness hastened to their appointed tasks. Death remained to speak to the Adversary. "I want this one. I want the life of the paramedic. He has fought me with only the knowledge that the Good One has given to Men in medicine and won. Now, with the aid of the Warrior of the Good One, how many will he steal from me? I cannot have it! I must have him!"

"So be it. Take him… if you think you can. How do you suppose we could get around his Warrior? Not to mention on what grounds do you think I can get the Good One to let us take him, now that he is in His camp?" Adversary was not pleased. Reminding Death of his limitations caused putrid vomit to rise within him. "Listen, Death, you must wait. All men come to you in time. You will have him, as well. How soon, will be determined by the success of our strategy.

Let me, the great Adversary, consider the matter. You go and make his job miserable. Take the lives of as many as you can in his work area. Weary him. Let this paramedic fight you for the lives of others, as we work to find a way to take his life. Maybe he will tire in his fight with you and forget about his new relationship with the Good One. I will find a way. We will win against this new Man. David will see your face, the face of Death. I shall drink his blood with you."

Rescue 12 arrived at 8780 Arena Drive within five minutes of being dispatched to the emergency call for "Shortness of Breath." The ambulance was parked in the street and left running. David and Jonathan grabbed boxes containing medications and oxygen. They entered the small mobile home rapidly.

David studied the woman sitting on the sofa, hands clutching the edge of the cushion as she leaned forward on her arms. Every muscle in her neck, chest, and back pulled with each breath in and pressed forward with each breath out. Over and over, the struggle continued, each muscle working to force air into her tired lungs. Her face dripped with sweat. Her body was exhausted, trying to get rid of the fluid within her lungs.

Jonathan took the stethoscope from the box. He placed the earpieces in his ears and the small metal plate against her chest. His eyes focused on the rising and falling of her chest and his ears heard the unmistakable sound of the mingling of fluids and air causing the bubbling crackles with each breath. In and out, the rhythm of the breaths and the melody of the crackles played their death song. At each location on her chest that he placed the stethoscope, the song continued.

As Jonathan took the stethoscope from his ears, his eyes spoke more to David than the simple phrase, "C-H-F" – congestive heart failure. Each man knew that this woman's heart was no longer able to pump the blood out at the same rate her body was bringing it to her heart. The blood was backing up into her lungs, and she was literally drowning in her own blood.

David looked at this seventy-five-year-old woman. Her eyes met his and begged for help. She inhaled deeply. Her mouth formed words that didn't have enough air to sound. "Out," she inhaled, "Of," she inhaled, "Breath." She gasped and lowered her trembling head.

David reached into his medical bag and came out with a long, narrow ET tube and the Ambu bag. "Ma'am, this is really going to be uncomfortable for you, but I want to place this tube in your nose and down toward your lungs," he held the tube before her as he spoke, and prepared it for insertion, "If you let me, we can 'breathe' for you so you can rest." He stopped working on the tube for a moment and looked again into her dark brown eyes, "Would you let me?"

She blinked her eyes and bowed her head. "Yes."

David coated the tip of this eighteen-inch-long tube with a non-petroleum-based jell so it wouldn't damage her nose. He knelt beside her on the sofa and whispered, "Ok, here we go." The tube was gently placed into her right nostril and slowly slipped to the back of her throat. She suddenly filled with fear as she sought the stranger's eye. He was too busy to notice. Thoughts raced through her mind. Was he going to block her only access to air? What if he failed? Her neck jerked back in defense at this painful attack on her only source of air. Was he killing her? Her head fell farther back. Suddenly, she realized she was too tired to fight him. Either way, for better or worse, she relaxed into his hands. She was too tired to care.

David waited until she exhaled. He felt the air escape from the end of the ET tube in his hand. Using this air to guide him to her windpipe, he quickly slid the ET tube into the proper place. The tip of the tube was only a few inches from the edge of her nose, and some air was moving in and out. He quickly secured it in place and then attached the Ambu bag to the tube. He placed the football-shaped bag within both of his hands, and when the patient inhaled, he pressed and forced air into her lungs. His eyes were focused on her chest wall. Each rise of her chest met with the slow, steady press of the airway bag. With each firm press, the resistance within her lungs became less.

The patient looked up at this young man who was staring at her chest. Her mind was already beginning to think more clearly. If only she could speak, she would say, "Thank you." But the paramedic was too busy to notice, and the tube in her throat wouldn't allow words to be said. Finally, she thought of a way. She reached up and grabbed David's hand. He was surprised by her touch and instantly looked in her face. With his attention, she took a long, deep breath, and her eyes, for the first time since their arrival, didn't hold the expression of one about to die.

David looked directly into her eyes and tried to explain why she was feeling better. "Your heart was backing up blood into your lungs. With each breath now, the fluid is being forced out, and oxygenated air is being forced in."

She nodded her head in understanding and seemed to relax a little further as David's attention returned to her chest and to Jonathan's efforts.

Jonathan captured a frail vein in her right arm with an IV needle and then attached a small blue cap to the end of the IV catheter. As soon as Jonathan had secured this IV site to her very sweaty skin, he picked up a small brown bottle labeled "Lasix" from his medical bag. He drew up the proper amount of the medication for this patient and slowly pushed the drug through the syringe and into the little cap at the base of the IV. Instantly the medication was within her arm and on its way to stimulate her kidneys. In about 15 minutes she would have a full bladder and hopefully, clear lungs. He smiled at his patient and said, "This medication should help you get rid of all that excess fluid in your lungs. It is Lasix, just like you already take, but at a much higher dosage. I saw that medication on your kitchen counter. Do you understand me?"

She looked up into Jonathan's blue eyes and nodded her head. He reached for her other hand and held it for a second. Her eyes lit up, and she smiled at him. He felt the tension in her hand relax further, and gently told her, "You are going to be just fine, now. We are going to be taking good care of you and get you to the hospital quickly." He squeezed her hand softly one more time before he let go. Jonathan looked at his patient's face. The blue-gray color that had moments before filled her lips was now being replaced by the bright red color of fresh, oxygenated blood. He wiped the sweat from her brow and continued to watch. No further sweat appeared. He smiled back at his patient and then up at David, who was continuing to press the air into her lungs. David's hand placement on the airway bag and the amount of reduced force needed to inflate her lungs showed that it was no longer as difficult to help her breathe. She was out of immediate danger, and they were now ready to go to the hospital. Quickly she was loaded onto their stretcher and driven to the hospital. Within twenty minutes the paperwork was completed in the emergency department, and they were back in service for the next call.

The ambulance left the hospital and began the drive back to their station. "Rescue 12," 911 dispatch called. Jonathan grabbed a notepad, ready to write down the next call. "Rescue 12, we were advised you need to come to headquarters for a quick maintenance check on your unit."

David looked over at Jonathan and groaned. Slowly he picked up the radio and replied, "Acknowledge, Rescue 12 now en route to headquarters."

"So at least we'll get lunch without interruption. What do you say we stop at the Tropicana restaurant on the way back from headquarters?"

"Sure, sounds great. I'd love to have a Cuban sandwich for lunch."

Jonathan's mind returned to their last patient. "So, how long were we on the scene? We really moved fast on that one." David looked down at his paperwork. It recorded the exact time of their arrival on the scene, departure to the hospital, and arrival at the hospital. "Only ten minutes," he said, turning to face his partner, "Good thing we got there when we did. Another five minutes and I bet she would have been dead. I'm amazed that she was getting any air into those lungs at all."

"Yeah, and you got the ET tube in quick. But, next time I'm going to intubate the patient. You got the last two. It's my turn next, ok?"

"Sure, got to be fair about the work," David smiled. Jonathan still got excited about being a paramedic and doing the glory work. "You still need practice walking on water, though, so if you don't get it on the first attempt, you tell me, and I'll do it." David's tone jested in friendly mockery of his partner's skill.

"What I can't do on water, apparently we're making up on raising the dead."

Ed was almost home. He knew his wife was going to be surprised to see him arrive so early. He had decided not to rest over in Atlanta, preferring to get home to sleep after unloading his semi at the warehouse on Hillsborough Avenue. He was now within a mile of home and turned the radio on to his favorite station, 88.1 WJIS. One thing about traveling around the country, he knew how hard it was to find a good station, especially the radio hosts like these guys. Ed had come to consider them friends and had listened to them talk more than any other people in the world. That was the life of a driver, though, always alone except for the radio.

The hot Florida sun blinded his eyes. He looked for his sunglasses and saw them on the floor beside the McDonald's trash bag. Glancing at the road while straining down, he realized the glasses were just out of reach. Unbuckling his seat belt so he could stretch just a little farther, Ed's hand pressed forward, searching. At that moment, the light at the intersection turned yellow. With the glasses in hand, he quickly sat up, looked over the steering wheel, and saw the warning light. Instinctively, Ed threw down the glasses and grabbed the steering wheel with both hands. Knowing he couldn't stop in time; he decided to punch it and slammed his foot on the gas. The mighty engine roared as he accelerated toward the intersection.

At the same time, two lifelong friends were on their way to the Eastlake Mall, a few miles from their homes in Temple Terrace. They were busy talking about the sale at Dillard's and about their walk near the Hillsborough River when they were finished shopping. Mary Dell picked up the magazine that

Waunda had lying on the back seat. "Hey, Waunda. I didn't know that Warren and Melody's pictures were in the Evangel magazine? They look really nice. Nathan is growing up so tall." Her pleasant strong southern accent drew her friend's attention from the road.

"I didn't show that to you?" Waunda and Mary Dell talked daily, and the magazine had been out for over a week. She took her eyes off the road for just a second to glance at the picture of her daughter and son-in-law. Her mind wandered to her children so far away as she was approaching the intersection. "Look over on the next page, they've got a small article about them."

"Waunda, look out! That truck ain't stoppin'! Dear God, help us!" Mary Dell's last words were lost within the noise of the crash.

"Rescue 12, what is your location?" 911 dispatch asked.

"Rescue 12, Hillsborough Avenue and 56th street," David responded, and then commented to Jonathan, "I guess they're in a hurry for us to get to headquarters. I wonder what they want."

Jonathan shrugged.

Seconds later, two tones pierced the silence in the ambulance cab, "Rescue 12 respond to a car accident on Sligh and 56th street," dispatch ordered.

"Rescue 12 responding." David reached over and pressed the three red buttons on the dashboard, turning the lights and siren on. He slowed down for a second to watch the traffic respond to his noise and lights. No one slammed their brakes in front of him, so he accelerated and headed toward their destination. "So much for lunch."

Driving up 56th street, they saw a light blue Mercedes that had been hit on the driver's side by a semi-truck. "Rescue 12, put the helicopter on standby," David said into the radio microphone. Dispatch acknowledged the helicopter status. David stared at the wreck as he spoke to Jonathan, "Damn, looks like work! You take the car, and I'll look in the truck." Jonathan nodded. David knew the odds of anyone surviving in that car were slim. He parked the ambulance as close as possible to the wreck, hopefully far enough out so that some inattentive driver didn't run into the back of their unit.

"Rescue 12 on scene," Jonathan notified dispatch as he exited the ambulance.

"Acknowledged."

Jonathan walked quickly over to the car. Instantly, he noted two women in their late fifties pressed against the dash of the car. The Mercedes had absorbed an unbelievable amount of the impact, but the weight and force of the semi had overcome this state of the art, safety-engineered construction. A pale white bag rested over the steering wheel. The driver's head lay upon the deflated pillow. The airbag had protected its driver from gross facial injury, but the door had been forced into the passenger compartment, causing bigger problems. Shredded steel from the front end of the semi-rested where the door had been. As Jonathan approached the car, he could tell it was going to take quite a while to free these victims. The car would have to be cut apart, piece by piece, just to get them out.

There was no time for that now. Jonathan slid his hand through the broken windshield and found the neck of the driver. He searched for a pulse and found none. She was not moving or breathing. He pulled his hand away and ran around to the passenger side of the car. The door was locked, and the windshield and window on this side were still intact. Jonathan pulled a small metal tool out of his side pocket. It looked like a ballpoint pen, but the tip was spring loaded. He placed the center punch against the window and pressed against the glass. The window popped, and the entire window pane cracked. He tugged at the hole he had just made, and the window crumbled in his hand. He pulled the sheet of crumbled glass back and slowly slipped his hand in to touch the top of the passenger's head. She didn't move. Jonathan frowned as he moved her cool body back against the seat to see her face. He touched her neck and again found no pulse. He glanced around her frame and noticed that the engine from the car was pressing against her broken legs and very little blood flowed from her wounds. Both women had died instantly, and there was nothing more he could do for them.

"Rescue 12 requesting a helicopter to the scene. We have at least one trauma alert. Will advise on other patients in a moment." Jonathan heard David's request from the portable radio that he wore on his side. He had a live one! Quickly, he pulled his arm out through the hole he had made and went to help David with the truck driver. Jonathan knew he would be needed there. Death already reigned in this car.

As Jonathan approached the truck, it was immediately obvious that the driver had not been wearing his seat belt. A large circle of broken glass marked the spot where his face had collided with the windshield. Bright red blood flowed down his deeply gashed face and filled his mouth. His head bobbed forward as his body unconsciously tried to bring in air through his bloody mouth. David was rapidly cutting the patient's shirt off. He noticed a large dark ring forming around the driver's lower chest wall. Each inhalation caused his chest to rise, everywhere except in that dark ring. There, the chest wall was pulling in toward his heart with each inward breath. David pressed softly against the ribs and felt the rubbing of broken ribs slide below the bruising skin. Blood ran down from the patient's face and began to cover the exposed chest. At least, David thought, he was still breathing for the moment.

David and Jonathan moved swiftly to save the life of the man. They began the fight with Death once more. The winner would have to endure a hard fight. The boxing match began. The champion would have to endure the punch and counterpunch of the other. There was much to be done, quickly, but the prize in this match was a human life. And David and Jonathan were champions.

"It is appointed unto man once to die and then the judgment..."

Mary Dell reached over to Waunda and shook her. "Wake up, Waunda! Look at where we are!"

Waunda sat up and looked at her friend, who, for some reason looked much younger than she should. "Where are we?" Waunda asked.

"Look, look at the clouds and the stairs, and look, up there is a great, white throne. Waunda, we made it. This is heaven. We're home!"

Waunda looked at the stairs and down at her hands. Slowly she rubbed them together. Just the feel of her own skin let her know whatever and wherever she was, was real. Her words were soft, an awed whisper. "I remember the truck, but that's it." She took her eyes off her hands and gazed with astonishment at her friend. "Mary Dell, look what's on your head." Waunda touched Mary Dell's head. "You have a crown! It's beautiful!" The sight of the crown seemed to make heaven more real, more believable.

"You have one, too," replied her awestruck friend. "Look at the stones of purple and ruby. Your favorites. Waunda, it's you. It's beautiful!"

Waunda ran her trembling fingers up to her head. Slowly she removed the crown that rested there. Her eyes filled with excitement and expectation as this new reality touched them. They reached out and hugged each other. There was no room in this wonderful place for tears.

"Well," mused Waunda, "There must be only one thing left to do. Let's go up these stairs and lay these crowns at the Lord's feet." She released her right hand from the golden crown and grasped the hand of her friend as they began their journey home.

When they reached the top of the stairs, they beheld the Lord on His Throne and His Son, Jesus. Then they saw at the base of the throne two large treasure chests. Each was open, yet each was empty.

Waunda's eyes moved around the scene, taking it all in. "Look, Mary Dell, our treasure is empty. Nothing we did mattered. I always feared that our work wouldn't be good enough! Now look, we have no treasure." Waunda's words were broken and whispered. "We have nothing of our own to give to Christ!"

Mary Dell smiled and spoke with faith. "We made it here, that's enough." She grabbed the shoulders of her friend, "It's ok! I really wish I had more to give to Christ, but this crown will at least be a token of my love. Come on."

Each bowed her head and humbly approached the throne. For a moment, they thought that nothing they had done on Earth had mattered. But, when they reached the feet of the Lord, Jesus spoke. His eyes looked into Waunda's eyes, penetrating her very heart, "Waunda, thank you!" Then, He turned to the left and looked at Mary Dell. His gaze touched her deeply, and His words were as soft as feathers, "Mary Dell, thank you!" Instantly, with these words, they received more than any treasure chest could ever have contained – unconditional love and acceptance from their Lord. He smiled at their understanding. Then, he spoke again to the two of them, "You have been faithful in a few things, come and rule over many."

Waunda let go of her friend's hand, and with trembling joy, placed her crown on the ground before her empty treasure chest. At the same time, Mary Dell turned again to see all that was surrounding her, then bowed down, took off her crown, and laid it before her empty treasure chest. Then the Father spoke, "Before you enter heaven, your works must all be judged." A chill ran up the backs of the two friends. He continued, "Fear not, for before each word and deed are judged, I will send my fire and consume all that is of wood, hay, and stubble. Everything that has no eternal value will be destroyed. And, each deed that would separate you from me, each sin, will be cleansed by the perfect sacrifice of my Son's blood shed for you—for you had called to me and asked for my forgiveness from your sins, and therefore are removed. Only those things done in My perfect love, and only those things that have been tried in the fire and endure as pure gold shall remain."

A great Light suddenly grew from behind the throne, its brightness grew until it was a fire that wrapped around the horizon. From as far as the eastern horizon is from the west, the fire raged. In the twinkling of an eye, the fire filled the sky and then it was gone. When the fire passed, Waunda and Mary Dell saw a host of angels filling the sky as far as their eyes could see.

Then the Father opened the book…

… each deed, each spoken word, each thought, each tear shed, each act was recorded within the book…

"Mary Dell, it is recorded that you organized, cooked, and served at 431 funerals, weddings, and other various events. Waunda, it is recorded that you organized, cooked, and served at 512 functions. Some of the funerals were for those you knew to be saints, yet, you also served others when you didn't know what they had believed, or what their end would be. You followed my Son's example and were truly servants, even to the very least of my children. And as you served each of them, you served Me. You served them because of your love, your love for Me, as well as your love for My children." The Father stretched forth his right hand and gestured to them to come, "Receive your reward."

Waunda and Mary Dell stood speechless. They looked at each other, their minds racing with this revelation. Had it really been so many? Questions pierced their hearts; they heard themselves, as they had on Earth, question the value of their service. "Was it really so important, that it was remembered by their God, and recorded in the Book of Life?" They remembered how often their efforts were not recognized by their peers, rarely understood by their families, and even more rarely thanked. Then it began – one by one the angels came. For every cup of tea poured, every salad tossed, every roast cooked, every card sent, every call of encouragement, the scene was followed by an angel's movement. One by one, they came, each holding a ruby, diamond, or other precious jewel or gold, each bowing down before them and placing the treasure within what had been their empty chests. Each woman saw the scenes of her life replayed so that all present could witness each act and thought that passed as a vapor on earth.

Waunda and Mary Dell watched with eyes of wonder. Their treasures mounted higher and higher until there was no room within the golden chests to contain it all. They held onto each other for support, overcome with joy. Truly, nothing was left for them to desire. Their joy was complete: they had entered their reward.

Then the Son spoke. "Mary Dell, Waunda, there is one thing I would ask of you."

"What could we give to our Lord?"

"All these years, I have seen you cook the roast, black beans, and rice. Because the food was cooked in love, each time the aroma reached the very throne room of heaven." Jesus stopped and rubbed his mouth with his hand, smiling. "Would you cook this meal, just one more time? Just this once... for just you and me."

Children played in the fields near the crystal river. The golden streets were filled with saints on their way to greet their newly arrived co-laborers. And joy filled the hearts of all... as the aroma of roast and garlic filled the hillside of heaven.

The helicopter circled once more overhead. The firemen below signaled the exact spot for the landing zone on the high school parking lot located near this intersection. The Florida Highway Patrol stopped all traffic on 56th street.

David and Jonathan worked with precision as they prepared the driver of the semi for transport by helicopter to the nearest trauma center, where the surgeons were standing by. The blood from his head wounds no longer flowed freely, and his pulse was weak.

A large ET tube hung from the patient's mouth, and Jonathan was compressing the Ambu bag, forcing air through the ET tube. The patient was no longer breathing on his own. Slowly his chest rose and fell at each compression of the bag. The helicopter team finally arrived, and Jonathan gave them a short verbal report. Within minutes, the helicopter was again back up in the air, this time racing toward the Emergency Department. Time, every second, counted.

Death followed their patient to the hospital. Doctors and nurses picked up the match with Death. IV fluid rapidly replaced the lost blood, and large tubes were inserted into the man's chest that helped drain the pooling blood pressing against his heart and lungs. With the regained space in his chest wall, his lungs expanded again to a reasonable size. A ventilator constantly brought a 100% concentration of oxygen to the patient and Death angrily watched as his fingers were pried off by this team of warriors. His grip would no longer hold.

Suddenly Death laughed and released his prisoner. "I could keep you if I wanted. But, I do not want you," Death turned from the room, but no one who could hear Death's boast believed him. They all knew he had lost. Angels stood guard over their ward and ministered strength to the exhausted human warriors. They watched as the patient was moved out of the emergency department and into ICU. The human warriors were tired, but somehow ready for the next patient.

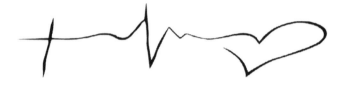

The traffic continued to back up on 56th street. David and Jonathan watched as the helicopter lifted from the street and began toward the hospital. The two men walked over to their unit and began to clean up the blood and used medical supplies off the floor. Each man looked over at the Mercedes, but neither returned to the car.

Fifteen minutes later, David notified dispatch, "Rescue 12 back in service."

"Acknowledged. Continue into headquarters."

An hour later, after the quick unit maintenance, they were released to return to their station, "Two calls already, and at least six to go!" Jonathan said as he sat back in the passenger's seat. "I think we better eat now while we have a chance. I have a feeling we better get it fast, if we are going to get it at all today."

David was too tired to respond to the implication that they might have six more calls. No sense jinxing themselves.

Nothing was worse than being hungry, paying for a meal, getting a call, and watching the food be dumped in the garbage can, so they ordered and devoured their meal quickly. Neither talked until they had finished. "Did you see in the paper that they are having a group memorial service tomorrow at the school auditorium for those three kids from Friday's cocaine overdose?" Jonathan asked.

"Yes, and I thought that we should go. The families might like to see us there. Maybe we can answer a few of their questions."

"Not like we will have the answer to the questions they will be asking! But you're right. I'll go, if you do."

"Ok, tomorrow we'll meet at the station and go over together." David sat back in his seat, ready to take a deep breath and relax a little. "I wouldn't mind seeing how Terri's doing, either."

David began to change gears mentally and move on to the more recent calls, "Those ladies in the Mercedes, I really got a feeling that they are going to be missed. Have you ever gotten 'feelings' about your patients?"

"Sure, I really 'felt' like we have been working too hard recently." Jonathan laughed. "No, seriously, I have gotten 'psychic impressions' of people before. Who hasn't?"

"Well, this 'feeling' is different. I can almost hear someone saying things to me, like, these were good ladies, they're in a better place. Like death wasn't the end for them."

Jonathan put down his soda and looked up at his friend who seemed determined to take today's conversation into uncharted territory. For some reason, Jonathan was willing to go with it. "That's an amazing amount of 'feelings.' Did you ever hear 'voices' before talking to you?"

"I am not talking about 'lock me up crazy voices,'" David said. "I am talking about the quiet inner voice we all have that tells us when something is right or not. I know you hear that. We all do. Any psychology textbook talks about it. Some call it your conscience, others call it your heart."

"Yes, yes I know. And Christians call it the spirit. Everybody has their own spirit within them that leads them, and once they become believers, the Spirit of God, Himself, is supposed to come and teach their spirit directly. That is how the theory goes." Jonathan smiled at the knowledge he had gained as a child that never seemed important before.

"You know, that is kind of exactly what Terri's mom, Mrs. Blake, told me," David remembered. "She said that the Spirit of God would be with me always, even in the back of our ambulance, and that He would teach me, and that He could teach me about God by things that happen. Do you believe that can really happen?" David's words quickened as he sought for answers to questions that he didn't even realize he had.

Jonathan shrugged his shoulders. "I guess anything can happen in the back of our ambulance. It gets pretty crazy back there."

"So then, if you think that, and obviously you have a lot of knowledge that you never told me about before, what is this 'better place that death has no part of?' And what else do you know that I should know?" David asked.

"Hold on, David! I don't know enough to answer these questions, and I really would feel guilty teaching you these things, especially if I don't walk in what it is you are asking about. Just because I know about this stuff, doesn't mean I believe it all. You need to talk to someone who walks what he talks. I'm not going to be a hypocrite. That's the reason I quit going to church. I got tired of all the people talking about this power and the presence of God, and then not being any different than me. No, you need to find someone who you think you can trust."

"Look, Jonathan, you are the only one I would trust with this. I don't know anyone to ask, other than you. I would rather have one honest answer from you than any answer from someone

I don't know or trust." David leaned forward and placed his hands on the table. "Please, teach me."

"Well, I guess that's fair. You sure have taught me a lot about the streets. I have seen you help me when you didn't have to. So, I'll be honest and answer any question you have, and if I don't know the answer, then you and I will search it out and find the answer. Just don't tell my dad, or else he'll think you're an answer to prayer, and we sure don't want that!"

David and Jonathan left the restaurant, returning to their ambulance and headed back to their station. "This will all start to make sense soon, right?" David asked with expectation. "So, where do we begin?"

"Ok, start with prayer. You do know how to do that, right?"

"Prayer. No, not really. Is there a book of prayers that I can buy somewhere?"

"Man, I'm going to sound like a master to you. You really are at ground zero. Prayer just means talking with God. It will grow to mean a lot more but start with talking to God. If you really believe He is in you, He will hear you, and you will hear Him." Jonathan had forgotten how good it was to think about God. "Ask Him your questions, and see how He will answer you, either in your heart or in some circumstance that shows you the answer."

Two strong warriors, angels of Light and Power, stood to the side of David and Jonathan. Michael and Sabbath were the angel's names. One name meant beloved of God, the other one meant Peace. They now had the strength to defeat the attacks of the dark ones, being strengthened not only by David's open and curious heart, but by the intercession of Mrs. Blake, a mighty prayer warrior.

Michael and Sabbath surrounded David with their shields. Jonathan's inner voice was being awakened by their presence. Michael spoke, "It is good to awaken the inner man of Jonathan. The Spirit of God is working on that one as well."

"Yes, we will see a great victory in these two men." Sabbath touched David's right hand.

David sat back and relaxed his grip on the door rest. It was beginning to make sense to him. He grinned at Jonathan. "It really helps to talk about this stuff. You're a good friend. Thanks."

Jonathan found the muscles in his back had begun to relax. His heart began to slow. He grinned back at David. "I know it won't make sense, but I really enjoyed going into all this stuff. It was fun to remember. Dad would be pleased."

Michael looked out of the ambulance window towards the western sky and spoke, "Let us seize the time. Death has prepared an attack against these two. We are strong enough to stop him. Let us approach the Spirit of God and see if we can bring Peace to this area. Let Jonathan and David have a quiet day and rest tonight so that they will be strong enough to bear the attack and struggle of tomorrow's battle."

These messengers of light stood before the Father boldly. Theirs was an easy task. Peace poured from the throne, surrounding the men and their area.

David quietly went to the bunk room and began to read. As the hours passed, Jonathan watched sports on TV then fell asleep. Later that night, they exchanged nervous glances as they prepared for sleep. The unspoken rule of thumb was that if they were quiet during the day, they would be up all night on calls. That didn't seem to be the case tonight.

Morning came with the sound of the oncoming crew kicking their beds. "Hey, you lazy bums, get up," Carl barked with obvious envy at their current condition.

David rolled over and slowly stretched his arms over his head. "So miracles still do happen!"

"I can't believe that we slept all night," Jonathan smirked in disbelief. "Well, I'm ready for today. What is it that we're doing again?"

"The memorial service for the teenagers, you are still going." David rose from his bed and prepared to end his shift. "I'll meet you back here at 2:00, that will give us plenty of time to get there."

Carl went to the log book that held the record of the daily emergency calls. "I see that at least you did work on the couple of calls that you ran. I hope that you enjoyed your little vacation."

David began to tell Carl about the equipment missing from the rescue unit, "Some spinal equipment went with the driver of the semi-truck to Tampa General by helicopter. We still have two boards, but if you get back to the hospital, pick it up."

"I don't think I'll want to, sounds like it will be pretty bloody. We'll just let them clean it first. I'm sure the two boards will be enough." Carl walked over and checked the controlled medications. Both he and David had to sign the log that these medications had been transferred to the oncoming team. David signed the log and gathered his equipment. It had been a long time since he'd had such a peaceful shift. He grinned and walked to his car, knowing he would remember this shift for a long time.

Chapter Three

TUESDAY:
WHAT'S THE POINT?

3:00 pm: The school parking lot was full of cars and students. Television cameras were set at the entrance doors with live reporters. Public intrusion was being forced upon the grieving mass of students and families alike. There were plenty of questions, but no one had any acceptable answers, so the questions continued. David and Jonathan headed to the side door, glad they had chosen not to wear their uniforms and could blend into the crowd, unnoticed.

The steel doors stuck against the jam. David pressed a little harder, and the door popped open. The sunlight pressed in, pushing the darkness back, but only for a moment as the door slowly closed behind them. David and Jonathan entered. Then there was nothing but darkness and dim, artificial light. The darkness surrounded them, and each felt the heaviness and stifling oppression permeating the atmosphere of the school gym.

Jonathan groaned. "The depression in here is about to strangle me."

"This service won't last long," David whispered. "Look at all these people. They all want out of here, too." There was quiet; no band, no cheerleaders, no mighty warring team. The hush of Death and Depression stifled each one's breath. Only an occasional sob was heard above the deafening silence. Each person looked within themselves for some light, some hope, some reason for this tragedy. Most only found the darkness within overwhelming. There was no hope, David thought as he began to remember each dead teenager as he had found them in that house. Their faces began to haunt him. He closed his eyes, this time imagining them laughing, being kids. Then he shivered as he remembered the tangible sensation of death and the eerie silence of being surrounded by so many who had just died.

David forced his mind to focus on Terri, the one survivor. He remembered her face as she lay unconscious in the back of the ambulance. She was at peace, and she miraculously lived. Yet faced with these two conflicting extremes of senseless death and eternal life, he struggled, and Depression tightened his hold.

He began to see the faces of other patients he had treated... the mother and child, killed by the drunk driver... the lonely old man who had shot himself in the head while David helplessly stood by and watched, begging the man to wait...

the young woman dead in her bathroom from the hands of her husband… One by one, each memory came. Each holding a clue to something that began to tear into David's belly. What was the point? What is the hope? Why try? Is there no hope? David bent his head forward and his eyes filled with tears. Tears were not unacceptable or unmanly now. He looked around and saw other men crying. He wondered if they, too, were overwhelmed with the hopelessness of life. He looked again, this time his eyes filled with anger. He wanted to yell out loud, You cry for these children, but I have seen hundreds die! The pain is too great… Death is too strong! The anger turned to sorrow, and he stood up. "I need to go outside and get some air," He left Jonathan sitting.

Jonathan would not, could not move. He yelled at the battle within him, screaming to himself, I am not going to break. I am stronger than these deaths. I will not cry! Paramedics take pride in the high walls around their emotions. How else could they survive? He didn't dare allow himself to feel or cry like David, or he might lose it. Jonathan let David leave alone. "I will survive," he spoke out loud, but under his breath.

The sun shone brightly. David wondered if it was mocking the darkness. He began to focus on the questions rising within him. He wanted to think about anything other than the teenagers. Light and Dark? He mused the question in his mind. Often in his college English class, they had pondered the concepts of Light and Dark, Good and Evil, Life and Death as deeper things, things of the inner man. That was so long ago. Yet the questions remained.

He pondered the issue of love. Love really was a beam of light. No one could deny its existence. If hatred, death, and destruction were darkness, then love was the Light. David's eyes dried of tears. He took a deep breath and began to walk about the courtyard. Everyone else was inside. He was alone. At least, he thought he was alone…

He heard a small inner voice raise another question within him, Did you feel loved when you read of God's love? Did you feel His presence? Wasn't his presence the presence of Love?"

Suddenly David remembered Terri's face as she looked up at him from the ambulance stretcher. She had seen the face of Love. David remembered Mrs. Blake at the hospital. What was that strength she had? Where did it come from? David looked up into the blue sky and spoke: "Dear God: I've been told you are always with me and will teach me," Now David's voice rose by the force of all the emotions raging within him, "So, what's the Point?" David took a deep breath, looked quickly around to see if anyone had heard him and chuckled at himself and the absurdity of standing outside a memorial service and asking, "What's the point?" He felt alone. Alone with only the faces of his patients past, the faces of death manifest. And, yet, not alone, somehow knowing his question had been heard.

David dried his face and forced himself to open the door of the gym auditorium and return to his seat. "This paramedic would be there to help the hurting." Paramedics weren't allowed to bleed or hurt, only to help others. He would help others. His mask was firmly in place. No more tears, he thought as he returned to his seat beside Jonathan.

The service had already begun. The audience was quiet except for the muffled cries from the observers. The minister spoke of the obvious sadness and loss, then said, "Choice. We all have the right to make our own choices. People can warn us, and God can warn us, but it is our choice. Do we ever stop to think that the consequences are not our choice? We choose, but the consequences are what? Random 'luck' or just 'bad luck.'? We have lost our friends. Three of our own have died from the evil of drugs? They chose to have a good time. They did not choose to die. We don't need to be angry at them any more than we judge ourselves for the choices and risks we take. We just need to learn from their mistake. And, in honor of that lesson, choose more wisely then they…" His message continued and clearly, it was intended to bring comfort and to foster change. However, the grief within the crowd was so tangible and the heartbreak so deafening, David doubted the words would have any lasting impact. Depression wrapped around him, and he found little reason to hope. David sighed and silently wondered why he had come to this memorial service. His attention shifted to watching the crowd for any sign of danger or physical distress.

When the memorial ended, many of the teenagers stood in line to walk by the display set up for each of the dead teenagers. There were pictures and trophies, and a table to leave flowers or gifts. David and Jonathan looked at each other. Without a word, they walked to the front and watched from the side. Experience told them both that their services were going to be needed.

Jonathan tapped David on the forearm then pointed to a young girl surrounded by a handful of helping friends as they were walking up to the display. She was a particularly pale girl whose face was swollen from tears. Her long, brown hair lay stringy on her shoulders. Dark lines of mascara streaked her face. Quickly, instinctively, she reached up and pulled her hair behind her ears. David smiled at Jonathan as they each noticed the quantity and shapes of the many earrings in each of her ears. The most eye-catching was a large silver cross that hung from her right ear. Jonathan whispered, "Hey, isn't that girl from the scene where the kids died?"

David nodded as he recognized her and remembered seeing her sit in the back of the police car on the night of this tragedy. He watched her closely as she leaned up and touched the large picture of Tommy. She suddenly paled and began to collapse. The paramedics rapidly slipped in behind this circle of teenagers, and instantly, Jonathan grabbed one arm and David grabbed the other and gently laid her down to the ground. Within seconds, the girl awakened to find herself staring into the faces of two strangers. "Where am I?" she asked, her voice cracking with exhaustion. Her head leaned against David's arm.

"You are at the memorial service. How do you feel now?" Jonathan took the lead with this patient's care. "What's your name?" he gently asked.

Debra's soft brown eyes, so full of emotion, looked up to Jonathan. She needed his strength. She sat up and straightened her clothes, "My name is Debra. I am fine, I guess it was too much for me." Her eyes filled with tears, "Tommy was my," she paused, "he was my friend," As she gained control of herself, her voice hardened as she realized everyone was staring at her, "Can I stand up?"

"Only if you let us help," Jonathan said, taking her hand.

Debra stood up, leaned forward, regained her balance and took a deep breath saying, "I am fine." She nodded curtly and quickly walked away. Embarrassed, as well as grieving, she just wanted to leave this service as quickly as possible. A young man had been watching from the shadows against the far wall. When Debra began to move forward, he quickly joined her. He looked around at all the teenagers coming towards them and cast an angry look at the approaching crowd, warning them away. He whispered something in Debra's ear, and she nodded at him. David watched as the two teenagers left the auditorium. She looked relieved to be taken so quickly from the gym, and the two paramedics returned to scanning the crowd.

"I sure hope these kids find a way to vent some of this depression or else we'll see some of them on our streets," Jonathan spoke softly, looking around at the assembly.

"Let's hope not. I don't think the school could take another heartbreak like this. But you're right. What's your bet? Suicide or drunken car accident?" David said and grimaced as he considered the reality of this real risk.

"My bet is we'll see both. But I will bet you on who it will be!"

"Sick paramedic street humor! You and me, we've worked the streets too long. I won't bet this time. These kids took too much out of me. My senses are shot." David looked around the room at the countless teenagers who were overcome with grief. He knew Jonathan was right. Which one or ones would it be...?

David left the memorial service empty and exhausted. He entered his bedroom for solitude, his emotions drained. The death of these teenagers weighed heavily on his heart, and in that weight, questions and doubts pressed against the foundation of his new-found faith.

Hopelessness was surprised when he found a crack in David's spiritual wall. Seeing the opportunity, he slithered in around David's mind, like a python moving slowly to entrap his prey. Hopelessness wrapped around and squeezed David's emotions. As he did, David heard the dark knowledge of the hopelessness of all people. He surrendered to the pressure of these thoughts and, like every person before him, asked, "What's the point? Was there no hope?" David cried as he lay alone on his bed.

Hopelessness began to revel in his new strength, when suddenly, the one he was a perversion of, showed up. Godly Sorrow entered the bedroom, "Leave, you have been done away with!" Godly Sorrow spoke to Hopelessness with the authority of his position.

"No, this man has let me in! I will stay." Hopelessness knew he had no right to be there, but bluffing was one of his strongest weapons.

"He has known you long enough. He shall know the truth and shall be set free."

"You…you will bring him more tears than me," Hopelessness scoffed at Godly Sorrow, "You don't offer freedom. There is only freedom in the Dark. Let us see which of us he prefers. The one he rejects will leave in shame. Let us see who he will understand better; the hopelessness of man or Godly Sorrow, which shall lead to Repentance." Hopelessness's words turned from scoffing to baiting Godly Sorrow. "Don't think for a moment that I don't know that Strength remains outside, just waiting to be called on."

Godly Sorrow, no longer speaking to the dark warrior, turned and gently touched David's shoulder. Suddenly David began to cry a little harder. A new part of his heart opened. David cried out to the God he was honestly trying to understand. He had never felt the weight of all the death and destruction he had seen before. His mental wall had always protected him from the emotional consequences of all he had witnessed. But now… now there was only sorrow.

He wept for all the lives he had seen destroyed and pain he had touched as a paramedic. Gradually his emotions were spent, his heart quieted. He laid still and started to think beyond the pain. He heard a new voice, the voice of Godly Sorrow, "If God is Love and Light – then whatever is not of love is not of God; then evil must be anything that separates from God…" David made room in his mind for these new thoughts, letting them take root and grow. He began again to consider the rescue calls in light of these thoughts. Good people have been destroyed by someone choosing to do something NOT in love. Rape, murder, drunk drivers, child abuse… all the worst calls have been done by someone doing something not in love but in self-satisfaction.

Again, Godly Sorrow turned David's thoughts away from the failures of others and back to his own choices. The images in his mind were cruel in their truthful rendering of David's decisions. The images were too real, too close to his heart. In his anguish, he again began to cry, and to cry out to God, "I'm so sorry. I'm hopeless on my own to do what's right, and I have hurt others. I don't have a right to your forgiveness, but please, forgive me…" David felt something inside his heart, like water washing over him. This sensation, like the tears he had shed, was cleansing his soul. Hopelessness closed his eyes to block the light radiating from one of the strongest spirits of the Good One. This warrior could defeat any weapon of darkness. Repentance entered on the wings of tears and joy.

Hopelessness turned to Godly Sorrow. "You have been strengthened. We will do battle again." He crawled out through the crack of protection around David and lamented, "Was I used to lead this human to recognize his hopeless condition without the Good One? I was used to bring a man to Godly Sorrow!" This thought choked Hopelessness and tormented him, "The Good One used me." He slithered back into his hole. The Adversary would not be pleased.

The victorious warriors sang a song of the heavens in unison, and David heard. Strange words came to David's mind.

He knew they were not his own words and spoke of things he did not understand, but he knew they were true.

"There is no one like my God,

From Hill to Valley,

I shall proclaim Your Glory;

You have lifted up the cup of Salvation,

You have filled it.

You shall speak your word to the poor,

And proclaim liberty to the bound,

Freedom and Joy are the wings of the Spirit.

By these two You can judge the Dark.

Whether it is of God or man,"

The Spirit of God spoke from within him, "Be at peace and arise. Go to the funeral of the two women. You will have your answer."

David knew he must obey that which he did not understand and could never explain. He would follow this life-changing adventure. Joy covered him like an oil. Every hair, every aspect of him felt God's presence. He slept in the arms of God and awoke with a plan, a direction, and he knew – an answer.

Chapter Four

WEDNESDAY: DIVINE CONNECTION AND DEMONIC CAPTIVITY

Wednesday morning sunrise found David awake and expectant. Life had become an adventure. His heart was full of gratitude, and his mind was at peace. He considered how he could share this with Jan, his wife. He could hear her moving around in the kitchen, so he slowly got up to join her before she had to leave for work. She was definitely going to be shocked.

"Good morning, sweetheart! Glad to see you up so early. I already read the paper. And, it is waiting for you on the table." Jan said as she rushed to their kids' rooms.

David sat down with his coffee and picked up the local paper and waited for her return. It was filled with the headline of the memorial service yesterday. He looked at the pictures of the three teenagers who had died, and the pictures of classmates, shown holding each other and crying. Did any of them get it? Would any one of them have the courage to stay off drugs? David wondered and then shook the paper as he flipped to the back section, and the cynicism of so many years as a paramedic caused the whispered answer, "I doubt it."

"Doubt what, dear?" a rushing voice was heard from the kitchen.

"Oh, I was talking to myself," David put down the paper and looked over the counter toward his wife who was busy fixing some cereal for herself and the kids. "I was reading the paper about the kids at the memorial service, that's all. It is so frustrating to face the death of these kids, knowing our own will be that age soon."

Jan walked toward David with coffee in one hand and a bowl in the other. They kissed as she sat down. "How are you doing with all this stuff?"

"It's weird. But, I have been thinking about a lot lately. I really want to tell you about it." A wave of emotions caught him off guard, and he didn't know where to start, "But, right now I just think I need some time to make sense of it all."

"You know, it might be a good idea for you to take off Sunday and just relax. I am here for you, when you are ready. I know it sometimes takes you a while to process all you deal with at work."

David moved the papers to one side and touched her hand in gratefulness, "I might just do that. Are you still planning on going to the beach?"

"Of course. Mom and I are looking forward to the weekend with the kids together. Dad doesn't want to go. Says it is still too cold for him. It has to be summer before he wants to get in the water. So, if you wanna just stay here, that's OK too. But, you are welcome to join us."

David looked at the faces of the teenagers staring from the front page, "Let me see if I can get the day off. Maybe I could get an extra day away from there."

"So, you didn't answer me. How are you doing with all these deaths?" Jan's deep blue eyes penetrated David's, and he quickly looked down and flipped the paper open to the second page.

"Well, I wanna really talk to you about all this. Last night while you were out, I thought about a lot of things. But you don't have time, the kids need to get to school, and you need to get to work. I promise that tonight we can talk, ok?"

"Alright, I'll let you off the hook because you're right. I don't have time. But, not tonight, I will be in late again. Promise you'll talk to me later."

David looked up at his wife of eleven years, "Sure, it's a date. Hopefully, I'll have even more to tell you then." With that look, she knew he would tell her when they had time, and that he would be alright.

His eyes returned to the paper. There, in the back section, was a small notice about another funeral. The paper stated it was for two women "fatally injured" in a car accident. "That sounds better than 'creamed by a semi-truck,' I guess," David mumbled. He knew these ladies must have died instantly. "I bet they didn't even know what hit them." He looked up, noticing that Jan had left, and he had again been talking to himself.

The hot steam from his cup reminded David of the steam from the truck's broken radiator. His mind replayed the accident, point by point. David constantly found himself replaying the rescue calls, to see if there was anything he could have done better. There was always at least one thing that he wished could have been done differently, but this call went very smoothly. However, to lose two women without even a fight was a shame. If only there were more ambulances, more hands on the scene soon enough. Stress lines forced their way across his brow, his mind was haunted by their faces. Would that have saved even one of the two women? He knew he would never know the answer to that question, and he knew it wouldn't be the last time he asked it. He continued to read the obituary. It stated that the service would be held at Crossroads Church to accommodate the large expected attendance, with the Reverend Timothy McDonald to officiate.

He knew where this church was, everyone in town did. They called it The Happy Church. Until yesterday, he thought that was a strange name for a church. But, if those people felt what he felt last night, no wonder they're happy. "Maybe it's about time for me to go to church."

"Daddy, Daddy! Good morning!" Tiffany ran to her father's lap and kissed him.

"So much for the paper," David said with a laugh, putting down the paper and looking fondly at his seven-year-old daughter. "Good morning to you, princess!" Tiffany loved it when her Daddy kissed her. She giggled and ran off to the next recipient of her morning ritual.

Sam, the large Doberman, looked up slowly, mocking the child's energy. Sam thought himself too sophisticated to show that much attention to the girl. His pointed ears stood up, and his brown eyes gave away his true affection for his young keeper. He would patiently endure her hugs and kisses. She hugged him so tightly that he stood up from his mat, lifting her from the floor, shook his head and licked the child. She had her kiss, and so she continued to the next person on her morning travels. Sam walked in a tight circle, and then returned to his place. The dog watched as she ran into the other bedroom.

"MOM, MOM, get Tiffany out of here!"

Tiffany had made it to her younger brother's room. David laughed, "Tiffany, leave your brother alone." His voice seemed stern. She knew better.

"Alright, Tiff, come in here and have breakfast," this voice was not one to push. She immediately left her brother's room and came into the kitchen. This time her mother had called.

"Good morning, Mommy. I – love – you," she said, stretching each word to the maximum as were her arms as she reached all the way around her mother's soft belly.

"Good morning to you, sweetie." The ritual was completed.

Sounds of the refrigerator door swinging open and shut, and Mommy's orders filled the kitchen. Kids ran in and out of rooms as they both hurriedly kissed their parents. The front door was left open as Matthew ran to catch up with his sister. Jan stood watching until her kids entered their school bus. "David, I'm leaving now. See you at 6:00. Would you get dinner started tonight?"

He got up and walked to the front door. He kissed Jan as she bent over to pick up her purse. "Sure. You got the stuff in the fridge ready, or is it whatever I want to fix?"

"Nope, nothing in there special. You'll just have to surprise me with whatever you want. I don't care." Jan reached into her purse for her keys. "Oh yeah, and don't forget to take the dog to the vet today. They said they need to keep him overnight."

"Well, I guess I can protect us tonight. Sure, I'll take him later."

Jan kissed David again as she ran out the front door.

David walked to the table with the newspaper and returned to his own thoughts. As he sat down, the emotional weight of the recent calls stirred in his mind. His eyes were drawn to his hands, and he noticed again the multiple small scars from the countless windshields that cut his hands as he reached for his patients. Staring at the scars, his mind focused on last night's mental war. "What is the point? That was the question. Today I'll find the answer." He rarely went to the funerals of his patients because it was too depressing. His job was hard enough as it was, but there was a point to all of this. David just knew there was some reason he needed to be at both services, but what? What would he discover? He realized he was looking forward to the funeral today.

An angry young man walked forcefully towards two ornately carved, mahogany doors at the entrance of an impressive office in downtown Tampa. A large sign stood above the entrance, R. Summerall - Imports. Joey's fists were clenched, and his body was rigid. He stopped at the doors and glanced quickly down the hallway, finding it free of observers. He pushed the heavy doors open and entered alone.

Two strong, well-defined and well-dressed men stood on alert just inside the office and immediately escorted him to his destination. The young man looked at these men as they hurried him down the corridor. Their handsome faces were lost in the darkness of their evil eyes. Apparently, pleasant interaction with the visitors was not the norm.

The spirits of Fear and Anger, while unseen, were also present with this angry visitor. Fear baited him to run, and his heart began to race. But, it was Anger who controlled his thoughts, and it was the voice of Anger he heard loudest. Anger enjoyed his control of this young man too much to allow Fear much volume. Anger reached over and blew into the ear of his toy. His voice was slow and hot, "He knew better. He set you up. You are in danger because of his error. The coke you sold Tommy will get you killed, and it's all his fault. He was careless, and they all died." The wind of Anger blew into the soul of this young man. Fear was immediately squelched by these strong thoughts. He waited, though, for he knew he would get to torment this fool soon.

Joey yelled as he approached the trim, perfectly groomed businessman sitting behind his desk, anger dripping from each word, "What happened? What went wrong?" Anger, the strongest tormenting voice within Joey, joined a stronger warrior of Rage, a voice that was familiar to the older man. Their two voices began to harmonize and play between the two humans, their voices were felt within each of their human toys, and each felt the surge of this emotional volley.

"Shut up, Joey!" angrily, Mr. Summerall returned the hostile verbal assault. He stood up from behind his desk and walked over to face his immature challenger. He controlled his voice, and his words became restrained, "The stuff wasn't supposed to be fatal. There was an error, and the coke wasn't cut before it was distributed. I would not have wasted that pure cocaine. I lost a lot of money! Hell, I would have cut it myself, if I had known. Do you think I am a fool?" He reached over and pulled out a white bag from his desk, "This; this is what they were supposed to have had. Accidents happen in our business; things are under control now."

"But that's not what they had! They are dead!" Joey, unable to quiet his anger, yelled at his affluent supplier, "We killed them. It's our fault, if you haven't noticed. If they find out that it was me they bought it from, I'll get the death penalty." He began to tremble in the onslaught of raging emotions. For a moment, Joey was blinded to the power of this middle-aged, red-haired man, then Fear gripped his heart when he saw his cold, dark eyes. Clearly, Mr. Summerall's expression showed no concern for the teenager's deaths and instantly, the young man knew he had spoken too abruptly. His fear was now strong enough to silence the anger raging within him.

The bodyguards moved forward waiting for the word to quiet this fool. The voice of murder was familiar to them. Silently they waited. Mr. Summerall threatened coolly, "If you are not man enough to keep yourself together, then we can take care of you, right now."

The young man's eyes dropped to the floor. He knew he had said too much and that this man could have him killed easily with a single word. Fear delighted at revealing a dark truth to his victim, "Die now, or die later. It's not for you to decide." The young, fearful dealer awaited his outcome. Death entered the room.

Mr. Summerall, enjoying the control and fear he wielded, lowered his voice further and sounded almost fatherly, as he placed his hands on the kid's back, "You're doing a great job. These things happen. Don't worry, the cops will never have enough information to pin it on you. Besides, it's not like cocaine is FDA approved. Anyone, including those kids, who uses this shit knows they are taking a chance. It is their choice. It'll blow over. Remember, this isn't the first time. People die all the time from drugs, and they know it. They can't stop us."

"But, so many at one time. It's hot out there," Joey whispered. He knew he would do whatever he was told. This risk of being silenced was real, and he just needed to get out of this place alive. He lifted his eyes and looked into the face of his boss. He sought hope but found only cold darkness.

Mr. Summerall taunted his captive. "Not nearly as 'hot' as where you'll be, if they catch you. I'm not afraid of death, but you should be." Death had been his companion and tool to control others for so long that he laughed at the thought of hell. He knew what death would be like for himself. The Voices within had convinced him that he was buying his place in Hell. He would forever be in control of fools like this one trembling before him. He had always won. His laughter grew.

The young frightened man didn't know why this evil man laughed, but he grasped for some reason to hope. His fear of death made him giddy, and suddenly he joined in the laughter.

They laughed together. All of them. Voices of Deceit and Lies danced at the foolishness of these men.

The voice of Control took over and suddenly, Mr. Summerall sobered and stopped laughing, returning to the business at hand. Mistakes cost money. Money was lost, and more was at risk if any other errors were made. His voice was as piercing as a knife. "With your high school buyer being killed by the cocaine, no one else knows you are the dealer who sold it," he paused, "Right?"

"I..." heat rose from the back of Joey's neck, "...don't think so." Fear taunted him again with the knowledge that he was in Death's grip. It was like a cat and mouse game, and he knew he was the mouse, and his life depended on him finding a way to escape. His mouth dried. He could make no mistakes. "There is only one other person who knew I sold it to the others," Joey said, carefully weighing every word. "I didn't know about Tommy and the others dying that night. And, after I sold the coke to Tommy, I met with a junkie who tried to cheat me. No one was around, and I shot him. I thought you would be pleased." Joey's words quickened. He knew he was speaking on behalf of his own life. "I knew you wanted me to make my mark on the streets. I did..." he forced his words to slow down, as he watched Mr. Summerall's eyes begin to glow red from a level of anger he didn't know existed. Joey grasped for a straw, "I thought it was what you wanted, but ..."

Mr. Summerall grabbed the young man and held him by the throat. His hands tightened, "But..."

Joey's voice trembled. "...but, somehow, he managed to live. I don't know how. I shot him right in the stomach. There was no way he should have lived."

"So, a bunch of good kids die, and a junkie lives. You had a fine night. It sounds like your luck has run out," Mr. Summerall enjoyed the feel of terror under his hands and decided he liked his pawn. He would wait till later to take this one. "So, who might this junkie have told?" He released his grip. He enjoyed the submission as much as he was enjoying the terror from this kid.

"No one now. He has already called me from the hospital. He wants me to give him some heroin. He is already feeling the pain of withdrawal and said that he knew it was his fault. He wants me to give him enough free drugs to last him for a while. That is all it will take for him to forget all about it." Joey rubbed the sweat from his face, his hands trembling with fear, then rubbed his neck. It felt as though the supplier's hands remained there. In some ways, they had...

"We can trust the junkie. I know their type. They will forget anything and everything just if you supply their need. It's amazing how little someone will sell their soul for, to possess this white death. There is only one catch. Was the junkie awake in the ambulance? Could he have talked? Fear of dying can make you say foolish things, things you would regret later." He sneered and then grinned at his pawn. "Find out and take care of it." The emphasis was on "take care of it." Joey knew he had been given an out. He could leave, but his life depended on what had been or had not been said at the moment the junkie regained consciousness. He rushed out of the room. The heavy office doors slammed shut behind him as he left. Anger taunted him as he fled the office, reminding him that he had been made a fool in there, Fear became silent with the reality that Murder had now been assigned to this captive. These three would be a mighty force to direct this pawn's choices.

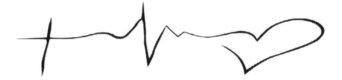

There were hundreds of people present for Mary Dell and Waunda's funeral. David arrived at the church and slid into a seat in the back. He watched as the people filtered in. The crowd yesterday was mostly teenagers, but today there were people of all ages. It was amazing to watch. The people would greet each other with a hug and a kiss. They were grieving, yet when they would look at each other, there was a joy in seeing one another, a joy in being together, a joy… It didn't make any sense to David at all. They were obviously grieving, but the heaviness that had choked David and Jonathan yesterday didn't seem to be in this place. Obviously, these ladies were loved, but to watch the people come in, you would have thought that they had just left and could return at any minute. Yesterday, David was overwhelmed, today he was just confused.

He leaned back just watching, and he grinned. He tried to be somber, but he could not. This was just too amazing, and his was not the only smile. He noticed that all the eyes in the house turned to watch as a large, distinguished looking man walked in. He knew from the paper that this man's name was Timothy McDonald. The man that stood before the congregation didn't even slightly resemble what David had imagined a minister of such a large church would look like. The creases around his eyes revealed a man who must normally smile, but the genuine sadness of the women's deaths was causing a strain to his normal demeanor. He was grieving, but there was strength in those eyes that David had rarely seen before. The minister walked purposefully to the front of the church and hugged each member of both families. His eyes rested for a moment on each one. They knew him, and David could tell by the looks, they loved him. The husband of one of the deceased women smiled as he hugged this large man who looked as if he had just whispered something funny. David's amazement deepened.

Music began, and the people gathered quickly. The beat was fast, and the message of the songs spoke of a better place "over the hillside...," and "...it will be worth it all when we see His face." David listened as nearly a thousand people sang of a hope that defeats death, of living forever with a Lord that they knew existed and they loved. Several songs later, the minister began to speak. His deep Kentucky accent was pleasant and his words intelligent and full of wisdom. David's mind settled, and he slowly began to recall the hopelessness that filled him yesterday, and then the release he felt when he prayed to this invisible God that he had just met. Gradually, he began to understand that what he experienced last night must be similar to what they have experienced and the source of their joy and their hope. "This is real," David mused and then grinned again, this time at the irony of discovering real hope at a funeral.

The service ended, and the minister announced that everyone was invited to the fellowship hall. "Waunda and Mary Dell would have liked everyone to have a good meal today. They would have been pleased to share in the abundance of food that so many of you have brought to share. There is more than enough for everyone, so come." David didn't understand the statement about all the food, but he had had enough surprises, so he stood up and started to leave.

"David, wait!" A voice in the crowd sounded familiar. He stopped and quickly scanned the crowd. "David, it's me, Terri." David turned around to see Terri standing next to some young male teen.

He was again surprised, "What are you doing out of the hospital already?"

"They couldn't find anything wrong with me, so they let me out." She smiled, and her eyes spoke volumes to David. He laughed out loud. He quickly looked around; he was, after all, at a funeral, but no one seemed to notice his laugh.

"Terri, did you know these women, too?" Her eyes instantly filled with tears. "I'm sorry," David gently added, "you have been through a lot. How are you doing?"

Terri squeezed the arm of the younger teen standing with her which seemed to comfort her and said, "This is my brother, Bobby." David nodded at the young man as Terri continued. "They were friends of Mom's. I've known them all my life." She paused to take a deep breath and shed a few tears. "It is really nice of you to come here. I saw you yesterday, too. You helped Debra, when she fainted at the memorial service."

David hadn't thought about Terri being at either of these memorial services. How could she be handling all of this? He had no idea what to say.

Suddenly, Terri reached over and hugged him, "Thank you for being here, thank you for everything." She seemed to be handling it pretty well, he realized, and he was glad. "David, you helped Debra yesterday, would you help me today?"

"Sure, what do you need?" He hesitated but was curious.

"If you don't mind, I told Pastor Tim all about you. Would you let me introduce you? It would be a real honor."

He shook his head again. Honor, joy, hope... this was indeed a strange church. "Sure, I would love to meet this man." David walked about two steps behind the two teenagers. Everyone was talking and moving around casually. He watched as they approached the minister and the good-sized crowd around this man. He noticed that the minister was also intentionally watching everything going on around him, and that he opened a space for them near him and motioned the kids to come in close.

Terri and her brother Bobby politely introduced David to Pastor Tim. "This is the paramedic I told you about. Isn't it neat, that he's here? It's great that you can meet him."

"Just call me Tim," the man said with a smile, extending his hand to David. His deep southern drawl seemed to fit this educated, but friendly man. He looked deeply into David's eyes and David grinned as he returned the firm handshake. He had earlier tried to imagine why such large crowds would come to hear this man preach, now he understood. He's just a man ... a real man, no pretense.

Tim must have understood the look on David's face. His countenance relaxed, "So, Terri has learned how to brag. She told me that she was dying and that she came back to life in the back of the ambulance. Do you often see people rise up from the dead?"

David recognized the play on words. He laughed softly, "No, not too often."

Tim's eyes widened and were full of delight. If he had laughed as loudly as his eyes revealed his joy, David was sure the walls would have come down with the sound of it. But Tim contained himself from laughing, and David instantly liked this man even more.

Terri grinned, then excused herself; she had to return to her family. When she had disappeared into the crowd, David asked softly, "Did she tell you everything she saw?"

"Oh, I guess so. Terri isn't one to go on about spiritual things, so I'm more inclined to believe her. It was quite a testimony. I guess the proof of it is that she is still here. Do you think there was a chance she really could have died?"

"Could have died?" He paused to consider what he was willing to reveal. "I can't believe she did anything else but die. No, she really was that far gone. I thought I was watching her take her last few breaths when suddenly, she just woke up. Just woke up! It was amazing."

Tim's shoulders seemed to stretch a little, he seemed a little taller. Obviously, David's confirmation of Terri's true condition pleased Tim to no small degree. "Did you pray with the girl?"

David thought for an instant about the boldness of this man. But so much had happened in these last few days, he thought, Why not? He smiled as he looked back into this minister's eyes. "Well, preacher, I guess I did."

Tim placed his hand on David's shoulder, "Listen, she must have really scared you, if you were willing to believe her then. But scared or not, the experience is real. How have you been since then?"

This question pierced David's mind like a light in a dark room, putting the emotional roller coaster of the last few days in perspective. "I was thinking last night, after the teenagers' memorial service yesterday, that if I came today, I would get a clue to what is going on."

"Was that your question?"

"Well, no… how did you know I had a question?"

"Let's just say that most of those who come to the Lord usually have questions."

David knew there was much more than that behind Tim's knowing. "I wanted to know what the point was in trying. We're all going to die one day anyway, so why even try?"

"So then, what's the answer?" Tim asked back, catching David off guard.

"Well…" David began, and paused. He had learned something. He would try it out on this amazing man, "Well, I think the point is just that. That we are all going to die. The point is to figure out what matters while we are living."

"Go on…" Tim's eyes revealed the depth to which he honestly wanted to hear David's answer, drawing David out further.

"Yesterday, I realized that the issue with the teenagers is that they chose something contrary to life, and the result was death. They obviously didn't want to die, but they did want to have the right to do what they wanted to do, even if they knew it was wrong." David paused as he thought of this answer. "Choosing to do something contrary to life is ultimately death."

"We call that sin. Did you ever hear the scripture that says, 'the wages of sin is death'?"

"That's it, exactly. That is what I was trying to say." David dropped his eyes to the ground. "No, I really hadn't heard it before. I have never been to church before. I didn't think I would fit in. Mrs. Blake did give me a Bible, though. I'm reading John. Do you think that was a good book, to begin with?"

Tim's eyes widened as he considered the scope of what was just revealed. "David, do you like to golf?"

David was not about to figure this man out. "Yes, I like to golf, why?"

"I have several firemen that attend this church. So, I know y'alls schedule, that you have time off during the weekdays. Well, you know what they say about preachers. We do love our golf. Would you like to get together with me next week and play some?"

"Sure…" David said out loud, while his mind thought, Amazing.

"Here's my card. My phone number is on it, too. You call me, or text me with whatever dates are good for you. We'll find a day when we can both get together, ok?" Tim reached over and placed his right hand on David's shoulder. "It would mean a lot to me if you'd come and hear me preach. But it would mean a lot more to me if we can get to know one another." David picked his jaw up from the floor. He had asked himself why so many people came to hear this ordinary man speak. He now knew why. "Will I see you Sunday?" Tim asked.

"Yes," David knew that somehow Tim would see him among the crowd that would be there. "Yes, you will."

Chapter Five

THURSDAY:
SOME DAYS ARE JUST TOO LONG

Thursday morning, David drove slowly to the fire station. The sun seemed to force its way into the morning sky. Darkness fought it but lost. The colors swirled across the sky. Light had broken through. Watching the sunrise over the interstate, David's mind raced as it tried again to sort all the different emotions. The last two days had been full, and his emotions had been taken from one extreme to another. How could so much happen so fast?

Lennie, the paramedic from the previous shift, was in the ambulance replacing the items they had used. Her hands were full of IV equipment and bandages. "Nothing major is missing. We did have a backboard go with the helicopter to Tampa General, so if you get by there, you might want to look for it.

But we still have two, so you're ok." Lennie continued with her morning report.

David slipped in beside her on the bench in the back of the unit and began his morning evaluation of the equipment and supplies. "Is the unit's a/c still not working well?" David asked. "They checked it out last shift but didn't find a cause."

"Yes, it still is kind of hot in the back with the patients. The mechanics said that it would have to wait until they could schedule it to look again. Hopefully, you'll get it fixed today."

Jonathan arrived to work a few minutes late and joined the crew at the ambulance. He spoke with anger as he came around the back of the unit and kicked the rear tire, "Well, I know what kind of day this is going to be."

"So, did you wake up on the wrong side of the bed this morning?" David tried to jest with his partner, even though he knew it wouldn't work to improve his attitude this morning.

"Wrong side. Ha! It's Robert, that bastard! He threw my clothes out of our bedroom. He's such a baby." Jonathan was not going to cool off quickly. Anger was just masking the depression in Jonathan's voice.

David stopped checking out the unit and turned to face his friend. Everyone knew that Robert and Jonathan weren't 'right' for each other but, that was for Jonathan to decide. Until then, David could only offer his friendship. "Boys will be boys." David again tried jesting. "So, what did you do this time?"

Jonathan sat on the back bumper of the unit and tried to calm down and control his emotions. "I didn't take out the trash. He threw my clothes out, because of the trash."

David chuckled. "That's gotten me in trouble before, too." He began again to check out the truck.

"Well, he said the only reason I keep him around is to be my woman. He says that I expect him to pick up after me. He can really nag and nag and nag. He's worse than my ex-wife!"

"No one is that bad!" Lennie joked as she came around the front of the unit.

Jonathan laughed, "You're right, no one is that bad."

"So, do you think you'll have a place to go home to tomorrow?" David asked.

"I don't know. He's so temperamental. I'll call tonight. Probably. I know he really cares. But, he gets so angry sometimes. Sometimes I don't know if it's safe to be around him when he's in one of his moods. He really scares me." Jonathan hushed, remembering how forcefully Robert had pushed him against the wall during their argument last night and the fleeting fear he had felt. Not wanting to continue that thought out loud, he tried to lighten the mood, "The truth is that he is the one who expects me to clean up after him. It will be ok. I have put up with him for five years - and he has put up with me, trash and all." Jonathan jested, "Boys will be boys... baby boys," he laughed as he turned around and opened one of the outside compartments. "I see we are missing a backboard. Do you know where it was left?"

Two tones put an end to this morning's equipment inspection, "Rescue 12 respond to a possible cardiac arrest at 10349 Highway 41." David immediately answered the call as Jonathan threw their personal medical bags onto the unit. The day was to begin early and go late, very late.

The two paramedics rapidly walked up to the door with their equipment in hand. Just as David began to knock, a little, eighty-year-old lady opened the front door, but only by few inches. She would speak to these men from behind the chain.

David looked at her curiously, searching for clues. "Did you call for an ambulance?"

"Oh, yes, I called." She spoke with hesitation and bewilderment. That answer didn't help.

He tried again, "Do you need an ambulance?"

"I guess so. Do you think I need an ambulance?"

David looked again through the small opening in the door. He couldn't see another person.

"Ma'am, could you try to tell me what is going on? We would like to help," he added gently. He could see nothing odd inside. He spoke to her with a warm smile, trying to win her confidence. "Is there someone else inside?"

"Oh no, I live alone. I called for me." she sounded surprised that David didn't know that.

"Could we come inside?"

"I don't know. Do you think you need to?"

"It depends. What's wrong?" David recognized the attitude. She wasn't comfortable with people inside her house. He put his equipment down on her front porch. He would take it as slowly as she needed.

"I called this morning when I woke up, and I didn't have a pulse."

"You didn't have a pulse? How did you know you didn't have a pulse?"

"I take my pulse every morning. With me living alone, I'm so afraid that I will wake up dead. I take my own pulse, so I know that I will be ok. Every morning I do this. But this morning, I didn't have one." She was so serious and slightly afraid.

Jonathan tried not to laugh and forced the mask of professionalism to cover his face that so wanted to smile. "If you didn't have a pulse, do you think you would have known to call for help?"

"I thought if you didn't have a pulse it meant you were dead. I didn't want to die alone." Her voice cracked as she honestly tried to answer their questions.

David and Jonathan looked at each other. They knew this was just another call for a lonely lady who just wanted some companionship and reassurance. Now they smiled; another crisis resolved. David looked at the woman. "Could I come in and talk to you? I would be glad to check you out, take your blood pressure and recheck your pulse."

She reached up and pulled the chain off the door. "Could I put some coffee on for you two?"

"That would be nice." Jonathan walked in behind David and adjusted the volume to the portable radio he was wearing. He would monitor the radio, and if he heard that another emergency call came in near them, he and David would take it. But, if it were quiet, they would give this patient the treatment she needed - someone to talk to.

A few minutes later, she returned to the front room with small china coffee cups and a small rose covered pot with steam rising from the spout. She sat with her guests.

David looked to his patient, "Could we take your blood pressure and other vital signs? It would help me a lot."

She seemed a bit surprised by this request. "Do you think it's necessary?"

Jonathan rose and walked over to her. Slowly he reached for her hand, her wrist. As he spoke to her, he held her pulse under his fingers. "It would help." Jonathan looked at David. The look told David that her pulse was fine. He began to examine his patient. David administered the cure; he had her just talk.

After they finished their coffee, David began the process of having their patient listen to him. "Do you understand that if you don't have any pulse, that you wouldn't know to call us? That if you are afraid of being alone, you should find someone to stay with you at night?"

"Yes, but I don't have anyone. I'm all alone." Her eyes filled with tears as she began talking about her late husband. For eight years he had been gone, but the pain was fresh as she faced each day alone. Jonathan again reached over and took her hand. She squeezed it tight; she drew strength from the touch of another person. Their patient was cured. She simpered, suddenly realizing they might need to go. "Could I give you some coffee to take with you?"

David stood and walked over to the front door. "No, but we do need to go. I'm surprised that we were able to stay this long. We need to get back to the station. Call us back, if you have any pain or other medical reason to call." David accented the "medical reason," hoping that she understood that today didn't offer an appropriate reason, but only time would tell. They walked out of the house burdened down with all the equipment they had carried in.

"Sure am glad we didn't need all this stuff."

"Yes, I can't stand a code first thing in the morning." Jonathan reached up and felt for his pulse. "Help me, David, I think I am dead."

"I am sure you are dead. I have known that for a long time - brain dead." Dispatch heard the background noise of laughter as David notified them that they were back in service.

"Rescue 12 return to your station," the dispatch voice calmly replied. A few minutes later, the unit turned into the station. Before they took their seat belts off, the next call came in. "Rescue 12 respond to a possible cardiac arrest."

"Rescue 12 responding," David answered.

"Well, maybe we will be lucky – twice," Jonathan said as he brought up the map for the new address. The ambulance responded immediately.

The crew ran inside the next house with all their equipment in hand. This house had no one at the front door, so they just entered. Cries were heard from the back bedroom. Jonathan reached the bedroom doorway first. He found an older man standing near his bed, looking down toward the floor. His voice was pleading to his wife. "Please, get up! Agnes, please get up…" His voice disappeared into the void that filled the room. Sobs were hushed as the two strangers entered.

Jonathan knew what he would find. He wasn't surprised. The code began…

David pushed past the husband. Quickly, the man left the side of his wife of forty-eight years and stood silently against the far wall watching and praying. David grabbed the pink silk nightshirt of this elderly female and with a single motion ripped the shirt, exposing her bare chest. Her pale warm body remained still. The EKG machine wires were quickly placed on her chest.

Three more firemen entered the small bedroom. The husband was pushed even farther away from his wife. Tears revealed the sorrow of this man's heart as he watched his wife exposed and manipulated by these strangers, knowing there was nothing he could do to help them. He could only watch.

One fireman knelt beside her small body and placed his hands on her chest bone. David grimaced as he looked at the straight line running across the small green screen of the EKG machine. He nodded his head at the youngest fireman. At that signal, the fireman compressed the rib cage about one and a half inches. The force of the compression broke a rib and the sensation of the snapped bone shot up his forearms. The fireman grimaced. He gritted his teeth and began the count. "One – one thousand, two – one thousand, three – one thousand, four – one thousand…" The cycle of compressions began. Bones continued to snap under the weight of his compressions. He hid the inner struggle of breaking this woman's ribs, keeping his face emotionless, focused on providing the blood circulation that might save her life. A life for a few broken bones, maybe. He concentrated harder, nor wanting to go any deeper than necessary. Another broken bone, and then another. The sweat from his brow dripped onto his hands as they worked on this woman's chest. Sweat was allowed. There was no time for tears. The compressions continued. "One –one thousand, two – one thousand, three – one thousand, four – one thousand…" All the while, he could feel the stares of the husband searching his expression for any sign of hope.

Jonathan opened the airway box and pulled out a hard-plastic curved shaped tool and an ET tube. He opened her mouth and found the airway passage. He inserted the ET tube, and with one motion he dropped the curved instrument he had used to find the air passage and grabbed the stethoscope. He inserted the ear pieces into his ears and then placed its metal end against her chest. His other hand grabbed the airway bag and attached it to the ET tube. He pressed the bag, forcing oxygen into the woman's lungs. He listened to the air exchange. It was equal in loudness on both sides of her chest. He checked the sounds over her belly. It was quiet. He smiled at the confirming evidence that the tube was placed in her airway and not her esophagus. It would be her lungs, not her belly that would receive the oxygen. His hand immediately went for the tape to secure the ET tube in place.

She didn't respond to their treatment; drugs, oxygen, chest compressions, there was no change. Her color remained pink, but her heart remained still. Ten minutes, fifteen minutes, and there was no change. The pace was fast. The time seemed like seconds to the ever-watching husband. Did he dare ask? Suddenly, before he even knew he had spoken, he asked the question that every paramedic dreads to answer. His eyes were dazed, like a dream, Did the question come from him? Again, he asked, "Is she going to be alright?" His voice broke, and the question ended more like a whisper than a request for information. David heard. He looked up at the frightened husband. The man's eyes begged for the right answer. Begged for his wife. "Please."

David stood up, walked to him, then looked him in the eyes. "Sir, it doesn't look good. She's not breathing, and she doesn't have a pulse." Instantly the man's eyes filled with tears. His silence had been broken only to discover what he feared. Not another word was spoken. He simply watched through dazed and tear-filled eyes. David knew the man understood. Now he needed to return his attention back to the patient. There was little left they could do that couldn't be done en route to the hospital. Quickly, they placed the woman on the stretcher and began transport to the hospital. They all knew it was too late, but all effort was given. David watched as the ambulance backed up to the Emergency Department entrance. He looked down at his patient. In the ambulance, the mechanical chest compressor provided perfect chest compressions and ventilations causing noise and rhythm without rhyme or reason. Why does one respond to treatment and medications and another remain untouched by the power of men and medicine? There was nothing left to do but the paperwork.

The exchange of patient and treatment were given to the Emergency Department staff. The husband was taken to a small waiting room nearby. He nodded at David and mumbled something about the doctors doing what the paramedics could not. There was no reason to remove the last layer of hope this man had, but David knew the only thing left for the doctor to do was stop "the code" and sign the death certificate. Quietly, David walked outside to his ambulance. The cries were hushed for a while, but David knew they would return and did not want to be there then.

Death stood silently near the door and watched. All must come through him. This woman passed through the door of death and entered a new life. She left her sickness behind. She saw her husband as she passed through this life and into the next. She kissed his cheek and said goodbye. He could not see her. He felt nothing but loneliness and began to softly cry. She continued to follow the path of life. She knew he would join her soon and she would be waiting for him. Her love for him began to grow, until all she could feel was love. Yes, she would be waiting for him, and he will like it here. With joy, she went into the light.

"Agnes, you can't leave me. Please, Agnes, come back." He sobbed, but she could not hear. Death turned and walked out of the waiting room. He had no control of the destiny of those who passed through his doors. His task was complete. His victory was hollow for he could not claim those who passed from death into eternal life. The sting of death could only touch the living for a moment. He left the task of suffering to Loneliness who stood and began to speak into the ear of the crying man. Death's appetite had been satisfied, but only for a moment.

David walked out into the sun. Jonathan had begun the process of cleaning the unit. Paper boxes, tubes, and wires covered the floor. David said, "So much for not starting the morning out with a code."

"At least, we got our coffee," Jonathan replied as he bent over and picked up the empty drug boxes. He dropped them slowly into the trash. "Do you need to count these boxes?"

"No, I have them all recorded. But I do need to finish the paperwork. I'll be in the nurses' lounge, if you need me." David returned inside, carrying a long trail of EKG paper. It stretched out for several feet and had a single, straight line running through the middle of it. The straight line recorded the stilled heart within the body of the man's wife. This paperwork would be quick.

The ambulance pulled out of the ER parking lot. Dispatch advised them to return to their station. David turned the unit down a small side street. Its tree-lined avenue was a beautiful reminder that life went on. Jonathan ran his hand through his hair, "Let's stop at the convenience store, I need a drink."

"Sure. Where did you get that scratch from?" David saw a large cut across the top of Jonathan's right hand. His curiosity was not only out of concern; it meant more paperwork, as well.

"I cut it on the screen door as we were carrying the lady out of the house. She was so light that I didn't say anything when it happened. We needed to get her to the stretcher," Jonathan reexamined the cut on his hand. It had only bled for a moment, and that blood had been trapped below the gloves he had been wearing. "Did you notice the broken screen on the way out?" Jonathan asked.

"Yes, I saw it on the way into the house. I thought you did, too. Sorry I didn't mention it to you." David knew that they both were on guard for dangers. Sometimes they saw them, sometimes they didn't. Paramedics all wear scars from the dangers not seen.

"I'll do the paperwork when we get back to the station. But I doubt there's any point. I don't need to go to the hospital. My tetanus shot is current, and the gloves protected me from any of her blood. No chance of AIDS on this one."

"Well, just don't forget; don't even come close to another patient without one pair of gloves on. And if it's a messy one, you put the gloves on – two thick." David's voice held the tone of command. Jonathan knew he had better comply.

"Only if you stop here for a coke. I'm thirsty,"

The unit turned into a convenience store parking lot. As David began to turn off the engine, the tones again pierced the cab. "Rescue 12 respond to a car accident on Bell Shoals and Bloomingdale."

"Rescue 12 responding," Jonathan replied. "So much for my drink."

David reached over and pressed the lights on. "Looks like we're going to make up for last shift."

"No rest for the thirsty, I guess," Jonathan joked as the unit pulled out of the convenience store.

The fire engine could be seen from several blocks away. They had beaten the ambulance on scene by several minutes. The unit stopped behind the engine. Captain Madden approached the paramedic crew. "We have one girl pinned in the Honda. The driver of the other car is fine. He's standing up over there." Captain Madden pointed to the thin, pale man leaning against the fence. "Says he doesn't hurt anywhere."

"What about the girl?" David grabbed the spinal equipment as well as his medical bag from the side compartment.

"She has a broken leg, but she can move her feet ok. She denies any back pain. Her driver's side door is crushed into the passenger's compartment by at least two feet. The men are getting the 'jaws of life' ready now. She'll be free in just a minute." Captain Madden's voice was full of concentration. The three separated from each other as they turned towards their own tasks.

Jonathan reached the young woman first. He crawled in through the passenger's side window and slid in behind the patient. "My name is Jonathan, I'm a paramedic. I'm going to be with you while we get you out of here. How do you feel?" His hands softly and gently took her neck and supported it while maintaining its position.

She looked over to him. Her eyes were full of fear as she looked at him and whispered, "Will I be alright?"

"Sure, I'm here now. You'll be fine." Jonathan's voice was full of enough confidence for them both. Immediately he felt the tension in her neck relax. "Where do you hurt?"

She paused and took a deep breath. "Only my leg. Do you think it's broken?"

Jonathan glanced at the leg that obviously was bent in the middle of her thigh. He spoke, not with detached professionalism, but genuine concern. "Yes, I'm sure it's broken. Does it hurt much?" His voice began to take on a friendlier tone. "What is your name?"

"Melissa," she said, now beginning to really relax. She felt like she was with a friend and no longer alone. She continued, "No, not really. It really doesn't hurt that much now. I guess I'm too scared to notice the pain." Her voice was slowly showing signs of less fear.

"That's it exactly." He looked at her so she could see his eyes as well as feel his support of her neck with his hands. He knew he was gaining her trust. Now he began to small talk with her about what was going on inside of her body. Resolving those questions would help to calm her down. His voice took on a more professional tone, but his eyes were compensating with compassion. She watched his eyes as she listened to his words. "You are scared. But, it's nice that if you have to be scared, your body releases natural pain killers. Hopefully, we will get you to the hospital before that wears off, and you start to feel any pain."

Melissa grinned, "Well, I'm glad something inside me is working right."

David peered in the front window, "Can I get anything for you two? They are ready to cut the door." He smiled at the young patient, watching for any hidden messages of pain or elevated fear. He knew she was looking at him for strength and confidence that she was going to get out of the car all right. He took a moment to look in her eyes and give her that strength.

"Nope, we are fine. Right, Melissa?" Jonathan's question added strength to her confidence.

"Sure, we are ready." She tentatively smiled at David through the window.

"Ok, let's do it then," Jonathan added reassuringly. His kindness meant much. She wasn't afraid anymore. Jonathan gently continued manual support to her neck as a heavy blanket was placed over them by one of the firemen. Darkness covered them, and instantly the air was hot and smelly. Melissa swallowed as the car began to bounce from the force of the large, loud metal jaws that began to open slowly. They had been placed between the driver's door and its post. The roaring of the generator allowed for no further talking. Nothing could be heard above that roar and the screeching of metal being torn apart in these jaws that separated, and ripped, and separated, then suddenly snapped the door open.

Firefighter Reynolds released the metal jaws and removed them from the doorway. Another firefighter turned the generator off. The instant quietness surprised Melissa, and her body trembled in the quiet darkness that held her under the heavy blanket. Jonathan whispered in the stillness, "It's ok. We'll be out in a second now." The quiet lasted but a fraction of a second. The emergency personnel began their hum of busy communication. David reached in and removed the blanket from the two of them. And Melissa breathed deeply. Jonathan spoke gently to his patient, "Still ok?"

"I guess so. What's next?"

"Well, let me tell you what we are about to do..." Jonathan began explaining the procedures that they would use that would not only keep her leg from any further damage, but also keep her back from moving. As he spoke, pieces of equipment were passed to him. She recognized them by his earlier quick descriptions. Within seconds, she was lying on a wooden board on the stretcher outside the car.

The thought of being completely strapped in and unable to move began to frighten her. She knew that was next, Jonathan had already told her. Her right hand slid up and grabbed Jonathan's hand. He squeezed it and looked at her. His eyes were full of kindness. Sensing his support, yet his obvious need for his hand, she reluctantly let go. He continued to put traction equipment near her broken leg. He was pleased at how easily she responded to his hand for support. "This will hurt for a second," he said, "but we need to straighten your broken leg so that we can put some traction on it. But then we will find just the right amount of tension, and your leg should feel better. Ya ready?" Jonathan looked directly at her as he asked.

"No, but go ahead." She tried to be brave, but he watched as her bottom lip trembled. "Ouch! Stop that! It hurts ... Stop!" Her voice rose, then suddenly she paused as she took a deep breath. Jonathan didn't know if she was about to scream or relax. He braced himself. Instantly, she deeply exhaled and whispered, "Oh, ok, it's starting to feel better." Then she looked up at him in utter surprise and spoke in a calm voice, "Hey, the pain is all gone."

"Are you ready to go to the hospital?"

"Sure, let's go. I'll race you there." She laughed with him, as the fireman rolled her stretcher to the unit. From her head to her feet she had been completely strapped to the board, but she was able to laugh with her new friend.

David left them and returned to the driver of the other vehicle. He had spoken to him immediately upon their arrival, but now he came to officially verify this patient had no medical complaint and his desire to remain on the accident scene. The middle-aged man was leaning against the fence. As his eyes focused on David's return, he dropped his cigarette to the grass and slowly extinguished it with his left foot. His dark gray eyes begged for answers to his many questions, before

David was even at his side. David knew these questions by experience, but those questions would have to wait till after his were answered.

"Are you still alright?" David's eyes began to take in much more information than this simple question would answer alone. From top to bottom of this man's frame, David began to search for clues. The patient's skin was dry, his eyes were of a normal reaction, he didn't seem to favor one side over the other. There was no obvious sign of injury.

"Yes, I'm ok," the man's voice broke with worry then bubbled forth with his questions and fear. "How is the girl? She pulled out in front of me, I didn't have a chance to stop. Is she ok?" His face began to pale as fear began to rip at his heart. The man stood up and walked a few steps closer to David, his hands swung out wide as his palms rose into the air. "I stayed out of y'alls way. But I have to know, is she ok?"

David stepped toward this man and joked, "She won't be dancing at the next party." The man's eyes stopped and focused on the paramedic as he tried to process the meaning of that statement. David continued, "But she'll be fine. It's only a broken leg." He stressed the term "broken leg," and then watched as the muscles in the man's neck began to relax, and he took a deep breath. "She is all right," David calmly said. He knew he would now have his complete compliance. "But I can't leave to take her to the hospital until I am sure that you are ok." David placed his medical bag on the ground and pulled out the B/P cuff and stethoscope. "Can I take your blood pressure?"

"Sure, but I'm fine." After a few minutes of examination on the side of the road, and at the man's denial of injury and insistence on staying at the scene, David returned to his unit alone.

The ambulance arrived with their sixteen-year-old patient at Brandon Hospital. Before David had completely stopped the truck, a large man grabbed the back door of the unit, pulled it open and jumped in. Jonathan stood up and blocked this intruder. "What are you doing? Get out of my truck!" Jonathan was ready to jump the man regardless of who he was. And every syllable of his words contained that message, loud and clear.

"Daddy!" Melissa called to her father. Instantly Jonathan relaxed.

"Please step outside so we can get her out," Jonathan's tone was back to normal, even if his own heart rate was not.

The father, having heard the voice of his child, regained his control and quickly got out of the way, "I am sorry." His voice held the tension in check as he stepped out. A woman stood watching at the door of the ambulance. She didn't speak, but just reached out and touched the foot of her baby as these strangers pulled her daughter out of the ambulance. At the touch of her daughter's foot, a tear gently ran down her cheek. She knew, like only a mother can know, her baby was going to be alright.

David quickly spoke to the mother. "She'll be fine, it's just a broken leg. It's not that bad. Your daughter is ok."

She didn't take her eyes off her daughter for even a second to reply to this stranger. She smiled, "Melissa, you're going to be ok. Mom and Dad are here with you now." Her voice was strong.

Melissa saw her mother and Jonathan knew he was no longer needed for this young patient. He pushed the stretcher into the Emergency Department entrance. He walked a little to the side so that there would be room for the mother at Melissa's head. His job was done, except for the paperwork.

David and Jonathan returned to the unit.

"So much for more coffee," Jonathan said. "Let's get lunch! I'll finish the paperwork fast, if you go find us some more backboards." In his voice was the challenge of a race. Who would be done first? They were both hungry. David took up the challenge, and the race was on. Food would be the trophy, and both men needed to win.

The ambulance pulled into the local hamburger shop. The two men quickly ordered a large meal. As they walked to the table with their food, the tones again pierced the air. "Rescue 12 respond, Car accident at 301 and Riverview Drive. Possible overturned semi-truck."

David took the portable radio from his side. "Rescue 12 responding." David and Jonathan watched as their lunch went into the trash.

Jonathan's eyes were so sad as he looked at David in mock pain. "I am so hungry."

"Oh, well." David laughed. What else could he do but laugh? They moved quickly. Within a few minutes, the unit arrived on the scene of a Chevy Caprice versus a semi-truck hauling sulfur. The smell burned their noses. David saw the small opening in the back of the trailer that was allowing the yellow molten sulfur to pour out into the street. The firemen were already working quickly to secure the safety of the emergency scene. One firefighter held a charged hose ready to put out any fire the molten chemical might ignite. Other than the local irritant to their nose and eyes, they were in no other danger from this spill, as long as they didn't get too close to the sulfur. It would burn fast and very, very deep.

David hurried to the car and asked the driver, "Are you all right?"

Each word was slurred into the next. "I am just fine." Even with the strong smell of sulfur in the air, David could smell the alcohol rise from the man's mouth.

"Do you know what happened?" David could see that this man appeared all right. He still wore the seat belt, and the deflated airbag rested upon the steering wheel. Except for a few scratches on his nose from the airbag, this man did not appear to have a single injury.

"Yes, I do. A dog ran out in the road and forced me into that truck. It wasn't my fault." His voice rose and fell in musical tones with each word slurring into the next. The man began to unbuckle his seat belt, "Let's get out and look for the dog. I'm sure he's around here."

David shook his head, and continued his exam, his voice contained professional tones and hid the bitter humor in the drunk's excuse. "Oh, I'm sure he is. That dog causes a lot of accidents around here. Usually a little later in the night, though. You stay in the car until I have completed talking to you. I don't want you to get out on your own, if you are hurt." David scowled at the man as he tried to mimic an appearance of concern. The driver of the car remained behind the wheel as David rapidly finished a more thorough medical exam of his patient and as anticipated, there was not any sign of injury. "OK, you stay here until the deputy is done with you. Do you understand?"

"Yes, I'll stay in here. But, I don't know why you won't let me out to look for the dog."

David walked away before the man's words trailed off. Aggravation and hunger were beginning to wear on him. He walked quickly and approached the Sheriff's Officer that was handling the report. "How is the driver of the car?"

"Oh, he's just fine, A little drunk, though. He was attacked by the mystery dog." David laughed. "I wish you guys would catch that dog. I really prefer it when the drunks are drunk enough to come up with an original story."

"The funny thing about that dog of his is that no one else saw it. Not only did it cause the accident, but it was invisible, to boot." They exchanged frustrated glances and silently laughed together. The deputy asked softly, "So, what do you say, will you draw a blood alcohol for me?"

"I guess. I hate going to court though. You'll owe me." David walked over to the deputy's vehicle and waited as the deputy unlocked the trunk of the sheriff's car.

Deputy Qualmann reached in and grabbed the small white sealed box, "Well, you'll see me there too, if that's any comfort. So, it's the system that will owe you. I hate court as much as you do." She released the box into David's hands and whispered, "Thanks."

Slowly, carefully the deputy began to explain to the drunk his rights. "You can refuse to have your blood drawn here, but if you do, your license will immediately, on the spot, be revoked. Do you understand?"

"I don't know why you want to do that. My drinking didn't cause this accident. I told you, it was a dog. Don't you believe me?" the drunk began to get a little agitated. "Honey, if you can't do a man's job and understand a simple story then maybe you should get another officer out here to help you. I already told you, IT WAS A DOG!"

"Listen, I don't care about your dog story right now. We are going to draw some blood. Will you stay still?" The deputy's tone remained professional. She wouldn't give this jerk the pleasure of seeing her angry or the opportunity to justify a fight. The man didn't take well to the tone.

"I will. But, it better be quick." Vulgar insults continued to escalate as the driver focused on David. The deputy returned to her vehicle to check on the license of the obnoxious driver. Maybe, she would get lucky and find something else to pin on him.

David hoped to calm the driver back down; but David was tired, hot and hungry and his patience was shot. "Give me your arm."

Immediately, the man rolled up his sleeve and seemed to honestly be trying to calm down, "Listen, why don't you let me out of the car, and I can stand up. Then you'll have more room and I'll be comfortable." David was too tired to notice that the man's voice didn't seem as slurred as it had appeared when he first arrived on the scene, nor did he notice that the driver was constantly watching the deputy hold up his license in front of her as she spoke into the microphone.

"OK, that's reasonable. As long as you are still. Will you be still?" David was too tired to see the nervousness building in the man's eyes.

"Let me out!" He said with a tense smile. His eyes darted around looking for the deputy.

David reached over and opened the door. The man stepped out as David turned to open the seal on the white box. The deputy looked toward the street with the semi-truck. Without warning, the drunk leaned back and swung. His punch landed on David's shoulder. David yelled as he fell to the ground, striking his head. The deputy turned around to see the drunk running into the field. Instantly she radioed in for backup and began running after the man.

Jonathan jumped from the semi-truck cab, leaving the driver there alone. He ran to his partner and friend. Before he arrived at the car, David was already sitting up on the road. A small cut on the back of David's head produced enough blood that Jonathan found his heart beating faster. "David, are you all right?" Jonathan was looking around making sure the scene was safe for the two of them.

"Yes, I guess so, a little bloody though. They better find that jerk. He hit me when my back was turned," David looked up at Jonathan and smirked, "Will I live?"

Jonathan pressed his finger's against David's scalp, probing with his hands, looking for glass or road sand. "I have good news, and I have bad news. Which would you like first?"

"Depends!" David responded to Jonathan's smile.

"The good news is that you're not going to die. The bad news is that the cut isn't quite deep enough to get you the rest of the day off. The department still has you for today."

"Oh NO, that's too bad." David reached up and touched the cut. "Well, hand me some 4 by 4's to cover the bleeding."

David's mind returned to the big picture. The sulfur still stung his nose as he inhaled, "By the way, what do you have in the semi-truck cab?"

"Nothing, some mild pain where the seat belt crosses over the collar bone. That's all. The bone isn't broken, barely even tender. Everything else is OK. He does want to go to the hospital, though."

David didn't try to hide the disappointment, frustration filling every word, "He does! What for?"

"I am sure it is to build a workman's comp claim. Insurance-itis at its finest. "

"Oh, no not that dreaded disease! The insurance company would love to know of your diagnosis. Sure is a shame we can't tell them." The diagnosis humor was enough to help vent David's frustration.

"I can take care of him." Jonathan turned his eyes toward the semi-truck. "The firemen can help me get him out of the cab. You go and sit in the unit. I'll handle the scene."

"I'll be in the back, waiting on you." He slowly walked to the unit, looking at the field. It was empty. Apparently the drunk was hiding well. The three deputies had already returned to control the accident scene. They knew the K-9 unit was on the way to search for the drunk.

Soon Jonathan returned to the paramedic unit. On the stretcher was a heavy set, a twenty-five-year-old man strapped tightly to a wooden board. His eyes found Jonathan's, begging for freedom, "Do I need all this? I'm really uncomfortable."

"Sir, if you feel like you need to go to the hospital, we will need to take all precautions against possible neck or back injury. As soon as the ER takes x-rays of your neck, they will let you loose." Jonathan seemed pleased with his patient care. Sometimes doing what is right has its rewards. This patient wanted medical care; he could have it in all its glorious, uncomfortable form.

David grinned at Jonathan. "I see the patient is receiving excellent care." David opened the side door of the ambulance and headed for the driver's seat. The cut on his head had stopped bleeding. David had cleaned his shirt with peroxide while he had been waiting in the unit. Now, if he only had some aspirin for his headache.

Another sheriff's deputy walked up to the cab of the ambulance and looked in on David. "We are sure the drunk is still hiding low in the field. King will be here in a minute. He'll find him."

David rubbed his head as he laughed at the fate of his assailant, "Yes, and I bet his pants will be wet when he sees King coming after him."

"You are right. Maybe even a bit more than wet! I would hate to have that dog on my trail. I'll come by later and tell you how it went."

"Bring King with you. If that dog gets the guy who punched me, he'll deserve a good back scratch."

"Oh, he'll love that." The deputy began to shut the door, smiled with a queer grin and joked, "So would I 'big boy.'" The two men looked at each other and laughed out loud, as the deputy tried to bring some humor into a very frustrating scene.

"I hate to disappoint you, but I don't have time for a back scratch. I have a patient to drive to the hospital." David's professional tone added to the deputy's humor.

Deputy Perez closed the door on his friend and walked away. He hoped he would see David later at the fire station, that is if the call load ever slowed down. As he walked away, he doubted it would. A tired frown slowly returned to his weary face.

The ambulance transported the patient to the hospital. Thirty minutes later, Jonathan and David finished the report, cleaned the truck and were available for more emergency calls. David's headache radiated into his neck and upper back. Jonathan was just hungry. Both knew they would be fine as soon as they got something to eat and got out of the sun for a while. They only hoped. Not a word was spoken on the way back to the station. They didn't want to jinx themselves, but also, they were too tired to talk.

The unit pulled into the station. David walked immediately to his locker and pulled out a bottle of aspirin, and quickly swallowed two in his dry mouth. At the same time, Jonathan walked to the food locker and pulled out the bread, peanut butter and jelly. Jonathan's hands moved rapidly as he applied the thick layer of peanut butter to the bread. They both hoped that this lunch would be completed before the alarm would sound again.

"So," David said while his mouth chewed the last bite of the meal, "did you cure the semi-truck driver of insurance - itis?" Sarcasm, more than concern, spawned the question.

"Oh yes, I don't think he will want to go in an ambulance again, unless he really needs it. I don't understand why people think they must go by ambulance to the hospital. What is it he expects us, or for that matter, the ER, to do about such a minor bruise? I mean the whole world revolves around their opinion of what will sound best in court and, more importantly, what will gain the greatest reward from some insurance company. It's a real shame."

"No, the real shame is that this drunk punched me, and got away with it. I must be getting too nice in my old age. I should have never let him get out of that car. I should have had him handcuffed. Next time, I won't be so nice."

"Neither will I." laughed Deputy Perez. David and Jonathan looked up in surprise at the door as he, Captain Mike Taylor and King, the K-9 officer, walked into the station. King always walked within a foot of Mike's left leg. His ears were standing straight up listening for a command from his beloved friend and co-worker, Mike.

"Good, next time I'll bang you in the head if I get hit, or if I even think I see you being too nice to a drunk." David looked at his friends and offered them something to eat, "Would you guys like some PB and J with some tea?"

"No, I think we can do better than that later." Mike laughed as he watched King walk up to the table and begin sniffing at David.

"I bet he smells that drunk on you." Deputy Perez waved his hand across his nose. "You could actually smell better."

"Whatever do you mean?" David forced an old Victorian accent and smiled in mocked surprise, then continued talking to himself more than to the men present, "I would like a shower, but the way today is going, I doubt I'll get a chance."

"Hi, King, are you my Hero?" King's ears went up at the mention of his name, and he looked up at David who instantly knew what King wanted. David reached over and began petting the back of this very large German Shepherd. King turned around so that David could reach him better. "Oh, so you heard I promised you a back rub, huh." David started scratching King's back.

Jonathan laughed at King, "He really knows how to play a sucker, doesn't he?"

"Well, let's just say he knows how to get what he wants." Mike never took his eyes off his dog. "King got pretty excited out there in the field. He did a good job."

"So, I guess you mean by that, you caught the man?" David stopped for a moment to look up at Mike. King gently reached over and grabbed David's hand with his mouth and gently pulled it from side to side. "Oh, I'm sorry. I guess I wasn't done yet." David returned to King's back scratch. King turned a little more to the right.

"Not me. It was King who caught him. He went right where the man was hiding in the field. Really, the idiot didn't have a chance. We found him hiding in a ditch. He was so drunk that he didn't even realize that he was being eaten by ants. He was covered in bites by the time we got him out of there. We told him to come out, before we went in with King. King started to growl as we got close. The man came out on his knees, begging us not to let King go. Works every time."

David reached over and grabbed the big dog by his face, turned King to face him and hugged him tightly. "Thanks, King, you can come by here anytime for a back scratch. I'm glad you caught that idiot." King stood there and took the affection, his tail wagging in approval.

Deputy Perez corrected, "Oh, he was no idiot. That license he gave us at first was a stolen one. He's wanted in two states for robbery and one count of attempted murder. He wasn't an idiot, he was really scared."

Jonathan shook his head "Man, we never know what we are dealing with. Even in the simple car accidents. If he had a gun, he could have killed us all. We were thinking a simple car accident, and he was trying to find a way to escape." Jonathan looked over at his partner. "We will be more careful next time, right?"

"Oh yes, much more careful. I don't want any more of these either, don't forget." David rubbed his head with his free hand. He looked at Deputy Perez, "Pete, I do want to add my assault to the charges against that man. It is a felony, right?"

"Oh, definitely, I think it would add in quite nicely. Don't you agree, Mike?"

"Quite well," Mike added.

Jonathan immediately called dispatch, "We will be out of service for a while; we have to complete some paperwork with the sheriff's officer. I'll call you back when we are in service."

Jonathan walked over and patted David on the back. "I am going to get a shower while you gentlemen do more paperwork."

"Fine, rub it in. I get punched, and you get a chance to clean up." David watched Jonathan turn down the hallway. "Don't have too good of a time in there. I want some hot water for myself, when I get in there."

Jonathan shot back, "Well, no promises about the hot water, but I am sure I will have a good time... " His laughter was heard as the bathroom door shut behind him.

David smiled as he turned to the men, "So what do I need to sign?"

Deputy Perez pulled out a small note pad from his shirt pocket and flipped to the first clean page. "First your life history. What is your full name?" The interview was officially complete in about ten minutes.

Jonathan came back into the room with a fresh uniform. He was about 6'4" and built to wear a uniform well. His rather long dark hair fell forward and dripped onto the floor. Jonathan reached up with his right hand and pushed it back. His strong jaw and deep blue eyes accented well his total good looks. His left hand contained his shoes and socks. He sat on the sofa and King walked over to him and licked his wet arm.

"Now King, I just had a bath. Go on." King turned his head sideways at Jonathan trying to imply he didn't understand the request.

"King, come." Mike's command was quick and firm, and so was King's response. Instantly, King stood erect at Mike's side. He reached down and stroked the dog under his neck. "Now boy, you are going to have to leave them alone for a while. GO, sit in that corner." Mike pointed to the area near the TV. King briskly walked over and sat down. His eyes remained on Mike the rest of the time they were in the station.

"So, did you save me any hot water?" David looked at his partner.

"Of course. You needed a bath worse than me. Hurry up, and maybe I won't tell dispatch we are back in service until you get out." Jonathan's voice offered no guarantee that he would indeed wait.

David turned to the two deputies. "Are we done? You, of course, are welcome to stay and take a break."

"Yea, we're done," Mike answered as he turned to Jonathan and said, "I am going to take King out back and let him run a bit. He needs to burn some of his energy. Want to join us?" King's tail began to wag as he sat in his spot. "Don't you, King?" the dog sat up straighter. He wanted to leap up and run for the door, but he waited for the command. Mike walked toward the door, "OK King, Come on." Instantly, the dog was out the door and in the park area that was located directly behind the fire station.

A few minutes later David joined them outside. The dog loved to run in the field, and after a few more minutes of play, Mike called King and instantly the dog turned and was at his partner's side. Their partnership was built on friendship and trust. Mike smiled at David and Jonathan and returned to his white Ford Bronco, "See ya later. Try and take better care of your partner next time. OK, Jonathan?"

David looked at Jonathan, "When am I going to have you, Partner, trained so well?"

"Never, never! I'm untrainable." Jonathan's laughed, "If you don't believe me, call Robert."

"Well, we will keep working on it." David walked back into the station and called dispatch "We are back in service. The sheriff's officer has left."

"OK, but your supervisor called. You are to complete an incident report on the call, and one on going out of service for thirty minutes." The dispatcher spoke in a monotone voice.

"Thanks for the good news. I love paperwork," David said cheerfully, trying to breathe life into the conversation.

"The computer has you back in service." Dispatch's flat response was typical.

David ended the phone call. "So, you were right, today is a great day," David grumbled to Jonathan as he sat down in the dining area. He was tired but was enjoying this moment to relax.

Jonathan joined David at the table. "Every time Robert and I have it out, you can guarantee it's going to be a horrible shift. I think he waits until the mornings I work to pick a fight." Jonathan paused and spoke just above his breath, "He'll be fine." He looked away. "You know, that memorial service we went to on Tuesday reminded me that it just doesn't matter anyway. You never know what tomorrow holds, so just deal with what is dumped in your lap. Make the best of it."

"I kind of had the same thoughts. I really began to think about the helplessness and hopelessness of life."

Jonathan snickered. "That's a little too metaphysical for me. But, tell me, what did you discover?"

"Nothing that night. But the next day..." David's voice trailed off in memory.

"But the next day what?"

"The next day I decided to go to the funeral of the two women who died on 56th street."

"Are you crazy? Two days of seeing our dead patients? Are you into depression or something?"

"No, I just woke up with this idea in my head, that it might help me to balance the teenagers' death. So, I went. I'm really glad I did. I saw Terri there."

"The teenager that survived the cocaine overdose! She was there? That's weird. So, what happened?"

"Mostly, I met this fellow. He invited me to play golf with him next week. I thought I might go. You like golf. Would you come along?"

"Oh no, I recognize that tone. You are setting me up. Who is this fellow that I need to protect you from?"

"If I tell you before you meet him, I know you'll say no. So just come, by faith?"

"Another clue, by faith. Let me guess, he's a preacher?"

David sat back in amazement. "Oh, you're good, you're really good. I didn't even know a preacher before yesterday, So, will you come? I might need an interpreter."

"No, I don't think so. In this discovery, you'll be on your own. But the first shift after the game, you can tell me all about it." Jonathan realized David didn't understand. His voice hardened.

"A preacher being seen with me on a golf course, I think not."
He would never admit the emotional pain that came from the
rejection of homophobic people and was not willing to take
that risk with him, "You go and have a good time with your
new friend. I am going to call Robert." Jonathan walked away
from David. He whispered, under his breath so that his friend
couldn't hear, "It amazes me that you don't understand."

Jonathan paused in the hallway on the way to the back office
to call Robert. He was frozen in thought and in the darkness
of his closed eyes, he remembered the face of his father when
he had first told him about Robert. The memory of his father's
heartbroken countenance but hardened voice as he said, "I will
always love you, but I cannot accept you, and I do not accept
this choice you have made." The Words burnt like acid to the
core of Jonathan's spirit. His father had been so proud of him
until that moment, but their relationship was forever changed.
He trembled as the sadness touched his heart, a sadness he
thought no one could fully understand.

He frowned as the memory of that conversation continued.
"I did the best I could, and it wasn't good enough. I can't change
who I am!"

His father looked at him in stunned confusion, "Son, didn't
you pray about it? Surely God would help you?"

"Dad, I tried, but I couldn't pray the gay away."

"But, you have a choice."

"Sure, a choice to be celibate and never know the love
of another person or to live with someone I am not sexually
attracted to. It wasn't fair to my wife. I couldn't love her the way

she deserves to be loved. And, it isn't fair to me, to expect me to live a lie. My choice is to be honest about who I am. Can't you accept that? Can't you accept me?"

The conversation continued to replay in Jonathan's mind. He knew it destroyed their relationship because there was no bridge of understanding or acceptance that could be found. Each walked away, knowing the bitter rejection of the other would not be easily or quickly overcome. If ever... Years later, and it still had not.

Jonathan shook his head and walked to the office. He tried to force his mind off these painful memories. He had hoped five years ago when he allowed himself to give in to his sexual attraction to men, that these feelings of loneliness and isolation would have ended, yet they had not. They had only increased. He knew his father's fears drove a wedge of rejection between them, fueling the lie that God also had rejected him. He keenly felt the damage his own self-hatred had inflicted upon his soul.

Jonathan sat at the desk trying to think about what he would say to Robert, but David's new-found faith stirred his own memories of his personal spiritual awakening and discovery of God. He lowered his head and drew a deep breath. Jonathan smiled as he began to remember what it was like to feel accepted and respected by his father, by his church, by himself and his own faith in a loving God that had been so important to him as a young man. Within him a Voice spoke, this One spoke of dignity and of truth remembered. It was only a whisper, yet Jonathan could hear this still small voice. He relaxed as the image of a conversation with other teenagers in his youth group replayed. "Religion is man's attempt to reach God, that God will love you if you are good enough, if you comply.... but Christianity was supposed to be about God's attempt to reach Man. That Jesus was about sin no longer separating you from God. That God wants a relationship, not another religion." Jonathan had longed to hope this was true. He had wanted to believe it then, he wanted to believe it now. Deep within, he felt a peaceful invitation to hope again; however, he turned his heart away because he feared that he would never know an inward acceptance of himself or his life as long as those who loved him could reject him so completely. He forced his mind to turn and listen to what he thought was the voice of reason.

The Voice of God's Spirit was quieted by Jonathan's choice, and Rejection jumped at the opportunity to stop this potential reawakening of his captive. It beat him, torturing his soul and it provided the entrance way to Loneliness and Shame. The Voice of Rejection and Voice of Loneliness stepped forward to whisper their deceit and lies into Jonathan's ear. One Dark force strengthened the other as they marveled at their strength and drank from the well of inner suffering caused by Jonathan's agreement with their lies. Rejection strengthened the lie that Robert alone accepted him and what he was born to be, and Loneliness bound him to the fear of what it would be like alone and rejected. The pain of the past and the fear of the future were always their greatest weapons of inflicting damage on the human mind, and their tactic had worked again. Together they continued the torment of memories relived. Jonathan believed their demonic lies and whispered in his shame, "My father is the one with the problem, but that doesn't matter. I embarrass him, and I can't change." Surprised at how much it still hurt, he decided to just forget about it.

He wanted to remember something satisfying, and his mind raced to the scene where he first met Robert and tasted of the sweetness of forbidden fruit. He remembered the pleasure and believed it alone was powerful enough to numb the pain of rejection and loneliness. Sexual Desire now spoke, and his voice was one that Jonathan recognized and had always liked to listen to. This time was no different. The addiction of sexual satisfaction numbed Jonathan to the cost of the destruction of his own soul and did it with the powerful intoxication of desire fulfilled. These strengthened lies blinded Jonathan to the control and manipulation of Robert and then reminded him of the pleasure that Robert offered. Jonathan knew he would apologize to the man who alone could quiet the raging thoughts within his mind.

The demons sneered as their attack caused Jonathan's decision to appear so rational. Jonathan told himself that he was in control, He called Robert. As Jonathan hung up the phone, the stronghold of depression gripped him again and advanced its conquest through the wilderness of Jonathan's wounded soul. The war within his mind left his self-esteem desecrated and his mind captive.

The alarm sounded for the next call. Jonathan arose from the desk, and instantly his own needs were forgotten. Within eight minutes, Rescue 12 arrived on the scene of a sixty-year-old man who was having chest pain. Jonathan knelt beside the man who was laying on the living room sofa grabbing his sweaty chest.

"So, tell me about the pain?"

"It started about two hours ago. I thought it was gas. I tried Rolaids, but it didn't help at all. I tried a nap, but the pain got worse, and I couldn't sleep."

"Do you feel short of breath, too?" David questioned.

"Yes, that's when I started to get worried, and I called you guys. Do you think it's my heart?"

"Could be, but don't worry. Let us check you out first. We can help." David stood over the patient and placed the EKG wires onto his chest. The machine revealed that his heart was ischemic, suffering without enough oxygen. Extra heart beats were being generated by his heart that was already beginning to die. David watched as the patient's heart would begin to race with wide unnatural electrical beats, then suddenly return to a normal rhythm. David looked over at Jonathan. "Let's treat him in here, before we take him out to the unit."

Jonathan nodded as he reached into his bag. Not a word of concern was passed on to the patient. They each wore a mask of confidence to encourage him. David placed on the man's face a small clear mask that flowed with oxygen. Jonathan established the IV in the bend of the patient's right arm. Blood was drawn into small glass vials for the hospital. Lab results of the blood would be done immediately to confirm any damage being done to his heart. The pain from the IV wasn't acknowledged by the patient. He just wanted some relief. David held a small aerosol can of medication, the size of a breath freshener. "Sir, I need to spray a little of this medicine under your tongue. Have you ever taken a Nitro before?"

The patient whispered, "No." His breathing was becoming more labored.

David's tone remained the same, "It can take about five minutes for this medicine to reduce the pain. Let me know as soon as the pain has changed, OK?"

The man nodded, but the movement made the room spin. His pain was growing worse. He grabbed his chest tighter with his left hand and tried to take a deeper breath. He looked into the eyes of these strangers in his home. His eyes were filled with pain and fear as they pleaded to these men to hurry with their treatment. The paramedics watched as their patient's color began to match the color of the white walls of the bedroom. The sweat on his brow was turning cold. Every second counted. Everything the paramedics did now could either save dying heart muscle or be the last thing this man ever heard or saw before he died. No one in the room knew which it would be.

Jonathan knelt, reached over and took the man's right arm and placed the patient's hand against his own thigh. He placed the B/P cuff around the man's upper arm and began to inflate the bladder within the cuff. When the gauge read 200, slowly Jonathan began to release the air. He was listening for the soft 'thud, thud, thud' that could be heard from the stethoscope he had placed on the pulse point found at the bend of the patient's arm. The sound began at 170 and continued steadily as the cuff deflated of air, until the gauge read 110. Then there were no further sounds. "B/P is 170 over 110. He's tolerating the Nitro well." Jonathan stood up and returned to the ambulance to get medication from the locked compartment.

"Are you allergic to any medication? How about Novocain, the stuff your dentist uses?" David asked.

"No. I don't think I am allergic to anything," the patient answered.

"I'm giving you something for those extra heart beats," David said as he slowly gave lidocaine through the IV, then he looked directly at his patient. "Is the pain better?"

"Some, not much. It is better, but I feel like someone is standing on my chest," the patient said, still grasping his chest with his left hand.

Jonathan walked swiftly to David with a syringe full of clear fluid and softly said, "Here's the morphine."

David took a moment and read the words on the side of the syringe to verify its contents. He gave the medication to the patient through the IV tubing as he said, "This should help your breathing, as well as your chest pain." The man just nodded. David touched the patient's arm gently. The patient thought that this paramedic was just giving some needed emotional support, and he began to relax. David silently noted that the patient's skin was already beginning to dry and wasn't as cool.

Rescue 12 continued the medical treatment as they transported the chest pain patient to the hospital. The paramedic's care had already begun to reduce the permanent damage done to their patient's heart. The patient may remember the care these men gave, but this call was quickly out of their mind. The routine paperwork was completed at the hospital.

As the unit pulled out of the hospital, David tried to pick up their conversation they were having before this call. "So what did Robert say?" David knew he was leaving the door wide open.

"I don't want to talk about it." Jonathan's tone was rather matter of fact. He didn't reveal any emotion.

"OK. So, why don't you want to play golf?" David was trying to change the subject. He didn't know that they were the same subject.

"You don't get it, do you?" Jonathan squirmed in his seat. Why was David stirring up these old emotions? Jonathan had thought this part of him was dead.

"Get what?" David wasn't about to let this one drop too. He knew it was his turn to be there for his partner and return the favor and explore Jonathan's emotions.

Two angels stood watching; Charis, the one who had been assigned to Jonathan long ago, and the other, Rapha, had only recently arrived. Rapha said, "Look at how well David is doing, He doesn't recognize the voice of the Spirit in him, yet he freely walks in this direction. He is naturally sensitive to the voice of the Lord." The strong warrior shared with his co-laborer, "We have been told that Jonathan will have a great war soon, between us and his own appetites. We need to find a way to strengthen him before battle. He needs the strength of intercessory prayer."

"Yes, but who? Who will pray?" Charis knew that this would be the first in many thoughtful considerations.

"How about his father?"

"His father, he has believed a lie. He believes it is hopeless. His prayers about his son, that I might add, are constantly going up to the Lord, are full of fear for Jonathan's soul and resignation for his own failure to help his son. His prayers are weak because they are filled with doubt and not faith. We know that prayer strengthens humans. It builds their confidence in God's goodness and sovereignty. But, prayer is also a weapon in Spiritual Warfare. Those prayers will help free us and strengthen us to accomplish their intercession to their Father. Without their faith in prayer, their words will accomplish little. Jonathan's father's prayers express love. And the Lord always listens to love. But, to move, for us to be made strong, we need their faith added to their prayer." His voice tightened. He considered the men before him, "Maybe, Jonathan could use the prayers of David."

"David? He is but a babe in Christ. How could his prayers give us the strength we need?"

"It doesn't matter how old he is in Christ. Christ is ageless. The only thing that matters is that he has the faith to believe that God rewards those that seek him, then the Spirit is free to bless them." The Warriors knew they had found the key, "It is God that makes us strong in battle on behalf of His children."

Rapha considered, "David, how will he learn to pray?"

"Let us teach him. Teach him through Jonathan. It will be a real stab to the Adversary for us to use Jonathan. And every time Jonathan remembers, it also strengthens him. This will work." The face of Charis glowed with anticipation.

"Get what? Boy, aren't we nosy today!" Jonathan snickered at his friend. He knew David wasn't trying to be rude. And they both knew he felt better after he talked about things. "Well, I told Robert that he was wrong. That if I wanted a woman, I would get one. He should just leave me alone, take me for what I am."

"What did he say to that?"

"He said that he thought I had a real problem. A problem too big for him to bother with. He told me I better figure it out fast. That if I didn't, I wouldn't like the way he handled it. You know, David, sometimes he scares me." Jonathan turned to look out at the view of the distant horizon. The colors were vivid with blues and purples as the sun began to set over in the distance. "Aren't the colors magnificent? I love the sunset. It is so beautiful." Jonathan lightened his tone. It would be easier to talk about it if he didn't have to deal with the heavy mood. He needed time to think.

David looked toward the west. The purple streaks swirled through the reds and orange. "It looks so royal with all that purple. I bet it's wonderful at the beach."

"The beach, that's what I need right now, especially with the warm gulf stream water. I could use a good swim in the ocean."

"Me too. Jan and the kids are going to the beach this weekend. I might join them on Sunday." David turned to Jonathan. "So, what are you going to figure out?"

"I figure I'm going to have to face the fact that I'm really not happy with Robert. I don't think I'm really happy with any of my life right now." Jonathan turned to David and questioned himself honestly. "Doesn't sound right, does it? Me, not being so sure of myself?"

"You haven't been sure of yourself in a long time." David couldn't resist the opportunity to jab at his friend. "Well, I'm not so sure of you either."

"Oh, OH! I'm hurt. Call 911 I have been cut ... cut to the heart ... " Jonathan grabbed his chest and fell forward in mock unconsciousness.

David reached over and pulled the imaginary knife out of Jonathan's back. "I've got it. I saved another one."

Jonathan sat up and laughed again. "So, you haven't been sure of me. Well, I'll bet tonight after midnight, and you can't even find an arm, let alone stick it with an IV that you'll be sure of me then, won't you?"

"Oh sure, bring up the fact I don't seem to wake up well after midnight. I do keep you around for something, that must be it. You do start a quick IV. Here, take the knife and use it on me tonight, if I miss one." David took his right hand and held it out to Jonathan.

Jonathan reached over and picked up the invisible knife and laughed. "I'll do just that."

"But, I won't miss."

"We'll see," Jonathan pretended to place the knife in his pouch he wore on his pants' belt.

"So, what are you going to do?" David again returned to the subject.

"I don't know. Maybe I'll use this knife and kill myself." Jonathan patted his pouch again.

"I don't think so." David took his eyes off the road for a second and faced his friend. "You better not. Don't even think about it." His eyes returned to the road.

Jonathan was quiet for a few seconds. "I just don't seem to have the heart to leave Robert. It took a lot out of me after I got the divorce and Robert and I got together. I lost people I thought were my friends, and most my family treated me like crap. The family are all ashamed of me; even now after five years. They just can't accept my life, and the reality of being gay. I just don't think I could start all over again. And every time Robert brings me to the point of breaking, he switches and then can be so charming." Jonathan smiled, remembering how attractive Robert could be. "Sometimes, it feels like a game of cat and mouse, and I am clearly the mouse. Sometimes, that scares me, other times it can be fun. Most of the time, I just feel crazy and too drained to make the changes needed. It is hard."

"Yes, but I know you aren't happy now."

"So, to change the subject, how are you doing on the 'happy now' category?"

David honored his friend's need to change the subject. "I don't know how to say it. But..." he paused and grinned, "I'm happy. Happy on the inside. I don't know how else to say it." David glanced at Jonathan, who suddenly was wearing a big smile.

"Happy on the inside. Wow, it really did happen for you!"

"Do you know what I mean by that? I don't. But, it seems like I don't understand a lot of emotions I'm beginning to experience. So, teacher, teach me."

Jonathan grinned at his student. "First, have you finished the book of John in the Bible?"

"Yep, finished it last night. Incredible book. I don't understand it all. But, Mrs. Blake liked it a lot. You should have seen all the underlined parts. It was great."

"What are you going to read next?"

"Well, what do you think? I still don't understand that prayer thing. Got anything that will help that?"

"Got it on both counts. Since my name sake did you well, why don't you read the book that was mostly written by a guy named David. The book is a collection of songs and prayers. As a matter of fact, the name Psalms means songs. Read Psalms."

"Hey, that's perfect. So how will that help my prayers?"

"Just find a chapter that best fits your mood and pray it. Make it personal, as if it really is from your own heart." Jonathan leaned back in his chair. "They are really beautiful. The thing I really remember most is not only their beauty, but that if David felt mad at God, he said so. And, if he felt angry with someone, he asked God to wipe them out. The honesty is great. Sure is a shame most people aren't so honest."

"So, God didn't get ticked at David for getting mad at Him."

"No, that's the amazing part. The prayers are often two-sided. Like, if David spoke his part right to God, then God answered him right back. That's how some of the prayers are recorded. Some of the other recorded prayers, you can tell, just flowed out of David. The key to prayer is to tap into the direction of God and then ask Him. God will even help you by giving you direction on how to pray and sometimes even the words to say. Prayer gets really powerful then, sometimes even prophetic. That's what I think happened to David. His prayers were not only poetic, but often prophetic."

"Incredible!" David remembered his earlier attempts at prayer that seemed so real but so strange. Suddenly he understood where it had come from. "Do you think we can just pray like that? Like it comes to us?"

"That's the point. Prayer is just talking and listening; basic communication. That's all."

"Does it make a difference?" David felt the answer to this question in his own heart. Suddenly, he knew it did. He looked at Jonathan to see what he thought.

"I guess. But, not always. It's not like you get everything you ask for. Good thing, I figure. If most people got what they asked for, then their God would be nothing more than a vending machine. And, who needs that. He is supposed to be in charge."

"But, then why even bother to pray at all, if you don't know for sure He will answer your questions, as well as your problems?"

"Well, there are certain prayers that you can really believe He will answer, and just trust that He will work it out for you. Do you remember reading about that in John?"

"I did. Jesus said that you could ask God for anything in Jesus' name and it would be done." David paused. "But you said certain prayers ... Like what?"

"Oh, like help to do what's right - like asking for help for a friend, or for that matter, even an enemy." Jonathan's voice began to trail off. His mind was beginning to remember, to consider and weigh his thoughts. "The key is to ask yourself, 'Would love allow this thing I want, and can I believe God will do it for me?' If you can answer yes, well then, just believe He will do it. He probably will."

"How about healing? Do you believe He will heal?" David remembered his first encounter with God and with prayer.

"I guess so." Again his voice trailed off.

Both men stared ahead as the ambulance continued up the road. It became very quiet as they silently weighed through the thoughts and questions that this conversation developed. Jonathan couldn't shake the thoughts about prayer for help. The thoughts kept coming to his mind, and he tried to keep pushing them back. But, deep inside his heart, he remembered and longed to be free again and to be the man he once was. He wondered if there was any hope, if he could ever find his way back home. It seemed such a long way.

David considered the matter, and suddenly had a thought, If God could heal, by such a simple prayer, then He could help Jonathan. David had an idea, a homework assignment. He laughed to himself; he doubted his teacher would like to know what he was going to pray about. The quietness allowed each man to strengthen his own heart. They were each listening to the voices within.

The unit pulled into the station. The two men walked to the supply room and began the process of restoring their supplies. The night hours continued, and both were quiet as they sat and considered the conversations of the day. The TV provided the diversion necessary to keep them from continuing their discussion with each other. They both watched the TV and at midnight, went to bed.

Jonathan looked over at David as he slipped into bed. "So, do you have anything you need to do in the morning?"

"Nope, just staying home with the kids. Why?"

"I just wanted to see what our odds were of a good night's sleep." Jonathan turned over in his bunk.

"They're great, just great ... Good night." David turned the light off. Darkness surrounded them.

Depression carried a knife. He held it out to Death. "I have cut him with the knife of rejection. He wants me to take him. Oh, Death allow me to take his life."

Death took the knife and touched the dull blade. It would pierce the man, but at great pain. "Go ahead. I will watch. Enjoy your reward. Take him."

Depression grabbed the knife. He walked toward the man who lay quietly on the floor in the small dirty bathroom. Dean awoke. He cried, again. Alcohol had drowned his reason. He was left with nothing but pain. "No one likes a failure. You are a failure. Save yourself the pain. Take your life, it is worth nothing anyway," Depression whispered as Dean cried. "Look in your pocket. Take out all that you have." Dean took out his wallet. Nothing was left. He had no job. His wife had left him. He had nothing. "But, you do. Look at that pocket knife. See how sharp the blade is. See how well it would cut." Dean held the knife in his right hand. The silver metal reflected the little light in the room. The knife was beautiful. It was carved on the blade with the images of deer and trees. "Wouldn't it be nice to go back there? Remember how peaceful it was. Wouldn't you like to be at peace again? There is only one place that will offer that." Again, the drunk cried. All he wanted was peace. Maybe, a little love ... understanding. Maybe, a job. Depression coiled his hands around the knife. He held it up before the drunk. "Do it. Do it now!"

Dean turned his eyes away from his left wrist at the moment he pierced his skin. The knife slid gently and was held steady by the determination to find peace. His gaze returned to his left wrist, and he watched as the scarlet colored fluid rolled down his arm. The stream fascinated him, "Wasn't it interesting?" He was surprised at how detached he seemed from it all.

"Take the knife in your left hand. Cut your right wrist deeper this time. It will be strong enough to go back and do the left arm right. You are able to do one thing right, aren't you?" Depression laughed at the drunk, laughed at his stupidity, laughed at the notion that death would bring him anything close to peace. Depression mocked and scorned, but the drunk heard nothing except the promise of peace to come.

Dean took his knife in his left hand and noticed a small drop of blood had stained the steel blade. This time, he cried at the sight of his blood. He could hear the laughter of all those who said they cared, only to watch them turn their backs on him. Their laughter haunted him, pressed him on. "They will be better off without me," he cried, then inhaled deeply, "And I would be better off dead." He held his breath and tightened his grip on the knife as he plunged it into his right wrist and drew the blade upward, toward his elbow. The dark red blood freely flowed. Quickly, he took the blade and repeatedly cut into his left wrist. He exhaled as he watched the blood pour into his hands. The warmth and wetness soothed his drunken mind, and he fell asleep, knowing he would die, and the heartache would finally end.

Guilt began to haunt him in his drunken slumber. Depression kept his grip upon his mind. Gradually these violent Voices awakened him, and he wept at his failure at dying quickly. Again, he picked up the knife from the pool of blood on the floor and placed it against his wounded right wrist and cut again and again and again. He would find peace he thought, "Surely I could do this one thing right," he cried in anger and disgust. The alcohol and blood loss gradually calmed him as the tears ran down his face. He whimpered and fell asleep against the bosom of depression. Depression laughed.

Two tones pierced the silence as the lights came on in the firehouse bunk room. David sat up in bed. His mind focused as he heard the call being dispatched. "Rescue 12 respond to a man down in the bathroom at the Showtown bar on Highway 41."

The two men rose and went to the ambulance. "Rescue 12 responding," Jonathan answered dispatch, turned the lights on and pulled out of the ambulance bay. "Another one." Frustration choked at Jonathan. "I really hate going to that bar."

David stretched as best he could from behind the seat belt. "Me, too. Look for the Sheriff Deputies. I don't want to go in until they get there. Last time we got into quite a fight."

"Absolutely." After a few moments, Jonathan pulled the ambulance near the front door of the bar, right behind the parked car of a Sheriff Deputy. The fire engine parked behind them and three firemen followed them inside.

David and Jonathan were greeted by a group of very drunk men and women as they entered the dark bar. One grabbed David's arm, but released it quickly when he saw the expression of impending harm. He bellowed out, "I was the one that found

Dean. He's my friend." His voice raised and slurred, and his spit landed on David's arm. "You gotta save him." Then he began to cry.

Another drunk came up behind Jonathan, "Get in there, what's taking you so long? He's dying!" This drunk grabbed Jonathan by his left arm and pulled him off balance as he jerked him into the hallway.

David turned toward Jonathan, and his arm immediately went around the throat of this drunk and squeezed. "You let go of my partner or your friend will lie in there and die! Do you understand?" His voice held no room for compromise. The drunk released Jonathan, and all the others backed off a few steps behind these paramedics.

"Now, lead us to the patient," David said.

The large, slightly embarrassed drunk led them through the dark, dirty bar. David watched the faces of the other patrons, looking for any further sign of danger. His adrenaline was making his heart pump rapidly. His eyes raced from face to face.

Four men in dirty jeans and baseball caps remained entertained by their game of pool. They did not look at the paramedics as they passed behind the pool table. One player reached across the table and casually made his shot. As David and Jonathan continued down a short hallway, they could see two deputies. One was asking a short fat woman, who had also had too much to drink, about what she knew. Both deputies stood with their muscles taut and their faces slightly pale. By their expression, David knew he was about to work on someone.

David turned into the doorway of the bar's restroom and found a man slumped down between the toilet and sink. His left arm draped over the seat, blood dripping, slowly dripping into the toilet, his right arm resting in a large pool of dark red-brown blood on the floor. It had the consistency of partially gelled Jell-O. The man's skin was sweaty and pale, slightly yellow in the poor lighting of the filthy restroom.

David quickly put his gloves on and felt for a pulse at the patient's neck. "He has one. It's weak though." Jonathan was already reaching into their equipment bag for bandages. "Hey, wake up!" David called to the man before looking to the deputy. "Do you know what his name is?"

"Just his first name, Dean. Do you think you can wake him up?" "It would make the paperwork a lot easier."

"I bet." David turned back to Dean. "Dean. Wake up!" His tone was forceful, attempting to penetrate the sleep. It wasn't working. David took his right hand and balled it up in a fist. He placed his knuckles against Dean's breastbone and pressed very hard. "Wake up!"

Suddenly, Dean's left arm rose from the toilet and swung at David. "Get off me, you jerk!" Dean's voice was angry and slurred. David's left hand caught Dean's wrist. The warmth of the blood passed through the glove. The blood did not.

"Back off. We are here to help you. Don't hit me." David wasn't surprised by the swing. As a matter of fact, he was pleased that the sternal rub had worked well to wake up their patient.

"If you wanna help me, leave me alone! I wanna die." Dean weakly continued to struggle to free his left hand.

"I am sorry, but I won't allow that now." He was trying to use a lighter tone to help Dean calm down. "We're here, and we're going to try and save your life."

Death watched. Depression looked up into the face of Death, "What is stopping you? Why is this drunk still alive?"

"I have my own time. I want this man to suffer. I want him to fight me. He will learn that I will win," Death's words were slow and deliberate.

"Who are you talking about? Surely not My token." Depression was not laughing anymore.

"No, you fool. That paramedic, look, over there in the comer. Do you see his strongmen, waiting to be called on?" Death saw Depression's expression grow weaker. "Don't worry. I got approval to take your pawn before we began. I knew before we started that I would win. But, not without working this fool paramedic." Death sneered. Depression found some strength from Death's confidence.

Dean continued to struggle, "I don't want your help. Leave me alone." He took his right arm and swung it at David. His legs found strength and kicked. David was trapped by the space in the little restroom. His arms took the punch. He fell back into the hallway. Jonathan and two Deputies jumped onto the thrashing drunk. One deputy took the left wrist, the other took the right. Each began to press until the pain stopped the drunk. "Let me go! You have no right to stop me." Dean wasn't calmed by his pain, just controlled for a minute.

"No! You don't have the right to make us watch you die. We'll help you, whether you want it or not!" one deputy yelled, "Stay still!"

Jonathan pressed his shoulder against Dean's chest. Blood covered Jonathan's clothes. His hands found another tender spot. "Now stay still." Exhaustion did what pain could not. Suddenly, Dean fell asleep, the sleep of unconsciousness. His head rolled back and hit the toilet. He did not respond to the pain. Sleep would bring him rest, for a moment.

"Come on, Jonathan, let's move while he's asleep. I won't wake him up this time." David reached behind the patient and hugged him. Jonathan placed the patient's arms into David's hands. Jonathan grabbed the patient's legs and they began to carry him down the long narrow hallway. One of the firemen went before them to pull the stretcher from the ambulance.

David and Jonathan carried the bleeding unconscious patient in their arms through the bar. Again, the men at the pool table didn't turn to look. They had no interest. The crowd at the door started to surround David and Jonathan. "Get out of our way!" Jonathan yelled at the one who had grabbed him earlier. "Get them all out of our way!"

The drunk jumped at the chance of redeeming his honor. He grabbed at his peers and threw them back, "You heard the man, get outta the way."

Jonathan looked up into the face of David and grinned. "Well, at least we have one drunk who learned his lesson."

"Let's just get this one tied down before he wakes up again." David's voice was strained under the effort of carrying the unconscious patient. Once outside, they placed the patient on the stretcher. The man didn't move at all. He lay still without the slightest bit of restraint. "I don't like that, not one bit. He should have woken up by all that moving." David reached up to the patient's neck and took a quick pulse. "Jonathan, it is really weak. Get the equipment ready to intubate him. "

"While you get the IV, I know." Jonathan looked at David and winked. He walked over to the compartment with the oxygen equipment.

David took a large bottle of peroxide from the shelf. He poured it slowly over the patient's upper arm, trying to clean a site for the IV from all the dried blood. Dean's pale arm revealed no blue veins. David felt for some small tube-like structure under Dean's skin, a vein. Nothing. David poured peroxide over the other arm, looking, again nothing.

Jonathan stepped into the back of the ambulance with their medical bag that the deputy had returned from the restroom. "Having any problems?" Jonathan noticed the one cleaned arm and the other looked no better. He turned and opened the sterile packaging from around the ET tube and placed it by the other airway equipment. "I've got the airway equipment ready now. He's still breathing well. Do you want me to wait and see or just tube him now? I don't think he would tolerate a tube, just yet." Jonathan was talking as much to himself as he was his partner. David didn't look up. He just mumbled something about waiting. Jonathan watched as David searched for a vein and in good humor mocked, "Just let me know if you need any help with the IV."

David twisted in the cramped space of the ambulance, and the open bottle of peroxide fell off the seat next to David and landed on Jonathan's foot. "Oh, I'm sorry, Jonathan. Did I get you?" David smirked as he blindly stuck a large needle into the upper arm of his patient. The patient jerked his arm back. The needle was pulled out by the movement and blood oozed out of that blown vein. "Well, I guess that's an improvement. We did get a pain response. Sure wish this one would help me a little and stay still when I stick him for the IV next time!"

Jonathan placed his hand on David's shoulder in playful condescension said, "Now, if you don't get it this time - I will."

David took another blind attempt at the patient's arm. Nothing was seen, but he could feel a small vein under the skin. The needle slid into the vein, and blood instantly filled the chamber. "So, I guess, I woke up," he said, enjoying the humor that eased the stress of watching their patient dying despite their best efforts. Once the IV fluid was attached and flowing into the secure site, David looked up at Jonathan and held out his hand expectantly.

Jonathan reached into his pouch and ceremoniously pulled out the imaginary knife that he and David had joked about earlier today and grinned. "You won, good job." He pretended to hand it to David and then more seriously said, "I just wish the patient would wake up again."

David nodded in agreement. Together, they quickly wrapped tight the patient's bleeding wounds with sterile pressure bandages and his arms were tied to the stretcher to avoid the risk that he would wake up again and want to fight. A fireman drove the ambulance to the hospital so that both paramedics could stay in the back with their patient. Each man was hoping for an improvement. Each watching the heart rate increase, but the blood pressure decrease. Their efforts weren't working.

"I am going to wake him up again. It might help raise his blood pressure." David placed his balled fist on the patient's breastbone. He pressed it, while he called to Dean, "Wake up, wake up!" Dean moaned and fought to move. His arms and legs were secured to the stretcher. His eyes opened. David and Jonathan were pleased, thinking the inflicted pain had worked to revive him.

Suddenly, while David was still bending over and rubbing the patient's chest, the patient sat up, and vomit was hurled onto David. The smell of beer and bologna filled the unit. David jumped back and cursed his patient who quickly had fallen back against the stretcher. The verbal assault fell on deaf ears.

Jonathan cleared the patient's mouth of all the remaining vomit with the suction machine near the head of the stretcher. "He has almost stopped breathing."

"But, he still has a weak pulse," David glanced at his shirt, as he rubbed vomit from off his own face and checked for the pulse with his other hand. "I guess I'll have to wait to clean up."

"Yep, and he got you good. It's all over your back, too." Jonathan laughed at David's predicament. The smell was awful, and their eyes burned in the presence of the nauseating odor. David grabbed the Ambu bag and ventilated the patient. Quickly, Jonathan reached for the prepared curved blade and ET tube and slid them both into their patient's mouth. The patient didn't respond to the tube placement. There was no further vomit. Jonathan took the Ambu bag from David and provided the controlled ventilations for his patient throughout the rest of the transport.

David started the second IV, and large quantities of fluid poured into the patient's arms. He contacted the ER by radio and advised them of the patient's change in condition. The trauma team was notified and placed on alert. "If we could get there in time," David murmured, "he still might be alive." There was nothing else he could do but watch the man die. David sat and watched and waited for the ambulance to arrive at the hospital knowing this would not end well for this patient.

Death watched. Slowly, slowly this token's blood poured out. There was his sacrifice. Dean's blood did not carry enough hemoglobin to satisfy his body's organs need for oxygen. The clear fluid that the paramedics were administering was flowing into his body, but though it contained liquid and minerals, it didn't contain hemoglobin. His brain and kidneys began to shut down. Organ by organ Death was claiming his prize.

The ambulance arrived, and somehow the patient had not coded and was still alive. The E.R. Doctor came to the patient with scissors in hand. He cut off the tight bandages. Blood spurted out and hit his lab coat. His gloved hands instantly grabbed the wrists, and with the pressure of his own hands, he held the artery from further bleeding. The blood oozed out past his hands and onto the floor. The ER trauma team continued the fight with Death for this patient's life. The battle was now theirs.

Jonathan removed his blood-soaked stretcher from the busy room. David disappeared immediately into the bathroom. He faced himself in the mirror. In his hair were pieces of bologna, and his clothes stunk of bologna and beer. He removed his shirt. He cupped his hands and filled them with water, letting the water wash over his arms, then he placed his head under the running water. The warm water only seemed to heighten the smell and burn his tired eyes. –

Slowly he finished the process of removing the obvious vomit from his body and breathed deep as he thought of the full shower he could get at the station. He looked at his watch and talked to his image in the mirror, "3:00 in the morning. What an awful time. No wonder I'm sleepy. Who could think at this time in the morning?" He rubbed his wet and tired face as he left the ER restroom. The hope of a shower and a bed was the only strength he had to draw on to get him back to the station. David walked out to the unit to find Jonathan cleaning the floor, and mumbled to Jonathan, "I am ready when you are."

"Give me five minutes, and I'll be done. The fireman who drove us to the ER went back to the station already." Jonathan picked up a sheet and threw it to David. "Why don't you make up the stretcher and help me and we can get out of here too?"

David was too tired to talk, so without a word, he placed the clean sheet on the stretcher. As they left the ER they heard a code called in the O.R. They both knew who had just died. Without saying a word to each other, they just walked to the unit. It was completely quiet on the way back to the station.

Jonathan fell asleep before his head even hit the pillow. Only the odor that clung to David gave him the strength to stay awake long enough to shower. The warm water splashed David's face. Over and over he scrubbed his head yet the smell would not completely leave, the odor reminding him of his failure to save the man's life. He stood facing the spout. His stomach turned. Sleeplessness and stench were causing nausea within. He could not completely cleanse himself of the smell of bologna even though the dried vomit slowly washed down the drain.

The sound of the water was drowned by the sound of two piercing tones. "Rescue 12 respond to a car accident at 1-75 and Big Bend Road." David fell forward onto the shower wall. He inhaled deeply as he reached over and turned off the water. Thirty seconds to get to the truck. Where was he to find the strength for speed? He rapidly clothed his mostly wet body and ran to the unit. Jonathan had already taken the call.

"David, it's for a car accident on Interstate 75 and Big Bend Road."

"Wonderful. What's the odds of that being minor?"

"Not much." Jonathan drove the unit to the call as David buttoned his shirt, then combed his dripping wet hair. David watched the fire engine drive down the road before them.

"Well, at least I don't have to map it. I don't think my eyes could focus on the screen." David rubbed his tired face, trying to rub off some of his exhaustion. These two men would simply follow the big yellow fire truck with their red lights on. They were awake enough for that. They hoped.

On a side street across from the fire station, sat a late model car. The young man behind the wheel watched, considering all his options. He rubbed his throat and knew he felt trapped on both sides. The police were looking for the dealer that sold the drugs to the teenagers that died, and his supplier had warned him that no mistakes would be allowed. He needed to escape the risk of being caught, and he had decided that inside that station was the key to his escape. The junkie he had shot, could have said something to the paramedics. *Why did I tell the junkie I was on the way to Tommy's party? Did he tell the paramedics? Maybe not, the cops haven't arrested me yet. I have time to make this right before they figure it out.* Joey sat and watched. He waited ...

The bay door opened, the ambulance and fire engine pulled forward, and the emergency lights were turned on. No one was left at the station. As the emergency vehicles pulled into the dark street, the garage doors began to close behind them, and a dark shadow slipped into the station. The intruder was able to enter unnoticed. On the dining room table was a large red logbook which was open. It contained the fire station documentation of who was working each day, and the location of each emergency call they responded to.

Within moments he learned all he needed to know. He closed the log book. The same ambulance crew had been sent to both Tommy's party and to the junkie, and they were the two paramedics working tonight. Joey sat back and took the first deep breath he had taken since this nightmare began. He could fix this. He could be safe. It was going to work out, he was sure.

"Rescue 12 cancel your call. Canceled by the sheriff on the scene. No injuries."

David grabbed the microphone. "Rescue 12 Canceled." David looked over at Jonathan, "Wonderful. The only thing better than no calls is a canceled call."

Jonathan laughed with exhaustion and agreement. "Yeah, but we're going to have to go all the way down to the next exit before we can turn around and go home."

"Just, take me home," David began to unbutton his shirt. He planned on beating Jonathan to sleep this time. "I have to get to sleep."

The sound of the garage door opening so soon for the returning emergency vehicles alarmed Joey and he quickly hid in a supply closet before he was seen. Anger seized the young dealer. He could kill two birds with just one stone. He hid in the supply closet as the two paramedics walked into the bunk room. He would end this threat and end any chance of his discovery. He could kill these men now and silence his fear. He took another deep breath and drew his gun out.

Neither of the paramedics knew who won the race to sleep. Their sleep came quickly but left almost as fast. The lights and tones again came on in unison, "Rescue 12 respond to a pediatric with fever at 9822 Gibsonton Drive."

David jumped up from the bunk by reflex to the sounds. His eyes began to focus after he was about halfway down the hall. His right shoulder hit the comer wall as he turned to walk outside to the truck. He rubbed his burning red eyes. The button at the top of his shirt refused to button because his hand refused to follow any commands from his hazy brain.

"Rescue 12 responding," Jonathan held the microphone and stared at the garage door as it opened. These few seconds allowed his body to dump just enough adrenaline in his system to provide him the hope that he would be safe to drive.

Joey watched as the two men left. He slipped out of the side door into the night. He was angry yet had the information to complete his task. He knew the names and addresses of these paramedics from their red log book. Angry, and determined, he left.

Not a word was spoken by the two paramedics. Maybe, they would get lucky twice. Maybe, the call would be canceled. The unit sped down the empty road, the red lights again reflecting off the morning fog.

"Rescue 12 on scene," David mumbled into the microphone.

The two paramedics walked into a small red brick house. Every light in the house was on. There were three cars in the driveway. One car was up on blocks. The other two were blocking the entrance door in the carport. David lifted his heavy boxes over the hood of one of them as he walked straight into the house.

A twenty-five-year-old white woman met them at the door then walked barefoot over to the kitchen table and sat down. She motioned for them to go to the back bedroom. The table was covered with dirty dishes, and dirty clothes were piled up high against the small dining room wall. She sat there, drinking her coffee, obviously drowsy and also intoxicated. David stopped at the table, "What's going on? Where is the child with the fever?" She just motioned to the back room and said nothing to David as he continued down the hall to find the reason for the call.

David looked around the house for any further clues to what he might find for a patient and for any dangers as he walked down the hallway to the back bedroom. As he entered, he found a three-year-old boy sleeping in his bed. He walked over to the child and noticed no sign of distress. Jonathan placed his hand softly on the back of the child. The child did not awaken. The child's skin was slightly warm to touch. There was nothing else out of the ordinary.

David put the heavy boxes of his equipment down and walked back to the mother. Before he fully reached the kitchen, he spoke out, "Why did you call us?" His tone was not as pleasant as normal, a little harsh.

"He has a temperature. Can't you tell?" Her tone was nonchalant.

"Sure. But, why did you call?"

"I ran out o' Tylenol. I thought y'all would give me some."

David took a deep breath. His hands tightened into balls. He forced himself to calm down, control his tone. "Ma'am, we don't carry Tylenol. And if we did, that isn't what 911 is for. Did you feel like this was an emergency? How high is his temperature?"

"I don't know. I can't figure out how to use those thermometers. But, I can tell he's hot. I gave him the last of the Tylenol 'round noon. Figured it would be enough. But, he just keeps waking me up. So, I figured I would call y'all. I need to get some sleep, you know." She looked at the two men and was slightly surprised that they weren't agreeing with her decision to call, and she couldn't quite figure out what their problem was.

David knew that remaining angry would not help him get to bed any sooner. He lowered his voice and slowed his words down. "Ma'am, has he had any other medical problems?"

"Nothing special, I guess."

"How about throwing up, lack of appetite, pulling his ears, diarrhea?"

To each question, the mother just shrugged her shoulders, no. Then she looked up over her steaming cup of coffee, surprised. "I think I saw 'em pulling on his right ear. But, he really didn't complain about it."

David looked at this mother. "How long has he had the fever?" Each word was drawn. He would remain professional.

"About a week, now."

Jonathan looked over at David and took a deep breath. They suspected she wouldn't follow up later with a primary care doctor, even if the child had one. "Listen, he needs to see a doctor. If you want, we'll take him to the ER." Jonathan paused, "or you can take him to his own doctor this morning."

"I don't wanna go the doctor. I only called for you to give me some Tylenol. I ain't got no money to pay a doctor. I just want some Tylenol."

David knew he needed to think of this child. "Listen, he needs to see a doctor. We'll just take him to the ER since you called, and we are here. Please." This might be the child's only chance to get the antibiotic that he may need. Now, if only he could just convince this woman.

"Well, if ya take him, which hospital will ya take him to? I don't want 'em to go to any other hospital but St. Joseph's. That's where he was born."

David's face paled. "But, ma'am, that hospital is forty-five minutes away. The one down the street is more than able to handle a prescription for antibiotics." He reached up and rubbed his face. The pain in his eyes was barely comparable to the steam in his ears.

She shrugged. "It's either St. Joseph's, or he'll just stay home."

"That's it?" he said, but by the look on her face, he knew there was no changing her mind, no matter how much it would be a risk pulling the rescue unit out of service for just a courtesy transport. "Is that your final decision?"

Frustration mounted as he faced this choice. They would be tied up on this non-emergency transport, and that would mean that if another emergency call came in for their response area, the arrival time would increase. The next available ambulance would be responding from a longer distance away. Someone may die because she wanted some free Tylenol. What a choice. She might not care, but David did.

"Yep. I guess I have to change my clothes. I don't want to go there wearing this. I'll be right back." She slowly got up and walked into the first room on the left side of the hallway. The door shut as Jonathan leaned against the kitchen table.

David walked into the back room, with each step frustration melted as he focused on his little patient. As he picked up the small child, the boy turned and hugged him. The child remained asleep, resting peaceably in his arms. David walked out to the ambulance slowly as to not awaken the warm and tired little boy. Jonathan followed quickly behind, loaded down with multiple medical boxes. At least at this time of day, he knew he could drive fast and with little traffic delay.

The mother came out of the house with a cigarette hanging from her mouth and an outfit that was no cleaner than the one she had on a minute earlier. David looked over at Jonathan and shrugged as she climbed into the passenger's seat in the front cab of the ambulance. She flicked her cigarette onto the ground as she closed the door to the unit. The only thing left to do now was to drive fast and hold on tight.

Two hours later, the ambulance pulled into the fire station to find Carl and Pete, the oncoming paramedics, sitting at the kitchen table, reading the paper and enjoying their coffee.

Carl lifted his eyes to watch two very exhausted men walk through the doors. "I see you got to make up for your last shift when you slept all night." He chuckled but then was genuinely curious. "So, what else did you do yesterday?"

"A code in the morning, a minor car accident, a suicide attempt..." Jonathan added, "that was apparently successful. We heard he died in O.R."

"Well, at least he didn't die on you. Two codes in one day would have been too much," Carl added. There was no comfort in his words.

"And, of course, a few abusers. One little old lady who wanted some attention, and one mother, who needed some attention." David added a caustic accent on the word attention as he thought of the mother who allowed for her son's suffering.

"Yeah, some attention and some gray matter. She has no brain," Jonathan added with sharp insult.

"So, you didn't like going to St. Joseph's?" Carl smiled.

"It would have been fine at 5:00 p.m. yesterday, but 5:00 this morning was just a bit much." David was too tired to hide his frustration.

"So, it sounds like a normal day. What equipment is missing?" Carl changed the conversation so these two exhausted men could finish and go home.

Jonathan answered, "Nothing. It's all restocked, just leave the back doors of the unit open for a while. It kind of stinks in there."

Carl looked up at David. "So what perfume are we wearing today?"

"Eau de Bologna," David smirked as he walked to the back office. There was too much paperwork to complete to continue this banter.

"Great! One of my favorites." Carl laughed as he stood to walk out to the unit to inspect it and prepare for his shift. "Well, at least you guys get an extra day off. Remember the shift trade. You are off til Monday."

Jonathan and David found the strength to smile at that reminder as they left the fire station to go home as quickly as possible. Hopefully, they were awake enough to make it home without falling asleep.

Chapter Six

FRIDAY:
LIFE AND NEAR DEATH

D
avid walked into his house past his wife, past the two
children watching cartoons, and he fell on his bed
asleep. The morning hours passed slowly as the two
little ones waited patiently for their father to awaken.

He tossed and turned in bed. His body was exhausted, but
his subconscious wrestled with rising emotions and struggled to
reveal truth to his mind that would remain when he awakened.
His dreams took shape; water flowed down the mountain
hitting the rocks below, each drop singing, dancing upon the
rocks. Clean, pure water flowed down and quickly became a
stream, then a river that gradually expanded into an ocean. The
sun burned against the sea, the water rose up to the sky and
clouds filled with water. A Voice in his dream spoke, "David,
David: My Love is like the water, going down to the lowest

places and returning to me. My love is like the water, it cleanses and refreshes. My love is life. My love always gives."

David awoke and barely remembered the strange dream, yet was amazed by the indescribable joy that remained. A smile crossed his face, not the smile he usually wore at work to hide pain, but this smile came from the warmth that heals pain. His habit was to quickly replay the emergency calls from the day before, then bury the pain, and remember the laughter. But, this morning he felt embraced by a tangible love that he could feel; its warmth touched his spirit, and his mind seemed drawn to the memory of his conversation with Jonathan.

"What is he running from? How could he know so much about this Christian life and still run from it? Why would he? Why does he feel such rejection?" David thought. He enjoyed this new spiritual sensitivity he was feeling and wondered why he had never known it was available to him. He wanted this for his friend, "Dear God: Please let Jonathan feel this. Let him feel this love, this acceptance..." he continued to pray. Faith entered the room and Peace greeted his friend. Together these ministering angels strengthened David as he interceded.

Later he noticed the time, "2:00 p.m. Did I sleep that long?" he whispered as he sat up and rubbed his face. His hands smelled of bologna and that smell, so soon after awakening, caused bile to rise to his mouth. Without thinking, he quickly jumped out of bed. Instantly, a sharp knife-like pain pierced his lower back and shot down into his thigh and ended near his left knee. He bent forward and stretched his lower back, trying to stretch the spasming back muscle. His right hand pressed against the small of his back as he reached into the night stand beside the bed, took out a pill bottle and placed two large, yellow, oval pills in his dry mouth. As he walked to the shower, his steps were measured and slow. He held the handle to the door, and then he questioned, "Why do I keep working a job that is killing my back?" David thought of his family and how he continued to lift the patients and heavy stretcher at work. "That was really the job of a younger person, one with a strong back," he paused and smiled to himself, "and a weak mind." As the shower water pulsated against his stiff back, David's body further relaxed, and his pain settled down. A few minutes later, he looked at himself in the mirror and grinned. He knew why he worked as a paramedic and knew it was worth the emotional and physical injuries. *We save lives and make a difference. And that is enough, it is more than enough.* He was now ready to face this day.

A few minutes later, as David opened the door from his bedroom and entered the family room, two happy children bounced toward him, "Daddy, daddy go back to bed! We are fixing you lunch!" Matthew reached up and jerked his father's arm. "Daddy, I am making you something. Go to bed. I bring it to you, OK!" His eyes sparkled in pleasure.

David smiled even as the pain shot down his back, he slid his son's arm off his in such a way that Matthew would not notice, "Now, Ace, what are you fixing for me?"

"Daddy, it's a surprise. Go to bed. I bring it to you." Matthew liked being called Ace, that meant he was the best.

Tiffany giggled as she grabbed Matthew and pulled him back with her to the kitchen and looked at her daddy, "Go on. Do as you're told," David recognized his wife's tone in the voice of his giggling little girl. He knew he better obey. He turned and walked to the room. He wiped mayonnaise off his sleeve as he shut the door. His stomach soured as he guessed at what his lunch would be.

A few moments later Tiffany opened the door to the bedroom. "Lunch is served," her back was stiff and her head straight, but as she said "served," she broke into laughter. David obediently walked to the table. He was ready for his feast. As he sat down, he saw his lunch. Before him were two bologna sandwiches. One had as much mayonnaise on the outside of the bread slices as it did on the inside, the other was placed perfectly centered on the plate. Beside this was a cold glass of beer, the smell of which sent bile racing to his mouth. David swallowed and rubbed his mouth in mock hungry anticipation of his lunch. His children were watching his every move.

He picked up a sandwich in each hand. The children watched to see which he would eat first. David looked at them and then looked again at their gift. He laughed as he stuffed both sandwiches in his mouth at the same time. A large bite from each sandwich was gone, as he quickly placed the sandwiches down and swallowed. The children laughed with joy and ran off to play with something else. David swallowed again. He picked up the beer and placed it to his lips. The smell reached his nose before the drink entered his mouth. He sat the glass down and stared at it. He knew that would be a bit much after last night. He stood up and walked to the sink, watching to make sure the kids were out of the room. The beer bubbled as he poured it down the drain. The smell lingered for a while. He rinsed the glass out and poured water into it. David returned to the table and finished his lunch. The water helped him eat the meal. He laughed as the kids returned to the table to see how he was doing.

A thought, a Voice, entered David's mind, "That is what My love is, I regard the greatness of the love that prompts a man, rather than the greatness of the achievement."

David stopped. He looked around. He had heard a thought. He knew it was a thought, but, it spoke to him, not from him. David looked at the eyes of his children. Their eyes revealed the same thought. They were pouring out perfect love, and he saw the answer in their eyes. They had given him the best meal he could have ever eaten, because it was out of the greatness of their love for him, not in the greatness of their achievement.

David looked at his children and thought to himself, Did this thought come from my mind or from their eyes? He called them to him. Immediately, Matthew jumped into his lap, and Tiffany ran to stand next to him. He held them tight within his arms as Love poured out of him and surrounded the children and himself. He felt that warmth of love again, and so did the children. They were quiet for at least two minutes enjoying their father's love. Then Matthew looked over at Tiffany and stuck his tongue out, pulling from his front pocket one of Tiffany's Barbie doll shoes.

The sight of the little pink slipper caused instant yells from Tiffany. "Daddy, Matthew stole my shoe and hid it from me!" Tiffany yelled at her little brother, "Matthew, I asked you where it was, and you said you didn't know!"

Matthew looked up at his father, then shrugged his shoulders, "I guess I just found it." He handed it to his sister with a bit too much pleasure.

Tiffany grabbed it from him and ran out of the room. "I'll get you for this, Matthew!"

"Ace, you are going to have to work on your acting ability. No one believed that one. Now, leave your sister's stuff alone." Matthew looked so surprised at David's correction, then laughed as he ran outside.

David was left alone for about one minute. Jan came into the kitchen carrying a box of equipment. "Do you want to go with me and the kids this weekend? Mom is going to meet us at Indian Rocks Beach at 11:00 a.m."

"I might. Jon and I swapped our shift, so we are both off on Sunday, but then work on Monday. Maybe I can join you Sunday afternoon."

"Why not come on Saturday?"

"I think I want to go somewhere Sunday morning, first."

"Oh, got a hot date?" Jan laughed.

"Yeah, actually I do. With a guy named Tim."

"Oh No! You've hung around Jonathan too long," she playfully responded. "Who is he? I don't know that name."

"If I told you, you would probably drop dead here in the living room. And, I worked too hard yesterday, to work a code on you this morning. Besides, the kids need their mother." David jested as he walked over and hugged her. He began to race through the possibilities. So much had happened recently. Where should he start?

"OK, who is he?" she grinned.

"I met the pastor at the funeral I went to on Wednesday. I liked him. He asked me to come this Sunday, and I thought I would."

"You told me Wednesday morning that you would let me in on what's going on in you. But, that is just weird. Why would you go to church? What is going on?"

David pulled her to the sofa and gently kissed her. "Ok, let me tell you from the beginning…"

Tiffany ran into the house, yelling, "Daddy, this guy came up to me while I was outside playing. He wanted to know if this is where you lived. I told him it was. He just looked real angry and drove off. Daddy, I didn't like that guy. He scared me."

David walked over to Tiffany. He had learned from too many years on the street not just to let things go. "Sweetheart, what did the guy look like?"

"He had on a yellow shirt, and he looked mean." Tiffany looked up to the ceiling and was trying to concentrate.

That information wasn't much help. "Did he look old or young?" He whispered to Jan, "Would you go out and check on Matt. I am sure he's fine."

"He is a big man, but not as old as you." Tiffany was honestly trying.

David could tell he wasn't going to get enough information to help, so he decided to just calm her down. "Tiffany come and sit in my lap." David held out his arms to her. He sat forward on the sofa as she approached him. Tiffany ran and hugged him. He reached over and rubbed the top of her head, playfully and comforting. "So, the man left, right?" She nodded her head. "So, there is nothing wrong now, right?" Again, she nodded her head. "And, I am here if he comes back, right?" This nod was larger than the others, and her grip was a little less tight. "And, I will protect you and Mommy and Matthew, right?" Tiffany smiled really big and reached over and hugged him tighter, realizing she had nothing to fear.

"I got it. So, we are OK." Tiffany started to squirm on his lap.

"No, not OK, you are about to be eaten by a big monster." David's tone changed. It held back laughter as it mocked danger.

Tiffany recognized the game. "OH NO, I see him now." Tiffany began beating the top of her daddy's head in mock defense. He reached around and grabbed her belly and began to tickle her. She laughed out loud. "Save me, mommy, save me." She laughed as she pulled away and ran a few steps toward her mother.

David acted like he didn't see which way she went. He turned and stalked her toward the kitchen. Tiffany seized the moment and snuck up behind him and leaped on his back. "I have you now, Monster. You're mine!" she giggled.

David reeled around and acted as if he was trapped by her weight. She began to tickle him on the neck with one hand

and beat him with the other. David yelled out in mock horror. The monster rolled over dead. Tiffany seized the opportunity to improve her position on her captive. She ran around and jumped on her daddy's belly. David gasped for air, it was hard not to laugh, but he controlled himself; after all, he was a dying monster. He growled and hollered, then laid still.

Tiffany laughed as she bounced on the dead beast's belly. She then got up and placed her little hands on his cheeks and kissed him on the nose. "Wake up, Now! It's OK!"

David partially opened his right eye while the rest of his body remained still, "I am so dead, I think I will need two kisses to wake up." Tiffany beamed and kissed him again. His legs shook, then his arms. Suddenly he was back to life, ready to take his next victim, which just happened to be his last. He growled. Tiffany giggled as she punched him in the belly and ran into her bedroom. David rolled over to his belly, then lifted himself off the floor. He growled and went toward the imaginary scent. As David approached her bedroom, the door slammed shut, and little giggles were heard on the other side of the door.

David turned to hear his victim yelling, "Daddy, where are you?" He let out a loud roar and entered her bedroom. The door remained open as the laughter and roars erupted throughout the house.

That night David's family went to bed early. Even the children went without much of a fight, anticipating the beach the next day. David tried to sleep; however, he had slept so late that afternoon that now it was impossible. He thought he might find the book of Psalms and read, hoping he might capture those warm feelings he had felt earlier in the afternoon. He slipped out of bed and walked into the living room. It was dark and private. No one would disturb him now. He went to the sofa and read for a few minutes, then he turned off the table light and sat quietly thinking. He enjoyed the dark as he mulled over all the events of the last few days, letting his mind settle before he returned to bed.

It started with the emergency call that had begun this adventure, then quickly moved to the people involved. First, he remembered the dead kids, then he remembered Terri and her mother. How could such an ordinary looking woman such as Mrs. Blake, possess such power? His thoughts slowly replayed the scene and the conversation. Terri had not only talked about seeing Jesus, but that she had seen demons as well. David paused as he began to consider that matter. All those demonic movies he had watched, they worked to scare him and the rest of the audience because no matter how educated you were, something deep inside lets you know that demons are more than a possibility, more than a probability, and definitely something to fear. *Could it possibly be that human beings are in a war with creatures that we can't see? Could it be possible, that Evil is a presence and a power? Could it be possible, that the evil we fight is not with men, but with the evil behind the men, controlling the men?* David was amazed at the possibilities. Could it be ...?

As he sat there in the quiet darkness, he heard a sound from the window above the washing machine in the laundry room. Instantly he knew it was the sound of an intruder. David's mind raced. In his bedroom, locked away, was his only gun. It was too far away. He was not in the kitchen, so he had no access to a knife. He sat there listening; the quiet and darkness were no longer a comfort. Slowly, David got on the floor. He began to crawl to his bedroom. He wanted to reach his gun and his phone.

The intruder entered the living room. David silently lay flat on the floor, hidden by the coffee table. He watched the intruder walk toward him, then past him, toward his bedroom. David's heart pounded. The adrenaline coursed through his veins. He remembered Tiffany's warning this afternoon. *Why didn't I take more precautions?* He was filled with fear as he watched the intruder, with a gun in hand, walk through the house. Sweat began to form on his forehead. He was trapped. He watched the intruder step into the kitchen, then into the dining room. The intruder was now far enough away that David began to crawl out from behind the coffee table and follow him into the next room.

The intruder felt the door of the bedroom. Slowly, he opened it up. He looked inside and saw the bed where Jan was lying, sound asleep. The blankets and pillows covered what could have been mistaken for David. David watched in horror.

He planned on jumping on the man as he entered the bedroom doorway. There the furniture and small space would somewhat control the intruder's free movement. David eased closer, closer, watching for the right moment. But, the man did not enter. He stood at the doorway for several minutes, watching, listening.

David felt nauseous, his head spinning for lack of a deep breath. Cotton formed in his mouth. He had to wait for the next move and hoped that the intruder would just chicken out and leave. He hoped that he would be able to protect his wife. He knew he would die trying, if necessary. David crawled a little closer.

The man slowly raised the gun and pointed it at the bed. Horror seized David. He stood and leaped onto the intruder a second after the gun exploded. David couldn't believe that the intruder shot the gun without even entering the bedroom. The intruder was obviously shocked by David's attack. David grabbed the gun in the intruder's hand and held the man's arm up toward the ceiling. The intruder's knee hit David on his side, knocking him forward, but David did not release him.

The light came on in the bedroom. Jan yelled in fear as she saw the death fight in her bedroom doorway. David, seeing the light, yelled out, "Call the police, NOW!" His voice broke, and his strength was giving way to this younger, stronger man. The light surprised the intruder further. Anger seized him. He had failed. He had to get out of there, now. The intruder freed his hand from David's grasp. The gun fell to the floor, and instantly David lunged for it. The intruder took the opportunity to run fast.

David reached the gun, grabbed it and followed him. He stopped and aimed at the back of the intruder. Shoot, Shoot. His heart demanded justice, Kill the guy! His mind tried to focus on this man's back. Suddenly, as his hand began to pull the trigger, another thought flashed in his mind: If you shoot, the bullet will go through the wall and kill Tiffany. She is awake and leaning against her door. David froze for a second. He wanted to stop his attacker, but he couldn't take a chance. David lowered the gun as he watched the intruder run through the laundry room door and heard him as he slid out the window. David returned to the bedroom. Jan sat on the bed crying.

David lowered the gun, but couldn't put it down, and walked over to her, heart pounding as he spoke. "Are you all right?"

"I called the police. They will be here in a minute," her voice was broken with her sobs. "Have you checked on the kids?"

"I saw the guy come in, he walked straight to our room." David held her hand. "He didn't come close to the kids. They are all right. I'll go look in on them now." David stood up, but she wouldn't release his hand. He turned to face her and said in bewilderment, "Jan, he was only a kid."

"I am coming with you." She had regained control.

David smiled at his wife. "So, you can protect me?" They stopped and hugged each other. Jan mumbled some nervous words as she walked to the kid's hallway. David held her hand tightly.

Jan opened Tiffany's room. Two large white eyes stared at her through the dark just behind the door. Jan grabbed her child and turned on the light. Tiffany's relief caused her little body to shake. David sighed deeply and then walked down the hall to his son's room. He slowly opened the door. The streetlight outside cast a pale blue light upon his sleeping son. David chuckled softly as he closed the bedroom door.

Returning to his wife and daughter, David held them both tightly as the tears flowed. "I love you," was whispered from one to another, with such depth of meaning that together all their fears began to flee.

There was a knock at the door. For a moment fear returned. Jan looked at David, then they both realized that it must be the police. David released his arms from around his wife and child. Instantly, Jan took one hand, Tiffany the other, and the three approached the door, turning on each light in the house as it was passed. The police identified themselves and entered. They immediately took the gun of the intruder from David and saw that the serial number had been filed off. The officers proceeded around the house, confirming their safety and looking for clues.

It was a standard 9mm Glock. Two bullets were missing from the clip. Two shells were found on the floor at the doorway to the master bedroom. One shot had struck the pillow and entered the bed. The smell of gunpowder hung in the air. A small hole was located in the ceiling above the doorway. The officers glanced quickly at each other. David recognized their look because he and Jonathan often spoke to each other with such glances. David knew that to these men this was just another call; nothing out of the ordinary and no one was hurt.

The two officers worked on their paperwork while sitting at the dining table, then tried to comfort David with their hollow words. One officer said, "The intruder was probably just some kid looking for drug money, and since he almost got caught here, he shouldn't return." The other officer tried a suggestion, "Maybe, you should consider a Security Alarm system." The officers didn't seem concerned that the kid shot before he entered the bedroom or tried to find things to steal. They just re-emphasized that the important point was that everyone was OK. Their paperwork completed, each officer walked around the house one more time, then they left for their next call.

David stood on the porch as he watched the officers drive away. Quickly, he walked into his bedroom and stretched to reach the box on top of the shelf in his closet. Slowly, he unwrapped his own 9mm Glock, realizing he owned this type of pistol for the same reason his attacker did. They were so reliable and easy to use. Looking down at his pillow, he thought, "*and so lethal.*" He held it up and fixed the sight on a flower arrangement in his bathroom. A grimace crossed his face as he slowly lowered the gun.

Jan returned from Tiffany's room and gently sat down on the bed and picked up the bullet clip. It was also wrapped in a soft yellow cloth. "Maybe, the kids are old enough now that we can keep the clip in the gun and keep it immediately available?" She spoke these words in fear. Her suggestion brought David away from his vengeful thoughts.

"Do you really want to?" David anxiously asked. He knew that most honest people and their children were shot with their own guns, far more often than by an attacker's gun. He had seen too many children killed by accidently playing with what they thought of as off limit toys. He repeated the question. This time the tone in his voice was not that of the fear of a returning intruder but the fear of continuous Danger from a loaded gun, "Is it worth the risk?"

Jan considered the tone in David's voice. She had heard him talk of what she knew was only a few of his calls involving gunshot injuries to children, "No, no. We will leave it up there," she said as she pointed to the closet shelf. "But, for a while, leave the clip in it. I'll call Monday about a Security System, though. I'm here too often alone, while you are at the station."

David nodded in agreement and then put the clip in the chamber of his 9mm semi-automatic pistol, "Tonight, we will sleep with it in reach."

Jan looked around her bedroom. The damage to their sense of security was far greater than the ruined pillow and bed. "At least, that was all that was lost." She rubbed her hand against David's pillow. "He would have killed you if you were in bed." She paused and looked at David, "Where were you? Why weren't you in bed?"

David placed his arm around his wife's shoulder. "I was up, thinking. You know, I started to tell you this afternoon about what is going on inside me. I wanted to tell you. You know I really love you and..." At that word, Jan reached over and hugged her husband. David continued. "I was up thinking about God." He paused, "About Evil and about the evil that makes men do evil things. I had gone to bed when you did, but I couldn't sleep. Something inside me kept drawing me to the living room, to think about these things." David stopped and took a deep

breath, it felt good to be honest with his wife. "I can't believe
that if I had stayed in bed, I would be dead. David suddenly
noticed his daughter standing at the doorway and spoke to her
gently, "Hey Tiff, you need to go back to bed."

Jan squeezed his hand for a moment. "I will stay with Tiff
until she sleeps then I will come right back. Go back to the sofa
and rest. This time, just do your thinking while you're within
reach of your gun. We will be fine."

Wide-eyed, Tiffany was staring around the damaged
bedroom while listening to her parents. She quickly took her
mother's hand and wondered if maybe in the morning she'll
wake up, and this will have been just another bad dream. She
was glad that mommy was going to sleep with her. She kissed
her daddy and slowly returned to her room.

David returned to the living room and lay on the sofa.
He stared up at the ceiling. Darkness, light, darkness light;
the light from the lamp caused the ceiling fan to project five
long shadows across the ceiling and wall which prompted his
thoughts of light and darkness, good and evil. He rested in the
freedom of thought and then he remembered a chapter in the
book of Psalms he had read just before the attack. That writer
had been sure that God would deliver His people. David picked
up the Bible on the end table and flipped through the pages
until it landed on the 91st chapter of Psalms. He read it again,
and this time he was amazed at how these words so perfectly
reflected what he had just experienced. He thought he should
do as the David of the Bible would have done; he would thank
his God with the knowledge that his God had protected him.

David sat up and bowed his head forward and clasped his hands together. He spoke out loud, "O God, you protected my family. Thank you, thank you!" David's eyes filled with tears again. He smiled at the thought that he had cried more in the last few days than he had in his entire life, then he whispered again, "Thank you." David looked up to see Jan standing in the hallway, looking at him. He rubbed his face and grinned at her.

Jan walked into this now holy room, speaking in a whisper, like she had done as a child, when she was in church. "David, what has happened to you? I have never heard you pray before. I didn't think you knew how." She came and sat beside him.

David took her hand. He looked at her; thanksgiving covered him like a warm blanket. He knew Jan would be pleased. He would share with her what he had discovered. He laughed in advance. David shared it all. He shared his heart.

Jan sat on the sofa and watched David as he spoke, never so amazed in her life. She listened. She began to remember. "David, I never told you this before. It never seemed important. But, when I was a little girl, my mom and dad went to church, but they got too busy with work. They got too busy, and I guess they thought it really didn't matter, because they always were morally good anyway. But, they never seemed as happy after we stopped going, like something was missing. David, when I was a little girl, when I was in a Sunday School, I asked Jesus in my heart, too. I just forgot about it when I grew up. But, deep inside me, I always remember. Kind of like a whisper you hear, coming from a far-off place, always calling me back, reminding me. David, I would like to have that voice as more than just a far-off whisper, more of a close friend. That is what they told me was available, something you have found, something I know is for me."

David was shocked. Were all those around him aware of God, yet unwilling to talk about it, unless they are pressed into it? David remembered his prayer that he had prayed with Terri in the back of his ambulance. If a teenager, nearly dead on cocaine, could introduce him to God, then surely, he could pray with his wife. It seemed logical. He smiled as the thought that nothing seemed logical to him anymore floated through his mind. He liked it better this way. David squeezed Jan's hand. "Well, let's do it together. Repeat after me: Dear God: ... I am sorry that I chose to forget about you... Please forgive me... Please be the Lord of all my life... of all my decisions ... Amen."

David added, "P.S. Thank you for protecting my family. Amen."

..... Another battle was won in the kingdom of Light.

Death left this house. He reeled in the knowledge of the significance of this loss. Failure produced the vomit of disgust in his mouth. How did his loss of another attempted murder end in the rededication of one of the Good One's lost children back to Him? Death went to find the human captive of Anger. He would die painfully. The intruder would die for his failure.

A few hours later, Matthew came into the living room to find his mommy and daddy sleeping on the sofa. He went over to his father and pulled his daddy's eyes open. "Daddy, is breakfast ready? I am hungry!"

David pushed his son's hand away from his face and eyes, "Matthew, it's not ready quite yet. Could you go back to bed for a minute, until it's ready?"

Matthew recognized that trick. "NO, I am hungry. I want to eat now."

David knew he might as well get up, before his son woke up the whole house. David slid out from under Jan. She rolled onto her side and remained asleep. David looked at his watch, 6:00 a.m. He rubbed the blonde hair of his little boy, "Matthew, what would you like for your breakfast?"

"Fruit Loops."

David was thrilled with this simple request. Breakfast cereal was poured, and David leaned against the chair as the coffee began to brew. David hadn't told Jan everything. He didn't mention that he was sure that this wasn't some 'kid looking for drug money.' He knew it was someone trying to kill him. But, he couldn't figure out why. Before Jan awoke, he called his friend. David thought that Jonathan might be in danger.

"Jon, you won't believe what happened last night. Some kid broke into the house and tried to shoot me while I was sleeping."

"What, are you kidding?"

"It was weird. You need to be careful. This wasn't a simple break-in." David continued with the details and Jonathan listened with genuine concern for his friend as well as the genuine concern for this possible threat.

A few hours later, David was pleased to see his family leave the driveway on their way to the beach. Everyone would sleep better knowing that they were safe. David spent the day fixing the drywall and painting the ceiling. It was a good project. It didn't take much thought yet kept him busy. He was pleased with the work he had done on the ceiling. The doors to the house were all deadbolted, and cans were strung along the windows to produce a poor man's security alarm system. All day, the phone and gun remained attached to his waist, and now that he prepared to lay in bed to sleep, they were each laid within easy reach on the nightstand. He was alone with only his thoughts. As the darkness of night filled his home, he began to wrestle with thoughts of protection and fear.

Chapter Seven

SATURDAY: NARCISSISTS CONTROL

M r. Summerall sat in his impressive office. His import-export business was successful in both legitimate and criminal branches. Supplying drugs through the legitimate imports he received was a very successful enterprise. It seemed all he touched prospered, and with money came great power. So much so, that he felt safe doing both businesses from his corporate office in downtown Tampa. He was in control of everything that he supplied and all those that worked for him.

His crimson colored chair blended tastefully with the mahogany desk and African antiques. Above his desk were a collection of exotic masks from around the world. Their wooden and painted faces seemed to follow all those that would enter and stand before the desk. No one who entered this office ever felt safe, and these dark eye-less orbs appeared to watch the decisions being made, and indeed they were. His men waited outside and watched through the cameras concealed in the masks, as well as those strategically placed around the building. They were ready to do whatever was asked by their boss. They knew those that didn't obey him, often met with a tortured death. They would always obey. In this office, his desires were all that mattered. Life and death were his decision. He left nothing to chance, and he would always be in control.

The door opened. A sober young man entered, his hands clenched and filled with sweat. The force of his own anger melted in the weight of the fear that gripped his soul. He tried to maintain an image of boldness, but he was scared, because he knew his boss exchanged failure with death.

Mr. Summerall drank in this fear. He liked its taste. Slowly he spoke each word, deliberately hiding his intentions from this captive. "So, you failed again."

Joey begged for mercy, "Mr. S., please! I can fix this!"

Death stood in the corner watching. He wanted a painful sacrifice for failure. The paramedic still lived. He was to have died, and this fool failed. He watched as this lamb was prepared for slaughter.

Mr. Summerall said, "So, you who have sold for me and aspired to become my student of power and wealth, you were supposed to take care of those paramedics who talked with the junkie. But, you failed. You are not worth anything to me." The demonic voice of Death spoke through him, fully possessing him, and he hissed, "I will be satisfied with nothing but your death."

"Can't I try again? Please, let me try again. Don't kill me! There's gotta be some way I can make it up to you! Please, anything!" Joey caught a glimpse of Mr. Summerall's eyes and knew he would die soon, and his voice broke as he whispered, "My death, nothing else?..." Joey dropped his head in stunned silence as Fear overwhelmed him.

Deep hideous laughter rose from behind the desk then slowly Mr. Summerall walked behind his prey. "I buy and sell, and don't tolerate failure or risk. You knew the cost if you failed me. And, you have failed!" he paused, and his words became condescending and cruel, "You bring me nothing but unnecessary risk. And now, nothing but your death will satisfy me." The insanity of this man's intent was revealed as his menacing delusion continued, "Death ... I control Death. He and I are partners. I give him the souls of men like you, and he gives me Power!" He placed his hand on the neck of the trembling captured fool, "One day Death and I will rule together in hell. You'll be my servant forever. Consider yourself my deposit for an eternity of power and authority!" His strong hand slowly ran down the back of his sacrifice. He was pleased and laughed again.

Joey suddenly understood that he had been working for a mad man and he would not escape. Tears flowed freely as he cried for mercy knowing he would be given none. These tears of surrender fueled the supplier's narcissistic control. His voice became toxic as he continued to pour out the vile evil from within his mind, "I think Death likes it better when those I send to him, suffer first. You failed me, and now you'll pay what

I'm due." He paused as he reached over and touched a button on the desk.

As the two men walked in, he looked away from his captive and said, "Make sure he's still alive when I get there in two days. But, please have fun with him. I know how you like to abuse the young men I give you. I give you permission, just make sure he is still alive and awake when I get there." His men didn't say a word and grabbed the young man who stood stunned by fear and unable to move. Their eyes were dark. Their task would not be unusual, and their captive would suffer.

Mr. Summerall looked again toward his captive as he was being removed from his office and sneered. "And, when you are dead, no one can connect me with those teenagers. You are nothing but a risk to be eliminated."

He no longer was interested in this young dealer, and his mind shifted to Jonathan and David. He spoke to the demons behind the masks. "They are both liabilities that are no longer worth the risk. I'll handle those two paramedics myself. Personally...Yes, this time it will be personal."

The stench of Death lingered in the office. His mind turned again as he stared up at the masks. Slowly, he began to hear, almost audibly, the Voices of Evil as they hissed, fueling the lie that whispered of his reign in hell. He needed to make many more human sacrifices before that day. Enough murder and his place in hell would be guaranteed.

The Voices quieted. They knew the easiest way to control any human was when the person thought the decisions they made were their own. Slowly, a smile, spawned by darkness, settled on the supplier's face and he knew what he would do. Jonathan and David could expose him, if he did not kill them first. But, he would wait until after he had enjoyed the kill of the young dealer. There was no need to rush, after all, he knew where these two paramedics lived and worked. That thought humored him and broke the remaining weight of torment that lingered on his soul. He enjoyed the power of knowing he was in control and could have these two anytime he wanted. Earthly power and wealth in exchange for hell's destruction was a fool's exchange. The Voices filled their fool with his reward.

The tearful young drug dealer was taken to an old wooden barn outside the city, blindfolded and tied down to await his fate. Anger and Fear tormented him. They had both worked well together to prepare Joey for his destruction. His soul would be eternally tormented by these two familiar voices. As worms, they would eat at the flesh of his soul, reminding him of his decisions made by their leading. He had chosen to obey their voices, and he would be tormented by that knowledge for eternity. It had begun. The torment of hell would begin on this side of Death's gate. The grapes of wrath and fear would continue to make wine for them to drink. They drank freely and deeply.

David couldn't sleep and got up to find some food in the refrigerator. He was hoping for some beer or anything sweet to satisfy the stress within but found nothing but carrots and celery to snack on. His family had gone to the beach and taken most of the food with them. Had he heard a sound? He looked up toward the laundry room door. He shook his head and moaned at his own imagination. He turned his attention again back to the refrigerator. This time he pushed the juice aside and looked for some hidden treasure in the back. There was nothing worth eating. David slowly walked over to the sofa, empty-handed. He looked at the clock; it was only 9:00 p.m. The house was quiet, too quiet.

"This place is giving me the creeps!," David groaned as his mind raced, "I need to get out of here!" He didn't like being here alone tonight, knowing he would never sleep and with nothing good to eat. He picked up the phone. "Jonathan, what are you doing?"

"Nothing. Just eating a pizza," came his friend's voice. "Don't want to be alone? Come on over. I don't blame you after last night's excitement. Bring your clothes. The spare bedroom is Robert's home office so you can sleep on the sofa, no prob."

David chuckled timidly. "Well, you're right; I don't want to stay here. I'm hungry. Got enough pizza for me?"

"Nope. But, by the time you get here they should have delivered the next one. Come on. I wouldn't want to stay there, either."

David drove quickly to his friend's home in Brandon. The large impressive condos in this gated neighborhood were well maintained and well above his pay-grade. Robert definitely had his perks. David paused at the front door and for a moment considered the wisdom of sleeping here tonight. Robert had been very odd recently, and he recalled Jonathan's frustration and growing fear of him. Spending the night at Jonathan's would be awkward, and he decided he would leave his bag in the car until he was sure it would work out. He took a deep breath and knocked on the door. After all, Jonathan was his friend.

Robert opened the door. His deeply tanned skin and dark red hair seemed to pale in the depth of the darkness of his eyes. He smirked, then gestured his hand toward the sofa. "So, where's your bag? I thought you were going to spend the night."

"I left it out in the car. I just wanted to make sure you didn't mind. You might want me to leave, after I eat all your pizza." David smiled at Robert and walked straight into the kitchen.

Robert shrugged and followed him. "Well, you can eat it all. I don't care. Just don't drink all the beer. I might have to kill you, if you do that." Robert went to the refrigerator and pulled three beers out. "A glass or out of the can?"

David took one, "Thank you. Out of the can will be fine."

Robert walked back to the living room with the two cans and two glasses. He was clearly in one of his better moods, and oddly appeared happy, "Go get your stuff. Come on, get comfortable. No sense waiting till later to get it out. I'm glad you're here. Jonathan is such a bore tonight."

Jonathan threw a cushion pillow at Robert. "Watch out, or it will be you on the sofa. And David in there with me."

"I don't think Jan would understand that one." David quickly interjected and looked at his friend. "The sofa looks quite fine." They all laughed.

The three men's attention was shifted to the football game playing on the TV. They talked about statistics and scores and yelled at the screen. The game was a great distraction, especially since David didn't want to think about what had gone on at home. After the game, Robert left to prepare for bed, and Jonathan and David walked into the kitchen to clean up the mess. "Are you going in the morning?" Jonathan spoke softly as he scraped the leftover pizza into the trash.

David was surprised that Jonathan remembered and brought the subject up. "Yes, I am. All by myself. Aren't I brave?"

"You sure are. You know I would really like to go with you. I don't know, but tonight before you called, I couldn't get my past out of my mind. I was wishing for a way to go but didn't know how to get with you. Really, I still don't. Robert would have a fit."

"You're right there. But, I would like a friend there. You know it's a lot easier doing something you're not sure about, if you have someone you can trust to do it with."

"Yeah, and it's a lot easier remembering your past when the present is not all that pleasant."

"Oh, so you guys didn't make up?" David whispered.

"Somewhat, but I don't know ... " Jonathan cut his last word off in mid-thought.

Robert returned carrying the sheets and a pillow, "So what great call were you guys talking about? All you ever do is talk about war stories when you get together." Robert placed the sheets on the sofa and walked into the kitchen.

Jonathan answered, "Actually, we were talking about some things that came up after we ran that call on those teenagers that died." Robert could always tell when Jonathan was lying. The best defense was just enough truth to keep him off track.

Robert saw right through it and instantly became angry and his words spiteful, "So, Jonathan said you were going to church for the first time tomorrow. Why would you want to do that? You don't need anybody to tell you how to live."

"Telling me how to live? I don't know. Is that what they do at church? I thought it was a place where people came together to worship God." David was surprised as that thought just seemed to pop out of his mouth. He had never thought about worship before.

"Worship God? Which god? What kind of church are you going to?" Robert's words taunted David with insult, and his body tightened in control.

David tried to ignore Robert's rapid mood swing. The journey of discovery and faith caused David joy as he spoke. "I met the pastor of the Crossroads Church. His name is Tim McDonald. Have you heard of him before? He's really an interesting guy. He seemed like a real man of integrity and very friendly. He even asked me to play golf next week with him. I thought I would. That's why I'm going there tomorrow." David shocked himself as much as Robert, when he asked. "Why don't you come with me? I really don't want to go alone."

"Are you drunk? They don't want me there. Never. Hell, no. I get enough rejection from homophobes, without going to church and getting more. It isn't 'If' but when and how their hatred is expressed to anyone not just like them. I will never be a victim!" His voice raised, became hostile and cold, "So better to just stay away from the conflict, unless, of course, I am in a situation to win." Then his voice became controlled and measured, "And if I'm not good enough for their God, and if they think they are, they can keep Him. They aren't any better than I am."

"Well, you're no worse than me," David said, not understanding the depth to which homophobia was a reality that homosexuals were forced to face. He tried to help Robert flip back into being calm again. "I was invited by Tim himself, and if I can go, you can too."

Robert walked to his desk and picked up a round black button pin in the top drawer. In the center was a bright pink triangle. "You know what, I think I'll go. Wearing my button. I wonder how many there will know what it means. The Hitler Christians marked Jews with yellow stars, and faggots, like me, with pink triangles, then they rounded up, tortured and killed them. Maybe, they should remember their heritage."

Jonathan spoke sharply, "I don't think many American Christians took part in Hitler's hatred. As a matter of fact, they fought him. Or did you forget that part? Not all Christians use their religion for an excuse to hate."

"No. But, enough do, so that the rest should remember their own guilt by association. Maybe, if they remembered, they would do a better job of loving and accepting others. The hypocrites, that is what they say they do. Love and accept. But, they don't. You KNOW they don't. They think they are OK. That their sin is more acceptable than mine." His words became bitter and poisoned. "I was born unacceptable to their God because I am gay. So, I am unacceptable to them. But, if there is a God in heaven, why would he reject me for being honest about who and 'what' I am? I have no choice in how I was created. So, what then? Was I created for Hell?"

Robert flipped the button over in his hand and in his anger he squeezed tight. "Maybe, I was created for hell, and I will be fine when my time comes." The sharp pointed pin stuck deeply into his hand. The pain felt good in comparison to the pain he felt within. The knife of rejection stabbed deeper than any pain that Robert could ever inflict upon himself, or others. "I didn't kill millions of Jews. But, murder is OK, murder their God can forgive. But, their God, I'll never forgive!" The Voice of Rejection revealed the depth of darkness in Robert's mind. The thought of death and murder momentarily hushed his verbal assault, and he stilled.

David knew that something deep in Robert was dying or was dead already. He could see it, and he wanted to help, but he had no answer for this level of rejection and anger, or if that was the source of this strange sense of death he was feeling. "So, are you coming, pin and all? I don't care if you wear a pin." David, simply offered, expecting Robert to say no and calm down.

"David, you are so naive. I just couldn't bear the thought of you going and being deceived by their lies. I would love to go with you! Will you come, Jonathan?" Robert quickly shifted tactics and let the soft melody of his effeminate words express his pleasure at protecting David from the lies of the church and his plan of playing an unashamed flaming homosexual at the service tomorrow.

Jonathan was leaning against the wall, trying to avoid this conversation by any means. "I would rather not," Jonathan stopped immediately when he saw the angry expression that Robert shot at him. "But, if you want to, sure, I'll go." Fear slowly tightened around Jonathan's heart as he looked at Robert and tried to guess what will happen if they went, then realized the depth of embarrassment he would suffer right now if he refused to go at Robert's word and Robert unleashed his wrath. Fear held his captive in an abuser's grip.

He smiled to mask his fear, "David, don't sit too close. Maybe you will survive the lightning strike and bring us back. I am sure Robert and I will be struck dead." Part of Jonathan knew he was being used as a pawn by Robert, but he also knew he wanted to be there for his friend. He took his eyes off Robert and exhaled as he realized that he also felt a real draw to go back to church tomorrow and embrace a lost part of his soul, even if he had no clue how that could happen. He thought in amazement as he looked at his friend, How in the world did you just pull that off? Miracle or a mockery, only tomorrow after the service would they know.

Robert stood and turned off the lamp. "I am sure I will survive. I always survive. I can't die, I have a deal with death." Robert smirked at his guest. "Good night, David. I'm glad you came. See you in the morning," Then he shot a glance at Jonathan that demanded he come to bed immediately. Jonathan obeyed in silence. Robert's voice quieted as they quickly walked down the hallway, and the bedroom door closed behind the two men.

David watched as they left. The large picture window let in the soft night light. He could hear faint mumblings from the back room, but he didn't want to pay attention. He reached into his backpack and pulled out his Bible. Tonight would be a good night to read. He prayed for help to understand what he read and asked for help to know where to read. He hadn't gone far in his prayer before his mind focused on the front cover page of the book and the phone number Mrs. Blake had written. David stared at the page, and he couldn't get her off his mind. He tried to think of something else, but over and over his mind went back to Mrs. Blake. David thought, or did he hear, Mrs. Blake knows how to pray. I should call her. David tried to convince himself that it was too late, it was after 10:00 p.m. Then he thought of Jonathan's fear, Why was he so afraid? Could they really be in danger, or verbally assaulted if they went to church tomorrow? Is homophobia that real today? David had no idea what to expect, reminding himself that he had never even been to church.

David walked to a set of beautifully fashioned french doors that opened to a large patio. It allowed the light of the full moon into the dark room he was standing in. This condo unit was on the top floor, and he was impressed with the location. He looked around and at the street below. There was a large oak tree in front of the entrance. Anyone at this window could easily hide from outside observation, and yet no one could leave or come in without being seen. The pool could be seen from here, as well, and David enjoyed watching two people swimming leisurely, appearing so carefree. He opened the door and stepped outside. He took some long deep breaths of the fresh spring air. In another month, the humidity and heat would dampen any pleasure night air would bring, but tonight he drank in the refreshing peace that nature offered. Slowly the stress of last night and the strange conversation tonight began to lift, and he gradually relaxed.

He looked at the stars and the moon and his mind filled with the thought of a God large enough to create all this. He thought of how foolish he had been to not realize the presence of God that was all around him. Why had he not seen it before? Suddenly, David understood that nature was a great proof and witness to the presence of God. And, that even if nature had just evolved, the sense of beauty could not have been designed by accident, nor simply evolved over time. Where would the sense of beauty have come from? Except from one who could have enjoyed beauty. David began to marvel at the depth of the lesson that nature was teaching him.

His mind returned to Mrs. Blake. Isn't that what she said would happen. That God, himself, would teach through the things around him, if he would but listen. Again, that Voice within whispered. David was quiet and still. He wanted to hear, and he stood there for a long time listening. He knew he should call Mrs. Blake. David smiled as he walked over to the phone. He didn't hear a voice tell him to call, but down deep inside he knew he should. He was unsure of what he would say or even why he was calling, but he didn't care. He was going to trust this impression. He picked up the Bible and turned it to the front cover page.

No one who cared could hear the sobs of pain coming from the old wooden barn. The tormentors had beaten their captive. Pain pulsated from the young dealer's broken and bleeding body. He had sold drugs to some high school teenagers, and they had died. Now, it is he who was being slowly drawn into death's grasp. He cried for mercy but found none. He cried to God, but in the painful silence, he thought that even God did not listen.

The two men came again to torment their captive. The taunts of hatred and disgust were hurled at this young dealer who had failed. "Hey, Joey, I thought you were a big powerful man. Looks like you're just a punk kid now." They laughed at him and beat him. Their fists pounded at his chest and his ribs that had already been broken. He cried out in pain and coughed blood that spewed out of his mouth, and his teeth shook, having been loosened by their abuse. His eyes were swollen shut from an earlier beating, and he could not tell with what or when the next blow would come. Now blind, bound and hurting, Fear and Hopelessness held this captive deeper in torment. The darkness of physical pain met the darkness of despair that overwhelmed him. He was alone, he was afraid, and only those to torment him remained. Their laugher pierced his soul with an even greater darkness. The young man whimpered in pain and cried out to die. But, Death waited and haunted him.

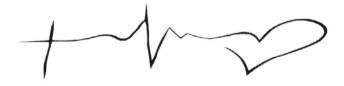

It was Saturday night, and Terri and Bobby had stayed home. Terri was in the living room watching TV. Bobby, her brother, was sitting on the sofa and reading his newest Science Fiction book. The thrill of a high school football game or a party never interested Bobby, who would rather read. Terri still shaken from her friends death last week, had no interest in going out with others. Binge watching TV at home seemed far more appealing. She flipped through the movie options and mindlessly stopped at a recommended new release movie. Within minutes, there were images of demons lurking in some creepy old house. Terri immediately turned off the TV.

"Hey, what are you doing? I was watching that too, you know." Bobby grumbled.

"You weren't watching that. You were reading your book. Besides, I just figured something out."

Bobby cut her off, "You? I doubt that." He smirked, looked up at her, then returned to his book, "You just got scared, that's all."

"I didn't just get scared. I figured out that if I don't want scary thoughts, I shouldn't sit here and watch scary movies."

"But, I like the background noise. It keeps the suspense up in my book." Bobby still had a hard time believing what Terri had told him about last week. "So, is this the new you? No drugs, no football, and now, no scary movies. Sounds like your turning into mom."

"After Tommy," her voice softened. "after Tommy, I'm just not going to be so stupid. The choices we make matter." Terri looked at her brother, "I've made some really bad choices, and

I'm just trying to figure out who am I now? This is all so weird. What do you think? Have I gone crazy?"

"I don't know. I always figured you were kind of crazy. But, I guess you are no crazier than mom." Bobby paused to think, "Mom is weird, but not crazy. She always seems to know when we are up to something. Do you think she ever misses? Praying for us, I mean?"

"Well, she thinks she almost missed it last week when I almost died. She said she fell asleep because she was so tired, but she had a feeling that something was wrong. She was upset that she didn't pray sooner that night."

"That's mom. Here she had a perfectly good reason to be proud of herself, and she thinks she almost screwed up."

"It isn't as easy as you think for her. The other night really scared her. She is fasting and spending more time in prayer. Mom says she isn't going to give the devil any room to hurt us."

"Well, if there are demons like you said you saw last week, I can't believe any of them can stand up to mom. I bet they are running. You know how she always says, 'Submit to God, resist the devil, and he will run away.' Bobby laughed but admitted, "I just don't know if I can really believe all that stuff. So, you really saw something last week, huh?

"Now you listen, it is real. It happened. I will never forget. It is more real than anything that has ever happened to me."

"So, you believe in what mom calls Spiritual Warfare now?" Bobby looked deeply at his sister. Had she really changed that much?

Terri looked at her brother. It was one of those rare moments when they would actually look at one another and talk. "Bobby, I don't know what it all means, but I do know what I saw. I will never forget. My prayers will never be the same. We are, whether we believe it or not, in spiritual warfare all the time." Terri's mind began to wander, "I guess, I'm ready to do whatever it takes to win the war. Bobby, I watched my friends die."

"You said you saw Jesus, too." Bobby wanted to hear about that part again. Maybe, it would be easier to believe this time. "What did he look like?"

"Do you think you'll ever believe me? I know I sound crazy." Terri's voice hushed. She was seeing again in her mind's eye, the vision that her words could never adequately express.

The phone on the kitchen counter began to ring. Bobby quickly glanced at his sister and then jumped up to get the phone. He didn't want to, and he wouldn't have, except that his mother was asleep, and he didn't want to awaken her. Bobby gruffly said, "Hello?"

"Hello, may I speak to Mrs. Blake?"

"No, she is not available." Bobby's tone was sharp. "Can I take a message?" He hoped not.

"No, I guess not. Just tell her David called."

"David, the paramedic?"

"Yes, that's me. Who are you?"

"I'm Bobby. You met me at the funeral. Remember, I was with Terri, my sister."

"Is Terri there?"

"Yes, she is. Would you like to speak to her?" Bobby looked at his sister and handed her the phone.

After the two greeted each other, David paused and drew a deep breath. "Terri, I'm going to visit your church tomorrow. My partner Jonathan and another friend are also coming. I remembered your mom had said I could call. I had hoped to talk to her. Could you tell her that I called and that I really do think I'm learning - just like she said would happen?"

Terri smiled, "Sure. We will be going out of town in the morning. Dad thinks we need some family time together. So, we won't be there. But, Mom will be glad you called. David, Mom is praying for you all the time. She will definitely be in prayer for you guys tomorrow."

"Your Dad. Was he at the hospital?"

"Oh, no. Dad was out of town. He came back immediately, but it did take a few hours. He's kinda ticked at me for what happened. Says I knew better than to be there. Mom, she's just thankful I'm OK. But, Dad, well I guess he's just worried."

They said their goodbyes and Terri hung up, "Bobby, I'm going to go to my room. I need to be alone for a while." She grinned at her brother, "I am going to pray. You're welcome to join me if you want."

Bobby watched his sister disappear down the hallway. For the first time, he truly realized that his sister had died last week, and it had changed her. His amazement quickly turned to awe. "No, I think I'll stay in here." He wasn't quite ready to let his sister see him awed.

Supernatural strength was added to the prayers of this new warrior of God. Terri paced the floor of her bedroom as she began to intercede for the two paramedics who had worked to save her life. She prayed and the Spirit of God was pleased.

Death stormed into the Adversary's Chamber. "How is it we only have human fools who run on our side? The coward of Anger's wrath ran! He shall meet me. I must have vengeance upon this young prey. I needed him, he was so close to killing that new warrior, and he ran. He shall die!" Death hissed at Adversary, "What has gone wrong? Why did this plan fail?"

Adversary waited until Death had finished, then spoke with contempt to his strongest weapon. "Death, when will you be appeased? This is warfare! This is not just our will that we must contend with. There are greater forces than our own that we must wage against. Remember we must live and die by the law of the Good One. We can only prevent and pervert it to the degree his followers will allow us. This battle involves one of his prayer warriors, and she has discovered that greater power is within her than is within our camp."

Death, not encouraged by the Adversary's tone, lowered his voice. "But, she is only one."

"One with the armor of God, Himself."

Death quieted and considered those images. "Then I will rise up an attack against her with a troop of darkness. Like a flood, we shall drown her."

The Adversary moved across the room and looked out the window. From this height, many nations could be seen. Softly he spoke, "She knows the contract. She knows how to use it, like a lawyer, reminding God of his covenant." Bile ran from his mouth as he spoke these words. "She will claim her right that God raise up a standard against you." The Adversary turned to face Death, "You know how he loves THAT. He loves to hear his contract returned to him. Like us, His word is eternal."

"No, His word is not like us, His word was before us. But we killed His word once. Adversary, find a way to kill it again."

"Are you going mad by your anger, Death? Have you forgotten that you lost that day? Look at your waist. Do you see the keys that locked men's soul eternally within your grasp? Of course not, the Word took them." The Adversary's words were bitter with defeat. Every day until the judgment was a curse to him, watching these mere humans given strength greater than his, seeing his plans fouled by simple prayer. Bitterness rose as a stench.

Death breathed in deep with pride. "But, I did not lose everything. All men must still pass by me. I shall attack this warrior of intercession."

"What weapon shall you use? None shall prosper. Look at the imp of pride. He bleeds. He has been beaten, and he left her house running. She holds the weapon of prayer and fasting. Not one in our kingdom is strong enough to stand against that."

"How is it that she learned of such a weapon? I thought you had sent teachers into the Good One's Camp to teach those fools to sleep, to tickle their ears, to worry only with occupying until I come. Where did she learn of these things?" Death began to hear the words of the Adversary. "Can you not send Sickness in?"

"Not to this one. The Good One has set his covenant in strength upon her. No sickness can get in. He won't allow it. Said it had to do with the finished work of His Son. I tried. I lost that case."

Death sat down upon the soft leather chair, "So I can't get to her, is that what you are saying?"

The Adversary nodded his head slowly.

"And the new convert, the one who has stolen from me, the Paramedic, I can't take him either?" Death was stilled.

Adversary sneered. "I didn't say that. You lost on one attack. Another could be successful. I have worked it out. There may be an 'accident.' There may yet be satisfaction."

"Well, I have a plan, too."

"Don't sidestep me. What is your plan?"

"I plan to use my human supplier. One who thinks himself my partner. One who is a great fool, but keeps my hunger appeased."

"Your hunger is never appeased. Satisfy yourself on Anger's slave, the young man who is being beaten. Just this hour, I heard him pray that you would come. Anger is giving him a taste of his eternal reward for following us. Take out on him your vengeance."

"This I will do. Anger is not done yet, and I must wait until my human supplier takes him in two days. In the strength of his death, I will go again to the Paramedic. I will find a reason for him to turn his back on what he has learned. I will cause him to come out from behind his wall of protection. When he's out, I will take him." Death leered at Adversary. "I will do your job. I will find the crack in the wall."

"Then go, do this thing." Adversary pointed to the door. Slowly Death stood up and walked out.

Chapter Eight

SUNDAY MADNESS

Robert's large white Cadillac pulled into the church parking lot. "Man, we should have gotten here earlier. I hate to park so far back. It will make a quick getaway tough." Robert frowned at his companions. "Maybe, this wasn't such a great idea. Let's leave." His voice broke with a rare tinge of fear "I don't like this place."

Jonathan ignored him, his eyes fixed on the full parking lot "I've never seen a church where the parking lot was so full. This must be a special service, I can't believe this many people come to church every week." Jonathan watched as two young men from another car walked briskly into the side door of the large tan building. "I guess that is the way inside." Jonathan pointed excitedly toward the door then to a parking space he saw in the back. "It will be good to be back at church. I forgot how good it feels. But, I am surprised."

David wasn't as surprised as the other two at the crowd. He had already met Pastor Tim. "That isn't the building they had the memorial service in for the two women. We were over there." David pointed to a smaller building to the left. "I bet there will be over a thousand people inside. This is going to be interesting."

Robert frowned again at Jonathan as he pulled the car into the space. The three men entered the sanctuary. The service had already begun. Jonathan searched the rear of the church for a place for the men to sit. None could be found. A large-framed man with cowboy boots on approached the men. He held out his hand and shook each man's hand with force. His blue eyes sparkled as he greeted the late comers. "Sorry, boys, but there ain't no seats back in the back. If y'all want to sit together, well, we'll have to find ya one up front. Walk this way." He smiled as he turned and began to search for a space large enough for three men. It wasn't going to be an easy task, even up front.

Robert smirked at the other two men. They followed the usher up to their seats, but his anger at the required forward seating manifested as he mocked the walk of the polite, but unsophisticated usher. David turned away from Robert and shook his head. It was going to be amusing to watch Robert complain and Jonathan's pleasure. Everything about being at church seemed so foreign and strange to David, and for some odd reason, this made his anticipation grow even more tangible as they found their seats and sat down.

The congregation sang songs full of energy and life. The words to the short choruses were projected on the large silver screen. Jonathan reached over and whispered in David's ear in a strong southern draw imitating the usher that had seated them, "This ain't how they sang it where I came from," He stopped to hush a chuckle rising in his throat, then in a controlled whisper, "It looks like these people actually are enjoying themselves here."

David laughed quietly at his friend's joke. He had no idea what he should have expected. Having met Pastor Tim, the energy wasn't that great of a surprise. What was a surprise, was watching Robert. His short red curly hair looked impressive against the expensive teal suit he wore, and he looked like he belonged here; he was relaxed and looked like he was enjoying being here more than most the other people present. He clapped his hands in rhythm to the songs and could occasionally be heard singing the words that were scrolling on the large screen. David just nodded his head and smiled at Jonathan, whose gaze was locked on Robert in amazement. Jonathan knew there was never any way to figure out how Robert would react, but somehow his freedom in church surprised him. Jonathan smiled back at David and relaxed as he assumed that it would be OK with Robert for him to enter the atmosphere of the service also. Jonathan clapped his hands and sang.

David was too busy watching everyone to learn the words to the songs. The faces of most present glowed, and they appeared genuinely happy. Occasionally, he would spot one who was softly crying, hands upraised, whispering some quiet words of prayer, yet their mouth turned up in a smile. Each song built upon the other, until the songs became almost militant in their cry against evil and their intent to overcome the enemy, Satan. Then slowly they turned soft and reverent. Now they sang, not about what they were going to do, or about what God has done, they sang about how they loved God and worshiped him. David felt goosebumps run up and down his arms as the atmosphere changed through worship.

He took his eyes off the people around him and looked up at the large screen that displayed the words to the song: "Surely the presence of the Lord is in this place, I can feel his mighty power and his grace. I can feel the brush of Angels' wings, I see glory on each face, for surely the presence of the Lord is in this place." The people repeated the chorus, and at each start, the atmosphere became more and more electrified with the sweet sense of Another's Presence.

David focused on these words. He wondered if this was what he was feeling. Was it angels' wings, that made the hair on his arms stand up? Was it the presence of God that made him feel so good inside, right now? Slowly he began to sing along with the crowd, and he enjoyed the experience. In the corner of his eye, he caught Jonathan singing, and he noticed the hair on Jonathan's arms standing up too.

The service continued. Pastor Tim walked to the microphone. As one, all those gathered prayed, and then they all sat down. Tim talked about unconditional love and acceptance, peace and contentment. Jonathan was shaken by words that seemed to whisper to him of the complete acceptance of a loving God, a Heavenly Father. Then Pastor Tim ended his message with prayer. He invited everyone that would, to come to the altar and pray. The music video with lyrics to 'Just as I am' streamed across the projection screen and Jonathan recognized the old hymn that they sang at church when he was a child and with his dad.

Angels of Light rallied behind Jonathan to encourage him. Their strength was mighty because of the intercession of friends in prayer. They surrounded him, and their shields knocked off the enemy's blows. Nothing could get at Jonathan from outside. He would be free to make his own decision. The word preached was like water to Jonathan's dry soul. He thought to himself of how miserable he had been, even though on the outside everything seemed under control. Jonathan wrestled with the revelation that the most important part of himself, the part no one could see but himself, was alone and empty. His eyes filled with tears and his wall of resistance began to break. The gate to his heart had been cracked, and light came in. His soul danced in the light of love, and remembrance. Could it really be true that I could come in the truth of who I am, gay and all, and God would accept me? His head was bowed as he stepped forward to pray. His mind was full of a love he had believed he lost.

As subtly as Jonathan's step forward had been, so was Robert's, who stepped to block him from leaving the pew. Robert's dark eyes sent messages of warning and rebuke as they met his partner's wet ones. Jonathan lowered his gaze as he remembered the cost to walk forward and pray, then he stepped back and sat down. He feared that for him to walk up to that altar would eventually require him to suppress the truth of his sexual orientation, and to leave Robert, the only person in the world, whom he believed, accepted him for who he truly was. He could not do that. He would not do that. He made his choice, he chose Robert.

Jonathan bowed his head as a tear rolled down his cheek. He hoped no one would see him dry his tears. David turned his head back toward the preacher and acted as though he had not witnessed the exchange between these two men, and Jonathan's desired hope destroyed. The angels of Light bowed their shields as the darkness rolled into the depths of Jonathan's heart. The embrace of angels that had been as close as the goose bumps upon his arms were now nothing but a fading emotion.

Another chorus, another quick prayer and suddenly the masses began to leave. The three men walked quickly and quietly to their car, no words were spoken. In the car, one man just laughed and mocked the meeting. The other two remained quiet. Robert's cruel mockery of the God Jonathan had known, pierced and tormented his soul, and his heart tightened in the failure to change his circumstances.

The voice of Loneliness and of Lost Destiny began to mock Jonathan as he suddenly realized that Robert had never truly loved him. He didn't even know him. The demonic voices continued to abuse him with the shame of his emotional captivity to Robert. His eyes drifted from this car filled with mockery and looked up toward the bright noon sun. The light of day seemed beautiful to him. He focused on the light and on the things passing by his window and began to hear the song "Just as I am" replay in his mind. Gradually, the mockery and darkness no longer touched him; and in peace, he whispered his desire to be free.

Robert became quiet and squirmed in his seat. The atmosphere in his car was unpleasant to him. He was not a man accustomed to feeling silenced by others. He looked over at Jonathan and saw a fool that would not mock this God. Slowly Robert realized how much he had grown to hate his partner, who was nothing more than a toy to be controlled. The illusion of love and acceptance that Jonathan had needed was easily taken and twisted for his own desire. But, he was tired of playing with this fool any longer. Anger shot from his mouth like a sword bent on death, "You make me sick. Why don't you just kill yourself and meet this God of yours. Do you really think there will be a place in heaven for a faggot like you? You're an idiot!"

Jonathan paled in embarrassment as David looked to his friend, offering support. Jonathan shook his head subtly at his friend, asking him to remain quiet. David grimaced, acknowledging that he understood. They both quickly looked away. Jonathan hoped that if they didn't say anything, maybe, Robert would calm down. Robert saw the exchanged looks of embarrassment of these two men to each other. Dignity had been destroyed. He was content. He pulled back his head and laughed with deep pleasure at the damage his words had caused. Power was his weapon with which to inflict pain. His perfect smile again rested on his face. His captive had remained quiet.

His control was maintained. Yet, somehow a deep uneasiness remained with him. He looked over at David and with a menacing sneer said, "Well, I hope you learned your lesson. Don't ever invite me to that church again."

David looked over at the driver of the car, "No, I don't think I'll do that again," then he looked at his friend Jonathan, "but, I will go back." Jonathan knew his partner had just thrown him a life-line. He smiled and wondered if he would ever be able to take it.

The memorial service had only been a few days ago. But, the raw pain of her friends' death pummeled Debra's heart. Her breathing was painful, her eyes stung, and her body ached from the sorrow that suffocated her. Debra stood at her mirror and mindlessly played with the large cross hanging from her right ear then pulled out the six earrings in her left ear, replacing them with multicolored stone studs. She looked again at the silver cross. She sighed, then pulled it out and replaced it with a big black feather. She stared at her image in the mirror. Her pale face was painted with bright lipstick and dark makeup. No matter how she dressed or wore her makeup she knew everyone thought she was perfect, and girls would have died to have her looks. She cried at this facade before her. It was a beautiful mask, and no one would look any deeper.

She yelled into the tangible void that filled her room and tortured her heart. She felt so alone yet overwhelmed with tormenting thoughts that kept yelling of her loss. Her real friends were all dead, and everyone else hated her or were jealous. There just wasn't any reason to live. The thought of suicide was never far. She could kill herself, and no one would care. "They would be better off without me, if they even noticed," she whispered in agreement as again tears ran down her face. She buried her head in her pillow and cried, and in a strange way, the thought of her death comforted her.

Her volatile moods were like a scary emotional rollercoaster; from angry to depressed, from numb to fear, and then back again to some other twisting, random thought and raw emotion. Memories of Tommy, Heather and Darien, her closest friends who had just died, and the life she used to live before her world fell apart, exploded in vivid detail then merged into the darkness of her next memory. She was out of control, spinning, and she felt so very alone. She used to be so popular when she and Tommy were dating. It had been several months since Tommy had broken up with her and he said he didn't care that she still loved him. He just wanted to be friends 'with benefits.' Depression smothered her as she faced that she did love him, does still love him. No, no! Died, he is dead. I did love him! Her mind thundered in grief and loss and anger as she imagined him standing in the corner of her room watching her. "I loved you! You were more than my friend. Why didn't you see that?" she pleaded in her mind. Debra turned away and stared into the mirror as she brushed her long brown hair. Gradually her strokes became fierce and hurt her. She cried, "Tommy, how could you be so stupid?"

Her anger then turned inward to self-hatred and guilt, "I killed him, it was all my fault! I should have told someone they were using drugs!" She curled up in her bed, took a deep breath and decided she would concentrate her thoughts on her date for tonight, hoping that would make her feel better. She remembered why she had agreed to go out with Joey, he was so very hot. His deep dark eyes and strong build caught the attention of all the girls. But, when she first met him, she recalled that she had told Tommy that no matter how cute he was, Joey looked like he was angry with the whole world because his eyes made him look so mean. He was a mystery to her, and not really her type; cute enough, but way too distant. "And, what was up with him? Why did he seem to stay in the shadows but still came to a lot of Tommy's wild parties?"

Again, her mind uncontrollably shifted away from Joey and spiraled to her friends, "Why is Tommy dead? Why am I alone? And, why is Joey the only person who wanted to help me?" Debra cried deeply as she again relived the memory of the memorial service. She remembered their faces as they laid there lifeless and her own life that seemed to be as dead and hopeless as theirs. Then her mind shifted back to Joey. Although she had not seen him in months, he was there for her when she fainted at the memorial service. It was Joey who took her hand when the two paramedics returned her to her friends. He felt strong and safe, and she didn't want to let go of him. His strength seemed to make her strong, and she needed that strength as much then as she did tonight. She remembered Joey's deep brown eyes seemed so intense and gentle when he looked at her at the restaurant, and he clearly wanted to be with her. She grinned as she realized that tonight she suddenly wanted to be with him too.

Now the memory of their conversation became more focused and soothing. When she stood up from the paramedics at the memorial service he walked quickly up to her and whispered that she needed some fresh air, and he quickly walked her outside, away from her classmates who were lost in their own sorrow. They were grieving for themselves and didn't seem to care that she was leaving with Joey. She almost laughed when she remembered how odd it was that she found herself sitting across from him at the restaurant, watching him eat ice cream and talk of college. The distraction was nice, and so was his company. He said that he had graduated last year from Hillsborough High School. She reminded him it was their rival school, but that was OK. He made her smile, and she enjoyed recalling their conversation, "I was surprised that you remembered me from Tommy's parties since you never talked to me."

"It's my job to notice who is at parties." His tone was so withdrawn that Debra didn't know what to think of it or why Tommy would have invited him to come. Joey quickly added, "Besides, Tommy would have killed any guy brave enough to talk to you."

She almost blushed then, and that thought brought a grin to her face now. At the restaurant, Joey was so determined and persuasive about going out on a date together that he almost got angry when she declined. She liked his effort. "He likes me. I am sure of it. I bet he just didn't want me to get away and thought he better ask now before we didn't see each other again. I kinda like that." Gradually she corrected the damage done by her tears and forced another smile as she spoke to herself in the mirror, "Well, at least Joey noticed me. Come on girl, shake it off and get ready for your date. He'll be here in two hours." She frowned, knowing it was going to take a lot more than heavy makeup and a large smile to cover the sadness in her eyes.

Debra walked to her closet and picked out her favorite pair of jeans. As she slipped on her jeans, her face tightened as she pulled on the zipper. She swallowed hard and looked down at her stomach that pooched out over her hand that held the zipper. She took her left hand and tried to stuff her belly into the jeans. It just wouldn't fit. Debra fell back on the bed and stared at the ceiling. She held her breath, arched her back and slowly she pulled the zipper up, till finally, it had reached the top. Debra exhaled, barely. She rolled over to her side and stood again at the mirror, this time focusing on her belly. "The weight returned with a little extra," she moaned. She looked at the soft roll that hung above her pants and began to gently rub her belly, somehow that comforted her. She took a deep breath and felt a little better.

As her mind relaxed, the dark thoughts immediately pressed their attack. Depression would not give her an inch of space to recover, this was his battlefield to win. And, he would take her mind. Another tear rolled down her pale face, as she faced that she was powerless against these overwhelming thoughts that smothered her, no matter how hard she tried to think of something else. Her mind began to cycle again as the depressive thoughts choked her. It was bad enough that Tommy had not stopped doing the coke, which was the reason that they had broken up, but he was doing more and selling it to others. She had begged him to stop. He just wouldn't listen. She had no choice, but to give up. Guilt beat her, "It's all your fault. If you had just told someone, all your friends would be alive. It's all your fault."

Debra fell on her bed, and her pillow muffled the loud sobs of agreement, "It's all my fault. It's all my fault." Her tears choked her, and her breath was hard to catch. Her heart ached, and she wished of a thousand ways she could die, and the pain could stop. The faces of Tommy, Heather, and Darien came and haunted her. Their voices called to her in condemnation. It was all her fault. She knew that they were doing drugs and she didn't tell anyone. She was guilty of their deaths. Depression wrapped his long arms around her and whispered to this wounded soul. She rested in his arms, and mumbled the words that poured from her broken heart as she continued to weep, "What's the point? I don't deserve to live. I can't live with this guilt. I shouldn't live with this guilt." She was the prisoner of depression and irresistible fatigue. She closed her eyes in exhaustion, expecting to rest for a moment, but she fell asleep and wrestled with her nightmares until morning.

Debra's mother was already asleep and didn't hear her daughter's sobs, and her father spent another uneventful Sunday in front of the TV. One football game was about over, and a row of beer cans lined the coffee table. At a commercial, he had a brief thought about his daughter and her date tonight. She had been so moody lately that he hoped a date might cheer her up and help her snap out of it. However, when Debra didn't come out of her bedroom, and no young man came to the door, he just assumed the date was canceled. He didn't give her another thought as he sat in front of the TV and pressed the controller to watch the next game.

Chapter Nine

MONDAY:
A GOOD DAY TO DIE

6:00 a.m. Monday morning, the alarm clock sounded. Jonathan rose from his bed on the first ring. Somehow, even in the early morning, the tension still remained in the air. Robert slept soundly, undisturbed by Jonathan's movement, who was careful to keep it that way. He didn't want to talk to Robert this morning. Jonathan hadn't slept well in the darkness of their bedroom and wanted to get out of there as soon as possible. His uniform was ready, and so was he. He shut the front door, and it locked automatically behind him as he rushed down the hall. Jonathan wished that he would never have to return to what had been his home but now felt like his prison. Depression held him as he decided that he needed more time to make his final decision.

At the station, he noticed the lights were all off. He

entered quietly. Slowly Jonathan reached over the bunk bed to the portable radio that rested on the night stand, and then he swiftly tiptoed out of the bunk room. The red pen still lay in the log book. Even with the lights off, Jonathan could see the multiple lines written in red. The early hours of morning had not been kind to the on-duty paramedics. He would give them a little more sleep while he checked out the ambulance.

David entered the garage to find his unit still wet from the morning dew. Jonathan was sitting in the driver's seat and motioned to him to walk to the front of the ambulance. Jonathan turned all the emergency lights of the unit on. The red and white lights danced off the walls and swirled around the doors. David walked around the unit, checking to see if all the lights worked. Wet grass clung to the rear wheel wells. The hood was still hot. David knew that meant it had recently idled on the side of a wet road. David nodded to Jonathan. The lights were working. Jonathan turned the lights off and got out of the cab.

"Are the guys still sleeping?" David asked.

"Yes, I thought we could let them sleep a little late this morning. Doesn't look like they got much sleep last night." Jonathan opened the back-compartment door and began inspecting the spinal gear. "Looks like they used the long spine board and the straps. We are down one complete set."

The door to the station swung open. Slowly Lennie walked over to the two men. Her eyes were swollen, her voice was scratchy. "Yes, we left it at Tampa General. The only boards they had in the back for us were bloody. I wasn't about to deal with cleaning up that mess this morning." She looked into the side compartment, then up to David, and then she turned and began to walk to the supply closet, "You do have two spine boards and plenty of straps and cervical collars on the unit."

David followed Lennie. She slowly reached into the cabinet with her right hand, her left hand rubbing her lower back. A slight gasp escaped her lips as she bent down to the shelf. She continued to move, handing David the supplies that they had used during the night: bandages and sterile dressings, IV fluids, and IV needles. David quietly held the supplies. They returned to the unit. David noticed the slight limp that Lennie had toward her right side. She didn't mention her back ache, so David respected her privacy. He recognized the painful limp and empathized with his co-laborer. She walked to the locked drug compartment and signed her name to the drug usage log book. She handed the drug box and book to him. David counted the drugs and then signed the book and returned it to the locked compartment.

The tired paramedic's morning had now officially ended. She could relax. "What a shift!" She rubbed her red eyes. "We were up all night last night. Some drunk teenagers drove their car into a tree on the second bad curve on Riverview Drive."

"Yeah?" David knew that curve well and remembered his own rescue calls he had worked there. "It is a bad curve. I've been there myself a few times. That tree has hugged a few cars that were going too fast around the curve. The last two times though, the drunks were dead. Were your kids OK?" He held his breath, hoping.

"It's a miracle; but yes, they were. You know, it's really neat how nowadays even when the teenagers are drunk, they remember to wear their seat belts." At this, her voice was cheerful, even in its tiredness. There was something to be pleased about. "As a matter of fact, one girl in the back said that they had all decided to go for the drive, but that they wouldn't go unless they all wore their seat belts. She figured they would be all right if they had them on." Lennie softly laughed. "They acted surprised that the seat belts hadn't worked like magic!"

Jonathan entered the conversation. "Well, at least they lived to complain about their injuries."

"Any real injuries?" David was curious.

"Nothing that will kill them; a few broken bones, and one of them really screwed up her leg. The driver's door had been impacted into the driver's section. The cut metal lacerated the driver's leg. It's amazing that she'll live to tell about her injury. She was a breath's length from death. You should have seen it. It was really gross." She sounded pleased with the visual images of this injury. "You could actually see the femoral artery pulsating. The cut was about ten inches long, and the skin and muscles were pulled back about three inches. All the muscles and the broken pieces of the femoral bone could be seen. The artery looked like a big balloon just waiting to be popped. It was just like a paramedic's idea of what a gross anatomy lab should be ... real interesting, real dangerous, and real important that we didn't make a mistake." She grinned with childlike wonderment in fascination of the human body, and then her eyes took on a mischievous twinkle, "When we arrived on the scene, I noticed this rookie deputy puking over the side of his patrol car. I acted like I didn't notice him." A small smirk crossed her lips, "But, I bet he won't forget that leg for a while."

Jonathan laughed out loud. "Some things never change. It's great to watch a rookie lose it on a scene. Something to break the stress of the accident. I bet he won't be first-in on a car accident for a while." His tone became serious. "Do you think the kid will lose her leg?"

"No, I don't think so. It was such a clean cut. The metal was sharp, and it missed the artery. Her blood pressure and pulse stayed well within normal range. We had the helicopter waiting for us. As soon as the firemen cut the door out of our way, we got her out, and she flew straight to Tampa General's trauma team. She was in surgery within twenty minutes of the accident. We drove the other two to Brandon Community Hospital. They were just banged and bruised. Rescue 33 drove the last one to Tampa General. The kid they drove looked OK, but he kept asking the same questions over and over again. We thought the neuro-team might do best to look him over. So, I think they will all survive."

"Good. Good. I would hate to think of another teenager dying right now. I don't think it would be too good for our business. One teenager's death always leads to another."

David had finished checking out all the compartments and boxes while they talked. He turned and walked into the station. The aroma of coffee had caught his attention. The thoughts of the teenagers were immediately replaced with thoughts of today's needs.

The two exhausted paramedics left quickly. Quietness filled the station. Jonathan welcomed the quiet. David wanted to talk. The two friends barely looked at each other. So much had happened in the last few days, neither knew what to say. David wanted to find out what happened after he left yesterday, but he waited. He had time to ask later. Twenty-four-hour shifts leave plenty of time to find the right moment.

Jonathan walked past his friend and hoped for a very busy day. He did not want to talk, and he did not want to think. He knew he had no answers for the questions that now plagued his mind. But, he did know that for some reason, he woke up afraid. Robert had made him feel like he was going to die, and those thoughts gradually strengthened within Jonathan until he believed it was true. Fear continued to oppress him. And for a paramedic who works the streets, where that risk was a constant reality, he knew this feeling was very ominous. Jonathan nervously rubbed his hands and felt himself tremble as he struggled to take control of his disturbing thoughts.

Death stood near the wall of the fire station silently stalking his prey and waiting for the moment he could strike. The eerie stillness touched David. He rubbed his arms, trying to warm himself, and couldn't understand why he felt so cold. Inside his head, he heard a thought, "Go talk to Jonathan, Now." Over and over the gentle thought came, but David ignored the inner leading. He walked over to the newspaper and opened it to the front-page thinking, I have time, I'll talk to him later.

Death sneered and stepped a little closer.

The school bus stopped and picked up the tall attractive teen girl. A large bubble of gum popped as Debra stepped into the bus. Her long brown hair bounced on her shoulders, and her sleek shape was accented by her tight jeans. She wore her tee-shirt on the outside, and she hoped that no one would notice her belly. Her dieting hadn't seemed to help much with her recent gradual weight gain. She swallowed and felt nauseated as she walked down the aisle. The boys stared at her but would turn their heads away when she approached, then back when she walked away. The girls tried to act like they didn't notice her. The sight of her caused envy in the girls, and lust in the boys. Debra pulled her backpack a little closer and continued her walk to her seat. She wondered if it was because she was so fat and ugly that no one seemed to like her or if it was because they knew she was guilty of her friends' deaths. She held back her tears as she heard giggles coming from the third row from the back of the bus.

One girl in cruel jest mocked, "Sure is a shame she is getting fat." They giggled and stared at her now. None of them would have admitted that jealousy fueled their verbal bullying. It was OK to hate her since she was popular and didn't seem to notice them. One girl whispered, "I would do anything to be like her, she is so pretty, even if she is getting fat."

The girl beside her punched her softly in the side. "You mean you would do 'anything' to be liked by one of her boyfriends," then laughed a little louder.

The third girl's eyes filled with tears instantly, "Hey, knock it off. Don't you remember her last boyfriend was Tommy?" Suddenly their envy was replaced by sadness, and the three girls quieted down.

Debra lowered her head so no one could see the small tear roll down her face, knowing they had been laughing at her but not knowing why. Her mind spun in confusion and sorrow. Why had she become someone to laugh at? And Joey, why did he stand her up? Two months ago, no guy would have stood her up, and she had her choice of dates, but Joey didn't even call. Am I just a joke now, to be made fun of and forgotten?

She knew they were laughing at her. Her friends were all dead, and now, no one liked her. She wanted, needed, someone to like her, but she had no one she could trust. She turned her head to the window and watched the world go by. She tried to find one reason to continue to try but found none. Depression flexed his strong muscles, and the other tormentors were jealous of his strength. "Why should I even try?" she whispered as she decided that she had no reason to live. I am gonna kill myself tonight and make this all stop. Her tears began to dry, and her heart numbed further as she accepted this decision and began to think of ways to do it.

The strong Voices of Torment spoke into this young girl's ear, thinking this captive was theirs alone but, to their amazement and horror, the Angel of Light entered their domain. She pulled Depression's arms off his captive. She poured oil into the wounds in Debra's spirit that these evil demons had inflicted on her then rubbed the oil into the girl's cracked and dry heart. Debra breathed deeply and once again looked out the bus window; this time she noticed the house with all the pretty flowers. She loved spring flowers then noticed more of the beauty that she was passing on the way to school. Debra took another deep breath as peace filled her heart and realized she could breathe again.

The angel took her sword and held it up to Debra's spiritually bound hands. Instantly, she cut the bonds that held Debra captive. She removed the cords and threw them far away. The dark voices screamed out in pain, horror filled their voices. "What are you doing?" The angel turned her back to them and continued to minister healing to Debra's beaten heart. The darkness was repelled further and further until only peace remained.

Debra dropped her gaze down to her tee shirt then with her right hand gently rubbed her belly. She didn't know why, but she had noticed recently that this simple act seemed to make her feel better, relaxed. The Angel whispered in her ear, "A part of Tommy still lives ... "

Debra looked down and stopped rubbing her stomach. Could it be? She wondered as she smiled and wiped the tears from her eyes. A part of Tommy still lives. Louder, the thought penetrated her mind with the light of hope. Like so many mothers instantly know, suddenly, she knew that there was a baby within her.

"What will you do?" whispered the angel.

Debra looked at her belly and knew from deep within herself that her womb held life and a reason to live. She had never thought of the possibility of being pregnant, but now, her weight gain and nausea suddenly made sense. She looked at her right hand resting on her belly and grinned, My right hand knew more about what was happening inside me than I knew myself. She looked out the window of her bus, as it pulled up to the school and smiled, really smiled. Laughter touched her lips as her heart filled with hope. She now had a reason to live. She wanted to live. She wanted her baby to live. She walked off the bus and beside her stood a strong angel of Comfort. Debra knew she was not alone. But, she had no idea of how close Comfort was to her.

Depression ran into Adversary's chamber. "Lord, I must speak!"

Adversary turned and faced his servant. "Why do you enter here?"

Depression bowed his head and spoke, "I had a captive. She was almost to the point of sacrificing herself to you, my great Lord. I had made my bed in her mind, and she was mine."

The Adversary walked over to his puppet. His hands dug into the flesh of his worker. "But ... "

"But, an angel of Light appeared. She was strong. She comforted the girl." He paused, "I could do nothing but watch her heal the wounds that I had inflicted on my captive. She had 'the Oil."

"Oil! That is only given to His Warriors when they have been strengthened by prayer." The Adversary released his pawn.

He spoke to one of his imps, "Go and find out who is praying for this girl." Immediately, two small bats flew out of the chamber.

Adversary returned his gaze to Depression. "Is there no door for you to enter into now? You did check that before you ran away, like a coward?"

"I did run away. I had to. The Light was consuming me. But, I did look first. All doors were shut to me. The angel told Debra something, it was horrible. Had I known, I could have used it for our purposes. But, I didn't know." Depression tried to find a way that his words could save him from the torment to come. He was afraid. It wasn't working.

The Adversary looked again at his pawn. "What was so horrible?"

Depression whispered, "She is pregnant."

The Adversary was shocked and angered. Life was his greatest enemy because he knew that as long as there was life, there was proof of his ultimate, as well as, present defeat. His victory could only be found in Death. "You will do me no good here. You have failed and will be punished." His words took on a sarcastic tone, "my dear co-worker. Hell waits for you ..." Depression left quickly, and as he exited the dark chamber, he noticed other strong men entering. Death, himself, was present in that group.

Terri met Debra at the bus. Her face was filled with concern as she asked, "Debra, are you all right?"

Debra was surprised by Terri's question. They hardly knew each other and now Terri acting like a good friend, "Yes, I'm OK. Why did you ask?" she answered hesitantly as they turned to walk briskly toward their classrooms.

"I can't explain it, but when I woke up, I couldn't get you off my mind." Terri didn't know how or if she should tell Debra that she knew she was depressed and needed prayer. She quickly blurted out, "I prayed for you."

Debra's face showed genuine gratefulness and a bit of confusion as she turned to look at Terri. "Well, that's real nice. Thank you." And then kept walking to class.

Terri was surprised at the response. Curiosity, as well as concern, motivated the next question, "Did it help? I'm new at this 'prayer for other people' stuff."

Debra turned to look at Terri, "You know what, I really think it did." Her mind raced as she remembered how her thoughts of suicide had suddenly left. Her grin grew as she realized that now she had a reason to live and a friend she could trust to share it with. They reached the hallway that would separate the direction the two needed to go.

Terri obviously was glad to hear that response and softly touched the shoulder of Debra. "I wanna talk with you later, OK?"

"I want you to. Come over to my place after school. I need to know how you knew..." Debra's words were full of hope. "So you really prayed for me?"

Terri nodded. Last week she didn't think she was good enough to know the "in" crowd. Now she knew she was needed and wanted. She walked to her classroom with her shoulders pulled back, and her head held high. She whispered a prayer. It formed upon her lips and raced to her God. "Thank You, Lord."

The Lamb smiled. The angels and the congregation gathered in the great throne room rejoiced. Joy and Love poured from the great throne and filled Terri's heart. She knew her whispered prayer had been heard.

Death yelled at the Adversary. "What is the problem now? I went to work with Alcohol, and we planned on taking five teenagers last night. Yet, none died. I can't believe it! I was robbed again. What are you doing up there? Sleeping?" His voice shook the room. The odor of death wrapped around the chamber.

Adversary grabbed the neck of Death, "I have had enough of you. Where is your reason? Settle down and tell me what happened."

Death pushed Alcohol before Adversary. "This wimp wasn't able to completely blind the teenager. At the last minute, the fool turned the car even though she knew she was going to take the full impact on her door. I heard the Good One ask if she would willingly die, that the others might live. The teenager became sober and chose to die. She turned the car at the last moment, and the tree struck her door."

"So, you were able to take one, then?" Adversary asked.

"No, NO! I was not able to take her! I cut her, pierced her flesh with the metal of the door. Her death was within my sight. Her artery pulsated in the night air. My presence was on her, draining her of life. Then as she began to pass out, she spoke those horrid words, so horrible I dare not mention them." Death's voice weakened.

"She asked for forgiveness." Adversary choked on the words.

Death cringed, "Yes, that is what she prayed for. I jumped off her. I didn't want to touch such a vile person. It made me sick."

"So, you don't have the stomach to fight the Strong One either? It's been so long since we have had to war with these Earth fools. They had forgotten that this was a war. One, that if they engaged, they could win." He turned and faced his co-worker. "Obviously, it has been so easy for you, that you too have forgotten that this is war. And in this war, we have no weapons that will prosper where there is prayer. That includes ... Death." Adversary went to the others in the room. They had slid quietly beside the furniture, hoping not to be noticed. "So, who prayed for these kids? Where is our gate open? Our gate of Hell remains intact against all those who would war against us in their own strength. Who has learned how to open the door, the gate? None can win against us unless they come through our gates with the weapons of our Enemy."

Slowly a weakened demon spoke to the Adversary. "It is the fruit of a great warrior. She has prayed that her daughter also become a strong prayer warrior. And this warrior shall be greater than even her mother, for she has seen us. She almost died. The Good One let her see the battle. She knows us as her enemies. She knows we are defeated in prayer. She binds us and casts us out. And, she listens for the voice of her Lord. Last week we almost killed her, and now, this week she is killing us, and destroying our plans."

Adversary choked on this revelation. "Terri, it is Terri! A child that does us so much harm?" Adversary looked at his messenger, "Who are you and why do you stand so weakened?"

"It is Terri. I came to her, to get her eyes off her Shepherd and onto all that had happened to her friends. I was reminding her of the party after the football game, and the other teenagers had been dancing and then screaming before they died..." Distraction stopped and slowly looked around this impressive office.

"Get back to what you were talking about! Why are you here? What happened?" Adversary would not become distracted.

"She saw me. I don't know how. I was simply standing in her room, blowing ideas into her head, then it was as if she could practically see me. She pointed toward me, and her voice deepened in HIS authority. Then she said, "Go in the Name of ..." Well, I'll not say, but you know who. He paused, "The next thing I know is that I am scattered to the ends of the earth. I shall never forget her strength. She tore me up."

Adversary slammed his hand against the desk. "Another real warrior. One who is looking for a fight." His mind raced, "Did you hear her pray for another called - Debra?"

Distraction didn't want to answer this question, "I don't know for sure. I heard the Strong One whisper something in her ear about someone named Debra. Then she began to pray, well, honestly, sir, I didn't know what she was saying, I didn't understand her prayer. She spoke in mysteries. It was then that she became so strong. I, well, left quickly after that. I had no choice."

"She has become like a cancer to me. She is spreading her cancerous cells all through my kingdom. I can't stop its spread either." Adversary considered his newest adversary.

"What we need is a little radical surgery." Death slowly added his desire. "One that she won't survive." Death's eyes lit up.

"She won't or ... " Adversary's voice whispered, "we won't survive." He raised his hands; all those present recognized the signal and immediately left the room. The war plans for the final fight were to be drawn up. Before Death left, Adversary turned to him, "I will need your pawn. The one who thinks himself your partner, the supplier."

"Take him, I don't care. I'll find another pawn. There are always fools to bed with me. I like to rape Humans, and then the fools think it's love with a commitment. He thinks we have a deal. I'll enjoy his face when he sees his reward." Death was pleased with the anticipation of another sacrifice to Hell's Gate. One he was sure he would gain. There was no protection for this pawn.

The TV occupied the attention of the two waiting paramedics. The emergency alarm pierced the stillness. The printer spat out the paper with the information. David took one more quick sip of his coffee, as he rapidly rose from the sofa. Jonathan grabbed his shirt off the hook and buttoned it up as he rushed out the door. The response paper recorded the time, 11:30 hours.

Over the loudspeaker, the 911 dispatch declared, "Rescue 12 respond to an 'unknown medical' at 7827 Indiana."

"Rescue 12 responding," Jonathan spoke into the microphone in the front cab of the ambulance, as he continued to button his shirt. "Great 'unknown medical.' That could mean anything!"

Minutes later Rescue 12 arrived on the scene on Indiana Drive. David grabbed his jump bag and ran into the small brick house. The stench of garbage caused the two men to gag as they entered. Their eyes watered and they took shallow breaths. The house was dark. David looked for a light switch on the wall. He could find none. He slowly walked into the dark, his foot searched for sure places to walk. Few were found. Often his foot would slip on the grease and filth that covered the floor.

"I'm in here," a faint slurred voice was heard from the back of the house.

David picked up his pace. Jonathan held his flashlight out. The light was searching for someone and revealed a dirty, yellow-eyed older man. His skin looked as though it had been painted upon his thin bones. Bright red sores covered his face.

Jonathan swallowed deeply and approached this elderly man. "Where are you hurting?" Jonathan's voice pierced the quiet.

"I'm not hurting anywhere, right now." The patient's voice was faint, "I called because I want to die. I want you to take me to the hospital. I don't want to die in this pit."

"What makes you think you are going to die, right now?" David asked. Curiosity, as much as anything else, prompted this question.

"I am. I know I am. The doctors won't tell me what's wrong with me. So, I don't know for sure. I've been losing weight for the last three months. Nothing I do helps. It just keeps falling off. I have no energy. I can't eat. But look at my belly. It's all swollen, especially up here on the top right side. It hurts when I push it too." The patient pushed his stomach. Suddenly he coughed.

The cough produced a green odorous mucus. The patient wiped his mouth on his dirty shirt.

"How long have you had that cough?" David inquired.

"About the same time, I started losing weight. I went to the clinic in Ruskin. They wanted me to go to the hospital. I told them I didn't want to. I didn't have any money. I just wanted some pills. They wouldn't give me anything." His voice turned angry, "They wouldn't even tell me what was wrong with me."

"Did they know?" Jonathan asked. "If you didn't go to the hospital for further tests, they may not have known."

"That's what they said. But, I know they knew. They just wanted to kill me, and I wasn't ready to die then." The patient bent his head forward, "I am ready to die now. You can take me to the hospital."

David began to feel sorry for this obviously confused old man. "What makes you think you'll die at the hospital?"

"Well, everybody I know dies at the hospital. My wife went in there last year for a cough and gas pain in her chest. They called me later and said she died of some alphabet stuff, I remember what they called it, 'CHF.' You tell me, I never heard of anybody dying of the alphabet. But, they tried to tell me she did." He bent his head forward and softly cried. "I got no one to take care of me since she died. I don't cook. I don't know how. For fifty years she cooked for me. Now, look at me. I am skin and bones. I can't live without her." He cried. It was cut short by the burst of harsh coughing.

David came to the man's side. "CHF means congestive heart failure. Your wife had a bad heart, that's why she died. It wasn't the hospital. I take people to the hospital all the time, and they don't all die. I want to help you."

"But you don't understand, I want to die, this time." His eyes met David's, they pleaded for understanding.

"OK, we'll take you to the hospital. Maybe, they can figure out what's wrong with your belly." David took one arm, Jonathan took the other arm and gently they walked the ill man a few steps to the stretcher at the front door. David and Jonathan breathed the fresh air in deeply, as they pushed the stretcher away from the house. Jonathan drove the ambulance to the hospital. David remained with the patient in the back compartment. He asked, "What is your name? Mine is David."

"Howard, Howard Reed." The medical examination continued while he patiently watched the paramedic work. The patient's heart rate was rapid, and his blood pressure was low. His arms were so thin that the veins stood up like small tree branches against the thin muscles. A syringe full of blood was collected for the hospital to examine. David started an IV fluid line in his patient's left arm. Slowly the fluid brought water and needed minerals to the patient's blood system. He then picked up the tablet to begin recording information.

"Will they let me die there?" Howard curiously asked.

"I doubt they will 'let you.' They will do all they can to keep you alive. Maybe, they can find out what is making you so sick and fix it. Wouldn't that be better?" David tried to encourage his patient.

"But, then I'll have to go home, all alone again. There is no one to help me. I want to die. Can't you understand that?" Howard was getting angry at his foolish caretaker.

David stopped his paperwork and looked up into the face of his dirty, smelly patient.

Howard reached over and touched David's gloved hand, each looking to the very heart of the other. David saw the loneliness, depression, and hunger for someone to talk to in the man's face.

David found himself whispering his thoughts out loud, at first his words surprised himself, but then he knew it was the thoughts of his patient. He reached over to touch the man's hand, and said gently, "Then what will happen? When you die, are you ready? Are you really ready to die?"

The words reached the heart of his patient. He softly cried. Finally, he knew his caretaker had heard him. He took a deep breath and squeezed David's hand, drawing strength from David. "I thought God left me too. Everybody I loved left me. There was no reason for me to believe that God hadn't too. But this morning, before I called, I thought I heard Ethyl's voice. I thought I heard her invite me home." Howard looked up into this young man's eyes. "Young man, yes, I am ready. I want to go to my real home. Ethyl is waiting for me in heaven." David didn't say anything. What could he say? He just let the man hold his hand. Some would think this old man was just confused. David wasn't too sure.

The ambulance arrived at the Sun City Center Community Hospital Emergency Department. The patient was transferred over to the ER stretcher. David said good-bye to his patient and immediately went to wash his hands while Jonathan decontaminated the ambulance from the germs the man's coughing produced. Bleach and spray cleaner covered the not too distant smell of urine and Death.

Thirty minutes later, the ambulance was back in service and ready for the next call, and the two men began the trip back to their station. Jonathan looked over at David, "So do you think this guy is going to get what he wants?"

"You mean, to die? I think so. Let's just hope we don't get to die of whatever he's dying of, too. I bet he's got hepatitis. Are you up on your hepatitis vaccine?"

"I sure am. Are you?" Jonathan asked.

"Yes. I think we are safe, I was careful not to touch any of his body fluid, and neither one of us got close to his face."

"So, will he get evaluated for his suicidal thoughts? I bet he won't. But he obviously waited to get help until he was sure it was too late. I don't see that as any less suicidal than the person who takes a hand full of pills. And he wants to die more than most of those who take pills." Jonathan tried to concentrate on the road. His mind was racing in the turmoil of thoughts that held no easy answers. Last night he had laid in bed and considered his own suicide. How easy it would have been to get up and take some of his own pills to excess. Hopelessness held Jonathan captive and surprised him with its strength. Jonathan felt bound and trapped by the decisions of his past, and now, he wanted to die. If it wasn't for his own fear of what might lie after death, he would have killed himself. The elderly patient's peaceful acceptance of death only worsened his own unrest. Death was not to be embraced, even though it called to him, and spoke of peace to come. The battle raged on within his mind. And, he knew he was losing. Jonathan hated who he had become.

David was unaware of the battle within the mind of his partner. His mind remained focused on their most recent patient. "I don't think the state forcing him to get psychological evaluation will help him any," David remembered his patient's words. "He said he was ready to die. Have you ever thought about that? Being ready to die? Are you ready to die?"

Often the hardest questions to answer are those that are asked with such innocence. A Sword of Truth pierced Jonathan's heart. The words had met their mark; not shot from David's knowledge, but from One whose wisdom is ancient and true. Jonathan turned the ambulance into a vacant lot and parked the unit. His voice changed as he faced his partner, and his face reddened. "Listen, I know last week I said we could talk about this stuff, but I didn't think it would bother me so much. If I didn't know that you didn't have a clue what you were talking about, I would probably punch you for prying so much into my personal life. Don't ask me about God, or life, and especially don't ask me about being 'ready to die.'" His voice was sharp and hostile.

David sat back in his seat. "Jon, I'm sorry. I was talking about the patient. He was alone, dirty, and sick but he thought he was ready. I thought it was odd that he looked at death as a reward, not as a curse." David controlled his voice, forcing it to sound non-confrontational. "I was talking about him, not you." David paused, "Are you all right?"

Jonathan looked over at his friend. "Listen, I am really sorry I jumped you. Robert really gave me hell when we got home last night. He threatened me!" Jonathan paused as a rush of emotions ran to his throat. He coughed and cleared his airway that seemed so tight, then continued. "He really scared me. I laid in bed beside him, knowing everything about my life was wrong. I have never felt that way before. I couldn't stand myself. Robert could tell, but he seemed to enjoy my suffering. He made me feel like his slave." Jonathan looked over the dash, "And, he was right. I just couldn't get out of there. It was like I was forced to see where I am, and where I was going. I really thought about killing myself to get away from him, and then I would look at him and see the sadistic pleasure in his eyes, and I knew that he could very easily kill me when I fell asleep. It scared me in one sense and brought relief in another. But then there was this real soft question that kept whispering through my mind," Jonathan paused as he thought. "For the first time in my life, I had asked myself 'If Robert does kill you tonight, then what will you do? Are you ready?'" Jonathan looked at David, "and then the first question you put to me is the same one, 'Are you ready?' It's just too much for me. The coincidence is more than eerie."

David had no idea what to say except, "Are you all right?" Again he asked the question. Now, he was afraid of the answer.

Jonathan frowned and put the ambulance back in gear. The hospital was about thirty minutes away from their station, and there was no fast way back to the station. Slowly, the unit progressed down Highway 301. "Let's get a Cuban sandwich on the way back." Jonathan tried to lighten the conversation, but he finished with the truth. "I just don't know what to think. That's why I don't want to talk about it anymore. My mind is like a battlefield. Does that make sense to you? One part of me wants to do what I don't think I can do, but I know is right, and the other part feels bound to the life I have chosen for myself, even if it will kill me. It's more than just Robert. It's a matter of who I am and what I have become. I feel torn apart. Until I decide, I don't know what I'll do. And, no, I am not ready for anything, especially death, right now."

David looked at his friend. "I won't talk about it anymore. If you want to, you bring it up. Is that a deal? But, promise me that you won't do anything stupid." David wanted to continue to press the point. It felt urgent inside of him to press Jonathan, as if it was the right thing to do and needed to be done now, but he chose not to offend his partner. He would let it rest. He was sure they would have time later to talk.

Procrastination whispered thoughts. Later, you have time. Jonathan has time. Later, he'll be OK. Wait until later. And, David believed these thoughts. The opportunity for Life passed through the window of the ambulance, and Death drew closer still.

"Sure." Jonathan reached down and turned on the radio. The music covered the strained quietness that both men still felt. The ambulance continued toward their station. Twenty more hours left to this shift ... Plenty of time, for anything.

The unpainted barn began to creak as the heat and humidity affected the old wooden beams. Dark clouds of an impending storm were moving quickly across the horizon. The air was heavy as the heat rose up toward the dark sky, but there was no breeze present to comfort the captive. The broken and bleeding young man lay against the post that held him. Unaware of the changing weather, he only knew he was in severe pain and just wanted it to stop. He wanted to sleep but the pain to breathe kept him awake as each shallow breath forced his lungs to press against his broken ribs. He shifted his weight against the ropes that held him, and he suddenly coughed violently, causing bright red bloody sputum and another tooth to be expelled through his swollen mouth. With each painful breath, he was reminded of his imminent death. He knew his drug supplier would be there soon and it would be over. He whimpered, "Please, just kill me." Tears ran down his broken and torn face. Helplessness held this prisoner. His captors just laughed. Death would come soon enough.

His mind drifted in and out of the delirium caused by his abuse. He watched fragmented pieces of his life slowly drift before him. He watched his mother making birthday cakes. Each year on his birthday, they would make one. He remembered the big black cake they had made. Batman. I remember. I was three. He tried to envision each year's birthday cake, and somehow the good thoughts of yesterday, eased the pain of the present. There before him was the dinosaur cake when he was five, and there was Spiderman. I was six ... What was it when I was seven, that's right, it was the race cars. On and on the memories rolled before his eyes.

"Joey, come in here, I have a present for you," he watched his mother carry his new Xbox video game system to him. The memory of his mother's voice and love comforted him. He forced his mind to concentrate on his mother and on her love. It was light in this dark place of tortured captivity. Suddenly, there were the tears of love that strengthened him emotionally, and the tears produced from the whip of helplessness gradually dried. His mind slowly found other good memories and moved away from the pain that throbbed throughout his body. He smiled as he thought of the beautiful girl he had spent time with a few nights ago. She had just sat there in silence, sad and detached from his attempts at conversation, but, gradually, she started to grin, and she was fun to talk to. Every so often, he could hear the faint Pop of the bubble gum she was chewing. Somehow the sounds of her simple pleasure of gum popping brought a smile to his face, then, as well as, now. "Debra," he whispered through his broken and bleeding lips, as he tried to picture every detail of the beautiful brown-haired girl he had taken out after the memorial service. Her memory gradually lifted him further out of his torturous prison, and he fell asleep against her imagined breasts. And, for a moment, like any normal teenage male might, he dreamt of her.

His pain only allowed for a short period of rest, and he awakened fighting against the ropes that bound him. And, as his mind cleared further, he wrestled not only with the ropes but now with the shame from the clear memory of the memorial service and why he was there. Somehow, the pain that racked his body comforted him, like it was a small price to pay for the damage he had done. He remembered all the people crying and the mothers and fathers suffering. He was going to use Debra to see if the students knew that he was the drug dealer that had sold the cocaine to Tommy. He didn't think Tommy would have told anyone of his source. Therefore, if anyone knew, he assumed it would be Debra. The thought of Tommy and the others at the football party and the reality of their deaths finally pierced his broken heart with truth. "I am so sorry!" he yelled as the guilt awakened further in him and, for the first time, knew he needed to make it right. Suddenly, he realized that he didn't care if the police knew and wished he could tell them. He whimpered in resignation and stopped fighting the ropes that bound him, knowing the opportunity to come clean would never be given him, and he trembled in the soul agonizing pain of that knowledge. "I am so sorry," he whispered, and again he cried, this time in deep sorrow for what he had done.

His evil demonic captors laughed when they saw him cry. They would not have laughed if they knew that the tears were washing his heart free of their hold on his soul. But the fools just laughed in their ignorance and arrogance. Anger didn't care that he was being replaced by remorse for a moment, for he knew Death was imminent and there would be no chance for the captive to clear his conscience. He would be sure of that. The inevitability of their captive's death gave Anger confidence to reveal his source of strength in Joey. So, he returned to the captive and picked up a knife of twisted truth and dug it into his heart.

The salt from Joey's tears burned as they ran down his face, and the dark brown mixture of blood, sweat, and dirt dripped to the dirty wooden floor. In his hazed mind, the color reminded him of the desk in his father's study, and he could see his father, sitting smugly in his office, reading. He watched as his memory focused to when he stood at the doorway, and his father yelled in violent anger, "Joey, what are you doing in here? I told you to never come in my office. Get out of here! I have to work." Torment raised his weapon and twisted Joey's mind as he saw himself standing in that doorway, crying and embarrassed by the warm urine that ran down his little leg. The memory swirled around his mind, stirring up the source of his pent-up anger and revealing the emotional wounds that tortured his soul. The young man looked down at his bruised body. I wonder if dad even noticed that I'm not at home. I doubt it. Joey yelled in anger at the vision of his father before him, "Money! That was all that mattered to you, Dad. Just your money, that's all you ever cared about! You didn't have time for me, and I was never good enough for you. I never mattered to you!" Joey cried again as he thought of his dad. Dad, I hate you! I hated you …

Anger stabbed his heart once more, but this time something had changed. Joey suddenly realized that he had allowed the anger of his father's rejection to control him. Tears again rolled down his face as Joey spoke to the shadow of his father before him. "Dad, I'm sorry. I am done hating you. I was so angry at you for being gone so much and being so cruel to me and mom, but I am just like you, but worse. My hunger for money and power controlled me, and I got angry just like you when I didn't get it." Joey wept that his father would never know how much he loved him. "Dad, I forgive you, and I am so sorry." The image before him vanished, and he rested in peace for a moment.

Anger had been a fool to reveal so much of his root strength and watched in horror at the loss of his own control. This young man had chosen to forgive, and there was no place for his anger in that environment. He had no option but to watch as this young man made his choice. Every human had the right to choose, always! Anger knew he would have to honor the choice. Everyone in this war did. Anger kicked and screamed in the face of the Warriors of Light that appeared, but then he quickly backed off. Again, he had lost. It was so unfair! He could no longer claim this one as His captive. He turned his fist up and held it within inches of the swords still drawn. "Well, you can take me off this fool, but I'll still win my reward. Death is coming to take this flesh and burn it, and You can't stop Him. I'll get my reward, you wait and see." He turned to leave, and the stench of his power carried the last of his venom, "I'm leaving, and I'll find another fool that will let me in."

With each painful breath, Joey was reminded of his imminent death. He knew his drug supplier would be there soon and it would be over. Joey tried to take his mind off his pain and focus on the wooded field beside the old barn. The land before him was barren of life, and the humid heat baked everything. No birds or rabbits could be seen. He had noticed them out there a few hours earlier, but now he felt all alone. Would they ever find his body? He doubted it and feared his mother would never know that he died and think he had just run off. He didn't want to die alone and wept as he whispered, "Mom, I am really sorry for all the pain I have caused you!" His mind swirled in the intensity of the images of loss and suffering, and then he thought he saw his mother standing before him. He rocked back and forth as he cried, "Mom, I am so sorry!" Joey took a deep breath, looked up at the dark clouds forming, and through the darkness that surrounded him, he whispered, "Oh God, please, forgive me." The last sounds he heard were of his captors' laughter as they mocked his cry. His exhausted body fell forward against the ropes that held him captive, the sleep of unconsciousness stilled him, and all became very dark.

Outside the barn, light broke through the dark sky, but dark rain clouds pushed back and rolled into the opening, causing darkness to once again cover the sky. Death came to claim his prize. A large white Cadillac slowly approached the barn. Quickly, two large men walked to the post that held their captive and cut the rope. Joey collapsed into the dirt. One man grabbed each arm of the weak lump of flesh and held Joey between them as they walked quickly to the car. He rested in their arms as he slipped into deeper unconsciousness. He thought he was resting in his mother's arms, and they didn't notice the smile upon his face.

Debra entered the school cafeteria and waved at Terri. She was not feeling well but was excited about spending time with her new friend. Debra blew a big bubble with her gum and walked quickly toward her.

As Debra approached, Terri noticed Debra's pale face and red swollen eyes. Softly Terri said. "What's wrong? You don't look good! Are you OK?"

Debra smiled and tried to sit down, but suddenly she stood up, grabbed her belly, and said "I don't feel good. I think I need to go to the bathroom. Will you come with me?" Her eyes pleaded with Terri and revealed the severity of the pain. The two walked to the bathroom at the far end of the hall. The closer bathrooms would be full of kids, and Debra said it was worth the walk to get to a private place. Halfway down the hall, Debra reached over and grabbed Terri's arm and squeezed as a little cry escaped her lips. "Hurry up, help me walk faster," she whispered.

Debra cried out again as the bathroom door shut behind them. Her forehead was now covered in sweat, and she pointed to her lower stomach, "My belly hurts, I feel like I am about to have the worst menstrual period ever! Which is weird because my period has been so strange lately." Debra grabbed her belly, crying out in pain, and slowly slid to the floor. "Help me get these pants off, I can't breathe with them on!"

"Not until I get some help. You don't look too good. I'll be right back."

Debra unwillingly released her grip from Terri's hand. Terri opened the bathroom door and saw a lone boy was walking the hallway. She called out to him to get help, and he ran for a teacher. Terri returned to Debra and noticed that her face was growing paler and that her cries of pain seemed to come and go. Terri didn't know what else to do, so she held her friend's hand and knelt beside her. She could see the blood and water begin to pool between Debra's legs and she felt nausea roll like waves inside her. Fear caused both girls to tremble as they sat there and waited. She whispered a prayer that help would get there fast.

Rescue 12 was continuing down the road toward their station. The radio music covered the uncomfortable silence. The two paramedics had ended their conversation about death. Jonathan filled his mind with thoughts about the great Cuban sandwich he was going to eat. He was driving the ambulance straight toward the Coffee Cup Restaurant on Highway 41. David opened his medical journal and began to read.

The 911 dispatcher asked Rescue 12 for their location. Slowly Jonathan picked up the microphone and confessed their actual location, "Rescue 12, Highway 41 and College Avenue." He hoped dispatch would have a closer unit to whatever emergency call had come in. He didn't want another call right now.

"Rescue 12 respond to unknown abdominal pain at Tampa High School. There will be a teacher to lead you to the bathroom with the patient."

Jonathan reached over and flipped on the lights. This was their call. Jonathan rubbed the palms of his hands on the steering wheel. He noticed that his hands were sweating in nervous anticipation. That 'paramedic feeling' was telling him that this was going to be bad, really bad. His eyes were focused on the road as they darted in and out of the traffic that rarely got completely out of his way. The air horn blew, the sirens screamed, and rapidly Rescue 12 made its way up highway 41.

David was surprised when he noticed that his own heart rate had jumped up a few beats a minute. He swallowed as he tried to calm himself. Cold chills ran up and down his spine.

Years of street experience had made him recognize that feeling. David knew he was about to fight Death again. He focused his mind for the battle.

The supplier walked to the trunk of his car and looked at his young captive. No one knew Joey was his dealer and he was the only link to the teenagers who had died using the lethal cocaine. Their deaths were not his problem, and one more dead teenager wasn't either. Joey lay bound and unconscious from the beatings his men had inflicted. The smell of blood excited the supplier. He laughed, mocking the bloody body he saw before him, striking him to awaken his sleeping captive. "So how do you like being my partner? Have you enjoyed your treatment so far?" His mockery was lost on the captive who remained still and unconscious.

The supplier looked toward his guards. "I told you not to take him too close to death. If he dies before I kill him, I'll punish you, as well." His men looked at each other. Fear gained strength in them and tightened his noose around their necks. "You know what I do to those that don't do as I tell them." His men nervously awaited their employer's whim, and he enjoyed their fear. It satisfied him for a moment.

"We'll take him to my boat. It seems like a nice day for a ride in the bay. I'm sure Joey will love a swim." He took Joey by the hair of his head, "Won't you?" There was no response. He dropped the head down with force, and it bounced as it hit the edge of the trunk. Blood stained the rear bumper area. The guards folded the crumpled body back into the trunk. The supplier reached over and touched the bright red blood that stained his white car. He stared at the blood on the tip of his finger and gently tasted it with the same pleasure he had in tasting the white powder of death he traded in so often. The sneer lingered on his face as he walked to the rear seat of his car. He was pleased to offer his partner, Death, another gift. Somehow, he thought it would add to his own eternal reign in hell.

Death reached in and touched the finger stained with blood. The sacrifice would be sweet indeed. The guards got back in the car, and slowly they left the wooded field, driving toward their destination called Death, Hell and the Grave.

"Rescue 12 on scene at Tampa High School," Jonathan spoke rapidly into the microphone as the unit came to a complete stop. Jonathan grabbed the airway bag. David carried a large box full of bandages and fluids in one hand, and the EKG machine in the other. Quickly, they followed the nervous counselor to the bathroom at the end of the long corridor. The fire department engine arrived behind them, and three firemen swiftly followed the paramedics to the patient.

The school administrator met them as the ambulance came to a stop and rushed them to their patient, "We didn't move her because she is bleeding. The parents have been called and are on the way now to the school. Hurry, I think she is having a baby. The school nurse is with her now."

David and Jonathan were surprised when the bathroom door opened, and they recognized both young girls. Each man swallowed deeply and maintained their calm, professional appearance while they looked for clues to what was going on. Both girls looked terrified and pale. Debra was trembling in fear, dripping in sweat and her bloody jeans were lying beside her.

"What happened?" David asked as he took Debra's arm. He found a weak pulse. His gloved hands were instantly wet by her sweat.

Debra simply cried, "I didn't know. I didn't know. I didn't know."

"Didn't know what? What happened?" Jonathan was concerned by the pool of blood between her legs.

Terri didn't speak. She just looked down at Debra's legs as she slowly held her hands up toward David. Blood hung from between her fingers, she was holding something gently in her hands, and stuttered, "It just came out. I just caught it. I didn't know what to do." She was obviously in shock herself, her hands trembled, and her fingers were frozen in position.

David opened Terri's hands and curled her fingers away from what she was holding. Because of the blood, he wasn't surprised that he found a baby, but he was surprised that it was still alive because it was so very small. He took the baby from Terri's hands and held it out for Jonathan to see. Instantly, Jonathan grabbed the portable radio on his waist and called for the helicopter. Each of the emergency medical personnel stood ready for action.

Joshua, the rookie firefighter, standing at the door, wanted to help the paramedics. He spoke up, "Can I help?" His pale face revealed the controlled fear that gripped him.

Without looking away from his patients, David answered, "The lights are bad in here. Get a flashlight and hold it over the baby so I can see it better."

Joshua complied instantly. The light flashed from side to side over the patient as the nervous young man tried and failed to keep his trembling hands still. Sweat dripped from his face as he watched the two paramedics treat their two patients, the teenage mother, and her new baby.

David looked up at the fire captain in the doorway and said, "Careflight is on the way. I'll need a landing zone ready. Would you have your men set up two IV's for us, and get the stretcher?

We need it yesterday." Captain Sawyer turned and rushed out of the bathroom. They would be ready for the helicopter.

David looked at the baby and began to speak to anyone who could hear this surprising report, "It can't be any more than two pounds. Yet, it is looking around. It is fully awake, and in no apparent distress." David was surprised, and his voice cracked, and he whispered, "The baby's color is pink, and looks very good."

Debra asked tentatively, "Is it a boy or girl?" Her mind was searching for something to hope in and something that would let this feel more real.

Jonathan was kneeling on the ground, next to Debra. He had rolled up her shirt sleeve, actively looking for an IV site but looked up and smiled at his patient. The question verified her level of consciousness as normal. He turned and looked at the baby that David held. David smiled as he picked up the umbilical cord that rested against the baby's body. The cord was almost as big and round as the baby's belly. Slowly he pressed the little legs down so that he could see the genitals. "It's a boy," David said, looking at the appendage, no wider than a piece of macaroni pasta, which was about right for a child who was almost as long as an ear of corn. He was so small, but he was definitely a boy. David delighted in the miracle he was holding and witnessing.

The baby rested in David's hand. Through his thin almost transparent skin you could almost see the organs underneath. David watched as the baby's chest bounced in response to his strong heartbeat, and his dark brown lungs filled and then fell, filled then fell, over and over. The breaths were regular and without a struggling effort. The baby was wide awake, and his eyes looked around in what appeared to be purposeful movement. David watched in amazement, and his throat felt like it was full of cotton in the face of this miracle. David continued to examine him, and it appeared that the baby was healthy and without any obvious distress. David inhaled deeply in relief and then wiped vernix, the white cream from the womb, off the premature infant. The baby kicked his legs at the stimulation, and simultaneously his right thumb found his mouth. He seemed genuinely comforted by sucking his thumb. A sterile warming blanket was wrapped around the infant to protect him from developing hypothermia. Otherwise no further treatment seemed necessary, for the moment.

David's attention returned to Debra as she lay on the bathroom floor. Jonathan had already started an IV and was giving his patient a large amount of fluid to replace the blood that she had lost. Terri was holding her hand and occasionally wiping a tear from Debra's face. Debra lay there crying softly. It wasn't the pain in her body, but the revelation of her new son that caused the tears. Her new son. Debra squeezed Terri's hand. "I didn't know. Today, on the bus, I had this idea that I might be. But, I didn't know." She cried, "If I had known for sure, I might have aborted it." Again, she cried and whispered, "Thank God, I didn't know. I have a son."

Terri reached down and hugged her friend, "Love won out this time. Your son is gonna have a great mom."

Jonathan opened the bathroom door as the firemen rolled the stretcher inside. Debra was gently placed on the stretcher, and the stretcher straps were applied. Her color was improving. Jonathan took a blood pressure reading, "100/60. It's better, but we still need to hurry." The baby was handed to his mother, and then the stretcher was rolled to the landing zone for the awaiting helicopter.

Excitement and fear filled Debra's mind. The helicopter crew only wanted to transport one patient, the baby. They wanted to have enough room to work, if the baby became distressed. David agreed. Debra trembled as she watched her baby being lifted into the emergency helicopter. "Debra, we'll get you there fast by ambulance. I promise," David said. Terri didn't want to let go of her friend's hand, and she started to step up into the ambulance. "Terri, I can't let you come." David's voice was forceful and allowed no room for debate.

Slowly Terri released her grip. "I'll see you at the hospital as soon as I can, I promise." As the men loaded Debra into the ambulance, she was fascinated by the surprisingly large compartment in the back.

David looked over at the eager firefighter, "Joshua, please drive us to the hospital." He looked at the rookie, "Use the lights, but please be as smooth as possible."

"I promise a smooth ride." sweat dripped from the face of this young nervous man.

David reached over and handed a flashlight to Joshua, "Here's your flashlight. You dropped it on the way out of the bathroom. I guess you didn't notice." David smiled a fatherly look at this new firefighter and patted him on the back as he stepped into the back of the ambulance with Jonathan and Debra. Joshua turned red at his own clumsiness and took the flashlight. As he walked to the cab of the ambulance, he determined he would prove his worth with the smoothest ride possible to the hospital.

David and Jonathan reexamined their young patient as the unit pulled out of the school. David knew life and death were again in battle in the back of the ambulance, but he didn't know why. Debra appeared stable; however, he could not shake the ominous feeling that troubled him.

As the ambulance screamed down Highway 41, David heard over the radio that the helicopter had landed at Tampa General and that the baby was still stable. He stood up and leaned over to tell Debra the good news. Suddenly, the air horn blasted through the air, and the brakes locked. The ambulance twisted. David lunged for the railing on the ceiling. His hand found it, as his feet left the floor. He held on, as the unit swerved to the left, and suddenly stopped, its metal ripping from the impact with another vehicle.

David found himself lying on the floor of the ambulance. Boxes of unopened drugs covered him because the drug compartment doors had opened, spilling all their supplies onto the unit's floor. The EKG machine rested on David's right ankle. He rolled over and bent forward to get the machine off but stopped because of the sudden sharp stabbing pain that shot up his right arm. He looked at his right wrist and hand that had held him up during the crash. It was twisted abnormally and was now obviously broken. He moved his right hand close to his body as he removed the monitor from his foot with his left hand and stood up to check Debra.

She appeared to have not gotten hurt by the crash, but she screamed in terror. She was struggling to figure out how to release the straps that held her securely to the stretcher that was locked to the ambulance floor while kicking against the medical supplies that had fallen out of the shelves on impact but had not actually injured her. He tried to calm her down as he turned his attention to the surrounding damage.

Suddenly, he saw Jonathan, who lay still on the ground between the stretcher and rear doors. He wasn't moving at all. Fear gripped David, and everything felt like it was moving in slow motion as he moved to get to his friend. His left hand stretched forward and touched Jonathan, but he did not respond, so with one hand, he grabbed Jonathan by his shirt and threw him up onto the flat bench seat beside the stretcher. David yelled, "Jonathan, wake up! Jon, wake up!" All the while his left hand reaching, touching, trying to find a pulse, trying to find some effort to breathe but there was none.

David grabbed the microphone from off the wall. "Rescue 12. Help us, we've been hit!"

Dispatch responded, "What is your location?"

David had forgotten to look. He peered out the window and recognized the entrance ramp to the expressway. "Highway 41 and the Lee Roy Selmon Expressway. Jonathan's hurt! I don't know who else is. Get the helicopter here quick."

David heard dispatch record the time "12:21 hours."

David turned his full attention back to his friend. There was no obvious injury, so David knew that meant it was probably something internal that was broken and bleeding. Immediately, he placed his broken wrist and hand under Jonathan's jaw to stabilize his head, and his good hand held the nostrils of his friend. David blew in four quick breaths into Jonathan's mouth. The chest rose evenly. His left hand shook with fear as he checked for a pulse and found none. David placed his broken hand upon his friend's breast bone and placed his left hand on top of the broken one. Slowly he began to count as he pressed into his friend's chest, "One - One Thousand, Two - One Thousand, Three - One Thousand, Four - One Thousand, Five - One Thousand..." He stopped and gave two quick breaths into Jonathan's mouth then continued the cycle of breaths and compressions. A puddle of tears and sweat formed in the hollow of Jonathan's chest as David stood over him and worked so hard to save his dear friend's life.

It didn't seem real, so he was surprised, when suddenly the back doors opened and the rescue crew from the helicopter stepped in. In a daze, he watched them push him back out of the way and carry Jonathan outside onto their stretcher. David sat on the bench seat and just stared at the helicopter. Its blades going around and around. Slowly he watched it rise from the ground as he heard the radio announce their departure for Tampa General.

Debra's whimpering cry brought David back to the continuing crisis at hand. David pressed his emotions into submission and forced himself to refocus toward the other potential patients from this accident. There was more to do, right now. He touched Debra, "You'll be alright. I need to see who else is hurt. They will be sending another ambulance for you quick, I promise. Just stay here and wait." She had no time to answer and swallowed in stunned silence as he stepped out and quickly disappeared around the front of the ambulance.

A white Cadillac was twisted and impaled upon the front end of the ambulance. David could see immediately that the driver and front seat passenger were not moving and were pressed against the windshield of their wrecked car. There had been no seat belt worn to protect them, and the airbag had not deployed. Broken metal pierced their flesh, and their heads rested against the windshield that encased their faces with shattered glass. Their death was caused by the blunt trauma they had absorbed at the impact of the accident, and they would require no immediate work to save them.

David immediately moved to check out the back seat for any other possible survivor. He could see a passenger laying still and twisted on the rear floor area; however, the broken metal and the front seat blocked a clear view of the passenger's face. Quickly, his left hand reached into the broken side window and stretched until it felt the man's head then slid down to his neck. David expected to find him dead, as well and was surprised by the strong pulse in the neck of the unconscious man. David heard sirens approaching and, in the distance, he looked up, and he could see a fire engine and second ambulance driving quickly toward him and knew there would be others to help this patient as soon as possible. He let go of this man's neck and continued to look for other victims.

As he rushed to check on Joshua, he thought that there was something about the damaged car and living passenger that seemed familiar, but his mind was blinded by fear for his friend and the need to focus on checking on the rookie firefighter. The hood of the ambulance had rolled forward at impact and now blocked access to Joshua. David's left hand pulled at the driver's door, but it wouldn't budge, so he jumped on the hood of the white car and slid himself onto the hood of his ambulance. He pulled himself as close as he could to the front window. David looked in around the twisted metal and saw Joshua laying still. His left hand grabbed the shattered windshield and tried to pull it back to see if he could somehow manage some entry into the cab that held Joshua. David couldn't budge the metal and glass, and his left hand began to bleed from the effort that was slicing it.

Captain Sawyer grabbed David's leg and yelled, "Where is Joshua?"

"He is in here! I just got up here. We need to cut the door off to get him out." David slid off the broken hood with the immediate assistance of Captain Sawyer, protectively holding both of his hands as he turned over the scene to the captain's care.

"Could you see him? Is he moving? Can he hear you?" Captain Sawyer demanded an immediate report, and he didn't attempt to cover his fear.

"I don't know. I could barely see him, and I couldn't hear anything. Let's just get him out quick. And, we'll need another rescue team to cut out the patient in the white car. I found one patient still alive in the passenger's rear seat, and two dead ones."

The captain glanced at the car. "If someone can survive in that, they'll wait until we get Joshua out of your unit, or until the second engine gets here to help. I'll get my firefighter out before I'll do anything else." Even as he was speaking to David, his men had prepared the equipment to get to their brother firefighter. The generator for the hydraulic tools instantly cranked on, and the Jaws of Life once again began the process of freeing a trapped victim. But this time it was the firefighter inside.

The noise of the generator for the Jaws of Life covered the muffled groans of the young pinned fireman. The sounds of his favorite piece of equipment somehow had awakened him from his distant dark sleep. He knew he would be out in a moment and he smiled before slipping back into unconsciousness. The driver's door of the ambulance ripped open slightly, and Joshua's hand fell out through the opening. The fireman on the Jaws of Life froze. His hands trembled as another man grabbed Joshua's arm. "He has a pulse." Cheers yelled out above the sound of the generator. The hand was held out of the way, and the mechanical jaws continued to eat the metal.

The door opened. One man swiftly grabbed Joshua's neck to keep it straight. Another man placed a firm collar around his neck. A third man reached around his brother and checked to make sure Joshua's feet were free. "He's free, let's get him out of here!" The helicopter crew had landed and had their stretcher ready. Joshua was carefully lowered onto their spine board. One paramedic began cutting off his clothes, while the RN from the helicopter crew stuck his arm with a large needle. They had brought universal blood with them from the hospital. The blood poured into Joshua's arm.

Rapidly, the helicopter team began to examine their young male patient. His face had multiple deep jagged cuts and blood poured from his nose and mouth. The flight paramedic grabbed the portable suction unit and cleared Joshua's airway. However, the bright red blood continued to flow from his wounds and filled the vacuum chamber of the suction unit. He needed to be intubated, but the injuries to his face were too deforming to attempt to intubate with an ET tube at his mouth. They didn't want to take the chance that it would land in the brain, and there was just no guarantee where the tube might end up.

The Flight RN began to use the Ambu bag to help force oxygen into Joshua's lungs. His chest rose and fell to her hand pressure on the football-shaped bag she pressed, but the stream of blood was still able to flow into the back of his throat, and into his lungs. The two flight medics looked at each other. In a flash of a moment, the decision was made. One paramedic removed the drying blood from the firefighter's neck. The Adam's apple of the neck was felt, and the location of structures just below it was confirmed, as the RN began to cleanse the neck with betadine and then alcohol.

Without warning the watching firemen of their decision, the flight paramedic took a scalpel and with one motion slit the neck of the unconscious fireman. Blood poured from the one-inch incision. Tears flowed freely from the watching fire crew. One man's face paled as he weakly stepped back. Immediately another slit from the scalpel was made to the incision. This time the sound of escaping air could be heard. The specially prepared ET tube was slowly slid into the incision toward the lungs. It was instantly secured in place. The Ambu bag was then attached to the ET tube. The patient's airway was now safe and secure. The bleeding from his face was no longer able to drain into his lungs, and a higher concentration of oxygen was able to be delivered to him. Within moments, Joshua was en route to Tampa General via this rescue helicopter team. He remained unconscious and unaware of the accident he was leaving behind.

David watched from the bumper of the fire engine parked close behind his ambulance. As the rescue scene continued to unfold before his eyes, he numbly thought it must be a dream. Men and women were rushing around to different tasks, and his mind continued to try and take in all he was witnessing. Police and fire department teams worked in perfect harmony. A second fire engine team had arrived on the scene, and they worked to free the patient trapped in the white car. The middle-aged man was pulled from the rear window, head first. He had been strapped to a wooden board to protect his back. His neck was being held still by a woman firefighter. The only feature of this patient David could see from where he sat was the red hair on the top of his head. The hair was matted by dark reddish-brown blood. He knew he was missing something obvious about the red-haired patient and white Cadillac. For a moment, he tried to remember but quickly returned to just watching everything around him in stunned silence. David decided he had seen enough and slowly walked to wait in the ambulance cab parked several rescue units away from the accident noise and chaos.

A fireman examined the front seat passengers of the white car. Their faces were ripped, their flesh and hair hung from the broken windshield. Dark blue bruises had already begun to form on their faces. The fireman threw a white sheet over each dead man. The roadside bystanders would be saved from seeing the images that nightmares are made of. The noises of power equipment began to quiet. Now, the voices of orders to be followed and plans to be made filled the air. The next rescue helicopter landed in the field.

Their flight crew ran over to the fire rescue team who were trying to control their patient. The redheaded man was somewhat conscious, but only awake enough to fight any help they tried to give. He fought the rescue crew and yelled, "Let me go. I won't die. Let me Go!" His fists flung out at anything they could find. Three firemen held him down as another one tied his feet and arms to the wooden backboard. The patient spat and bit at the man holding his head. "Let me Go. I won't die. I want out of here." His screams horrified the bystanders who had come up close enough to watch. "You can't do this! Don't you know who I am? Who are you?"

The flight nurse walked over to her patient and gently said, "Sir, I'm going to give you medicine that will paralyze you from the neck down. You'll remain awake, but you won't be able to move. It is for your protection. If you broke your back in this accident, all your moving around may kill you." As she spoke, the patient felt a warm sensation run up his arm. When he felt its heat touch his neck, suddenly he could not move. Horror filled his eyes and his spit out abusive insults to the team.

The fireman who had been holding the patient's neck and head as straight as possible leaned over and whispered in this abusive man's ear, "Now, we are in charge. You're not. Just shut up!" His words pierced the man's pride. He had never lost control before, now he watched as it was snatched from him.

The nurse reached down to his foot and took off his shoes. She checked for response. He knew what she was doing because he could see, but he couldn't move. "We need to see what other injuries you have so we are going to have to remove your clothes," she said out loud as she grabbed his pants and instantly cut them as the others pulled the clothes out from underneath him. For a split second, he lay naked in the middle of Highway 41.

The bound patient watched as he was stripped and examined by these emergency personnel but suddenly realized he didn't care anymore. He took his eyes off the caregivers and stared at the blue sky beyond the activity around him. He enjoyed the quietness that was rapidly replacing all the sounds that had been bombarding him a moment earlier. The clouds drifted overhead, and he rested as he noticed what a beautiful day it was, and his mind drifted further and further from the car accident. Up through the clouds, into the sky, into the darkness of space, he felt himself rise free of all earthly restraint. He could no longer see the road upon which he had lain. He tried to return his thoughts to the accident; however, where he was now seemed more real than that distant memory of the life he once knew. Gradually, he realized that darkness was fully saturating him, and this darkness was colder than anything he could imagine. He couldn't move his hands to warm himself, nor could he open his eyes. He was falling further into the darkness of eternal silence.

The earlier flight crews had already taken Jonathan and Joshua to Tampa General, so they diverted this helicopter crew to St Joseph's hospital. The rear seat passenger had become an unresponsive, unconscious patient who was secured to the spine board with IV fluids running. His blood pressure and pulse remained stable, and hopefully, he would remain alive until the emergency department trauma team could evaluate him.

Captain Sawyer leaned against the trunk of the wrecked white Cadillac. He was finally able to relax as he slowly inhaled his cigarette. His emergent tasks were done. Debra, the girl on Rescue 12's stretcher, was the only one without injury from this accident and she had left earlier by another ambulance to go to Tampa General to be evaluated for her recent delivery of the preterm baby. The last ambulance on scene was now pulling off to drive David to Tampa General to get his wrist treated. Within seconds, he and his men would have to return to duty and await the next call. Right now, all he could think about was the critically injured firefighter and paramedic. He looked down at the trunk as he bent his head to light his next cigarette. He noticed a streak of dried blood that stopped at the trunk. Richard looked up at the damage to the car and tried to figure out how there could be blood at this corner of the car. He bent down to look at the damage on the back of the car. He thought he heard something. He placed his head against the trunk and held his breath.

"Help!" came the soft broken whisper.

The captain's eyes grew wide as he yelled to his firefighter, "Kevin, bring me the Halligan bar. I think I found someone!" Kevin leaped from the fire engine and ran to the captain with the large metal tool. With one strong thrust, its pointed end was struck into the trunk lock. The trunk snapped open.

Joey looked into the face of his rescuers, each had the same shocked expression of both pleasure and worry. Joey's eyes returned to the darkness as unconsciousness covered him like a warm blanket, and his blood pressure slowly began its descent to zero.

Captain Sawyer picked up the portable radio, "Dispatch have Rescue 33 return to the scene. We have found another patient." David heard the radio, was surprised and wondered where they could have found another patient. He was frustrated at the delay in getting to Tampa General to see Jonathan, but he had no choice as the unit turned around and headed back to the scene.

The captain examined the young beaten patient sleeping in the trunk of the car. The bruises were obviously old. The patient's face was swollen and purple. Large green rings had formed around each eye. A large gash with dried blood was on top of his head. The men were slow to pull him out of the trunk for fear of a broken or damaged spine. Every precaution for spinal injury was taken. The few extra minutes might save his life.

David watched as the rear doors of the ambulance were opened again and the rescue crew rolled in their newest patient. Steve, the paramedic, assigned to this unit, offered an apology with his explanation. "David, I'm sorry, but this kid is beat up bad. We can't take him to Tampa General. They are full. We've got to go to St. Joe's."

David grimaced. He knew his friend was right. Tampa General couldn't handle another critical patient. He put his own concerns aside. His attention turned to the unconscious male now being attended to by his fellow paramedics in the back of this unit. The broken and bruised face of this young man was swollen, but suddenly David recognized him. He yelled out at the deputy standing near the ambulance, "Get in here, Quick! I know this guy!"

The Supplier of men's lives heard his name spoken from a hideous voice, "Robert, Robert, my purchased token, wake up." Robert saw the unveiled face of a thousand horrors, and he closed his eyes. Fear held him captive as Death grabbed the fool and sneered, "Don't you want to see your partner?" Pain pierced Robert's flesh as the words penetrated his mind.

Robert knew he was looking at the one he had moments before thought he controlled, but now he understood that Death was not one to make partners of humans. However, he clung to any chance that his deal on earth would matter now, "I thought we had a deal. I thought you promised me that I would live," he paused on these words, "Forever ... "

Laughter pierced his ears as scorching pain shot through his head as he heard, "You shall live forever. You shall live forever yet be dead." Again, the voice laughed at his tormented soul, and the darkness increased until Robert could again see nothing but the utter darkness that enveloped him.

"What do you mean? I don't understand." Robert turned to the left and then the right trying to find the location that this voice was coming from. He saw nothing but darkness, even the stars had disappeared in this eternal void.

Hideous laughter rose around him. Robert hated to be laughed at, and his hatred erupted beyond his fear and spun to the memory of the first time he killed someone. As clearly as a movie playing in front of him, he saw the scene replayed before him. It was morbidly interesting and pulled his mind further away from his fear, "What is going on? I remember what happened. Stop this!" He yelled into the void, "I remember, I was at a bar, and some redneck made fun of me because I was looking for a male date. I taught him a lesson though, and a lesson for all his friends. I stuck a knife in his belly, and he died in my hands. I'll not be laughed at! Whoever you are, stop it!" Robert's voice rose higher as he screamed into the darkness filled only with mocking laughter.

Robert tried to move his legs and arms, but he could not feel them, and fear came quickly again as his anger found no response to his screams "Death, you are my partner," Robert's voice whispered in the darkness. "I thought we had a deal." Darkness enveloped his words until Robert knew he was totally alone.

Suddenly a bright light appeared. Robert fought to leave the darkness and find his way back to the light. Robert gradually felt the intense throbbing pain in his broken body, and his eyes squinted from the bright light of the emergency department exam room. He looked up at the doctor wearing a blue face mask and goggles who was actively exploring the wounds on his chest, then turned to see the nurses moving rapidly around him. He took a deep breath in relief believing the darkness had only been a dream. For a moment, fear gripped him when he realized that he still couldn't move, but then he recalled that he had been given something to keep him from moving at the car accident. "It's just the drugs. I'll be fine," he whispered, but no one noticed. The intense brightness from the overhead light caused Robert to close his eyes, and again he detached from the activity going on around him.

He found himself standing, watching himself during the church service he had gone to yesterday with Jonathan and David. The words of the sermon could not be ignored, so Robert began to mock the sermon and reject this God who would offer forgiveness. "I don't need you!" he said and laughed as he thought that Death's laughter was surely only a drug-induced dream. "See, I have a deal with Death. I can't die. And when I do die, I shall reign in hell as his partner. I laugh in the face of God. Death is Mine. I am the supplier for Death, not his sacrifice." Robert rested in the knowledge that the brutal truth of his choice was as complete as it was perverse.

"I will reign in hell," his words drifted through his mind as he watched a bright light form before him. He began to rise into the light until it completely enveloped him, and he drifted toward its source. Robert found himself standing in a long white tunnel. He looked at the surroundings and said, "Huh, I must have died. This must be the tunnel I have heard about. Funny thing, how being here, I'm not afraid. Death isn't so bad" He smirked as he began to walk down the tunnel. The source of the Light was definitely at the other end.

The first few steps were full of peace, yet, as he continued farther up the tunnel, the memories of his own life and his decisions returned. As he took each step, he would remember another day. His decisions were seen in the Light that surrounded him. Fear had no place here, but sorrow did. His memories began to haunt him as his mind exploded with the knowledge of how evil his acts had been. Robert, not wanting any more light on his life, sought to return to the entrance of this place. Behind him, he found no tunnel, and no light to lead the way back; just darkness. He waited as sorrow dismayed him in the weight of his choices. From within the darkness, he heard a voice he recognized. "Go and receive your reward." Robert knew this voice. This voice called to him to kill. It was this voice that had given him wisdom and unnatural success in his business endeavors. This voice hissed and pressed him; however, no path appeared into Hell, the kingdom in which he had expected to reign. There was not a kingdom of darkness, only the void of darkness eternal.

Robert waited at the divide between light and darkness until he knew he had no choice but to follow the only way available. He slowly took each step toward the Light; this time it was not the past that haunted him, it was the knowledge of his future. He knew he was about to face the Judge of all men's lives. The tunnel ended into a large room with an ascending staircase. The Eternal Voice spoke, "You have seen your life in the revelation of My Light. How do you plead?"

Robert's mouth was dry, he was thirsty. He could barely speak. "I, ah, I thought I would stand with another. I would rule in . . . " Robert stuttered and thought about the foolishness of these words. He wondered why they didn't seem foolish before. "I thought I would be a ruler in the . . . " he paused again, "the other kingdom."

Before Robert, stood the men and women he had killed or destroyed. The dead teenagers stood silently before him. The drugs that had killed them suddenly rested at Robert's feet.

Robert stood trembling. The Voice of God spoke, "Their blood cries out to me for justice. I am Just."

Robert screamed, "But, I didn't know for sure about you. If you are just, how can you judge me? I did not know!"

The Voice again spoke, "I have written my laws upon all Men's heart, and the whole Earth declares my Glory and my Presence. Do you deny the knowledge of me and of my law?"

Robert would have loved to have lied, but he couldn't. Tears formed in his eyes and he fell to his knees because he knew that these words would be the purest truth he had ever spoken, "I knew, but I chose the darkness."

The Voice deepened, "Depart from me, for I never knew you."

The Light intensified in the room until even with his eyes closed, he could see light, and the brightness continued to increase. Robert's eyes burned from the brilliance, and he cried out, begging for darkness. Though he could not see, he knew he began to fall. He fell further and further from the light. At first, he rejoiced at his separation from this Judge. He was able to open his eyes as he watched the light slowly disappear into the void of the increasing darkness and separation. His skin began to tremble with the cold as he moved further from the source of all light. He continued to watch until he could no longer see the Light. He looked around to find another source, but there was none.

Darkness continued to increase until he was completely blind. Fear seized him as he realized that he could no longer see his own hands before him. He reached out trying to find anything, anyone who could help him. There was no light; there was no one, not even the voices of evil to torment him. There were no voices here, only the quiet of eternal death. He was alone, in the dark, drifting farther and further from what he remembered to be Light. He could still feel. He felt the cold as it pressed against his flesh. For a moment, it brought comfort, yet even that comfort became a torment. The freezing cold continued to increase and began to burn, like fire lapping at his flesh. Yet, there was no flame of fire. Flame would have brought some light.

He was aware of only two things, the pain that assaulted his body and the darkness that blinded him from all but his memories. He remembered he had arms and hands, yet he could not see them. He remembered he had plans, yet he had no power to fulfill them. He was blind and helpless. He screamed into the darkness. "Where is this dark kingdom that I was to rule in? Why am I alone?" He was thirsty. He cried out for something to drink. But, no one heard his cry. He wept to buy a drink to quench his thirst. But, there was no one to come. He yelled and yelled until his voice was gone, and only silence answered him, convincing him that he was all alone. Eternity began, eternal death ...

The doctor placed his hand upon the shoulder of the orderly doing chest compressions on the redheaded man. "He is dead. Let's call the code. What time is it, for the record?"

A nurse spoke as she wrote it down, "13:04 hours."

Robert lay dead and naked on the ER trauma table. There is no time for honor or words for one who dies in an ER. There are other living patients that wait to be treated. The curtain was drawn around the patient whose body was already becoming cool. The staff slowly exited the room. The light was turned off as the last one left. Robert was left alone in the darkness.

"Rescue 33, out at St. Joseph's." said the driver of the ambulance as he quickly exited the front cab.

"13:20 hours," dispatch responded.

The doors to the back of the ambulance were opened. Steve, the paramedic, assigned to this ambulance, pressed the bar on the floor beside the stretcher. The hook released and he pulled the stretcher out. David followed closely, and his eyes pierced into the young man that lay upon the stretcher.

Steve looked up at David, "Who is the kid?"

"I don't know. But, I do know, he's the one who tried to kill me Friday night. And, now Jonathan is probably dead, and this jerk was a part of it." His tone did not hide his frustration or anger.

"Well, I would hate to see another teenager die, but if one has to, I guess you won't cry too much if it is this one. He doesn't look good." Steve's attempt to use stark reality to shake David into the appropriate attitude didn't work. He moved his young patient into the Trauma Room.

David continued to walk into the ER. He was deaf to the words of his peer as his own thoughts began to torment him. Anger and Revenge locked arms around David. They searched for a crack in his armor as they pressed his mind. Anger spoke, "He deserves to die, and yet he lives. He tried to kill you, and now Jonathan is dead; it's his fault." David's eyes turned red as Anger filled him. The crack had been found in his mind for the Dark Voices to abuse him.

Liar ridiculed, "It's God's fault that Jonathan is dead. He let it happen. That is," the liar paused, "...if there really is a God."

David took his eyes off the patient on the stretcher and thought of his friend, Jonathan. His heart sank, *What if he is dead?*

Mockery's voice was heard loud within this human so beaten by grief and worry, "If there is a God, he let Jonathan die. He said he wasn't ready yet. Why would God allow someone to die before they had a chance to get things right? What kind of God do you serve?"

"There is no God. Turn your back on what you have learned this week. Give Him no room. Listen to yourself. You are going mad with this God delusion," Foolishness sneered.

David's mind receded in thought until he could think of nothing except the image of Jonathan dead at the foot of the ambulance stretcher with no pulse, and not breathing. He walked to the nurse's lounge emotionally drained, wanting to rest and be quiet for a moment. The voices of Deceit and Lies were stilled as the Quietness of God surrounded David and he was left alone to think for himself.

Destruction laughed with Death. "We did it. He let us back in. The Good One has lost his warrior. Our plan worked. David is again ours. He is lost in the darkness of Death and Destruction."

Death stretched his long arms. His sneer revealed the blood of his last meal. "I did get to kill my pawn's slaves," Death turned to face the Adversary, "and my pawn died to make this battle ours. When will I be able to keep Jonathan within my grasp?"

Adversary looked over the vast horizon. "The wall of protection is still around him. You have touched him, but he's still being strengthened."

"What? Anger, where are you?" Death yelled. Anger appeared before his Lords.

"Isn't David lost in our maze yet?" Adversary asked.

"He is confused... " Anger measured his words, his last failure still stung his back. "But, Quietness was there at the hospital and got to him before I was able to finish my attack." Anger said as he grew red at the thought of his interruption and failure.

Adversary turned to Distraction, "Make sure he doesn't hear that Jonathan is still fighting Death. If he hears, he'll be sure to pray for him." Adversary whispered, "We can't have that."

The warriors left their council. Hope was not one of their strengths.

"David, David," Christina, the nurse who had entered the lounge, whispered, trying not to startle David, who was clearly lost in thought. "David, let me look at your wrist."

"Oh, OK go ahead." David held out his right arm. She cut off the temporary splint that held the wrist firm as David moved his hand and winced. "The fingers still move, see?" He tried to make light of his obviously fractured wrist.

The nurse handed David an ice pack. "We'll do your x-ray as soon as they finish with the person in there. Do you need anything?"

"Yes, I need to get to Tampa General," David said sarcastically then paused and looked again at Christina. He knew her. There was no reason for him to be rude. He softened his tone. "No offense, Christina, but my partner and the firefighter driving the ambulance both went to Tampa General. We had to come here because of the young man they found in the trunk." David knew he really didn't want to ask, but he had to. "Have you heard anything about Jonathan?"

Tears came to Christina's eyes as she said, "No, I'm sorry. I haven't heard. We are all waiting for news. Last we heard, he was on the way to surgery. But, I did hear that the firefighter, Joshua is going to be OK. Apparently, he just was trapped. A simple concussion is all he's got. His face was cut deeply, but everything life-threatening is OK. He's tubed but breathing on his own. He's really lucky. See, there's hope." Christina continued to talk, but suddenly the weight of her words came to David. His mind cleared and focused on one word ...

"Surgery," David looked up at Christina. "Surgery, then they got him back. They got a pulse back?" David tried to take a deep breath.

"David, I heard that they got it back, two or three times, but he kept losing it." Christina knew honesty was best. Her voice softened and was muffled to stop herself from crying, "It doesn't look good for him."

David returned his stare to his wrist. "I'll wait 10 minutes. If you can't get me fixed by then, I'll hijack your helicopter and go over to Tampa General myself. I can't wait."

Christina winked at her friend. "I know the pilot. I bet I can get him to take you over there. Just don't tell anyone, OK?"

David stretched his wrist toward her. "The clock's ticking, let's go."

Christina walked with him into the x-ray room. As soon as the pictures confirmed the right wrist fracture, the ER team placed a volar splint to secure his wrist, and then a bandage was applied to his left hand, once the x-rays confirmed no glass had remained from the windshield lacerations. David appreciated the speed and care his co-workers were giving him. And as he waited, he noticed that the pain medication had the effect of not only relieving the pain but calming him down. He decided he wanted to look once again at the young man that had tried to kill him only a few days before. There were so many questions that this patient could answer. "Why" was the one question he mumbled as he stood up and walked into his intruder's room.

David entered the patient's room quickly then slowly took a deep breath. "What is your name, kid?" He took the medical band on the patient's wrist and read, "Joseph Harris, age 18." He looked closer at this large, muscular man. "Is it possible that you are only eighteen? What made you try to kill me?" David examined Joseph closer. His black eyes were swollen shut, but his pupils were reactive to light and equal so his brain could be alright David thought, then he quickly reached down and touched the bruised chest of the young man and could feel the rib bones shift as he breathed. Tears formed in David's eyes as his compassion dissipated his remaining anger. "Come on kid, fight this. There has been enough death already. Please kid, hang on." His mind shifted in thought to Jonathan who also was fighting death, and he quickly left the room to get to his friend's side, praying, "Come on, Jonathan, fight! Please, live."

Christina ran to David with good news she couldn't wait to tell him. "They found cocaine under the rear passenger's seat of that white Cadillac. The one trauma victim they flew here from the accident is dead. He died a few minutes ago. We got him over in the back room. We are waiting for the Medical Examiner to come and get him. The Sheriff's Office is excited. It looks like it is the same coke that killed the teenagers last week. It has the same kind of packaging that the coke in the teenager's home was in. Sure is a break that we found out who did it."

David stopped and turned toward the source of so much information. He took a deep breath and tried to focus his mind, "The coke that killed the kids. It was in the white Cadillac?"

"Yes, that's what the Deputy said. He said it was easy to recognize because of the packaging. They are sure it is the same stuff."

"So, this kid must have thought I knew something and was trying to protect himself." David stood at the doorway and looked at the kid with detachment. "I was the first one in at the teenager's house where they all died," David said. "I bet that is why he attacked me. And the dead guy probably was going to kill the kid, because he failed." David walked over to the side of the patient's bed. "So kid, that's why you're beat up like this?" David focused on the boy's injuries, trying to remain detached. "They beat him really bad. Didn't they?" he whispered to Christina.

"Yes, they did. We figure some of the wounds are at least two days old. They must have tortured him for a while before they planned to kill him. I don't think he'll make it. They will be taking him to surgery in just a few minutes, trying to find where he's bleeding from."

"Too bad. But, if he does survive he'll just face life in prison or possibly a death sentence for the deaths of those other teenagers." David changed the subject, "And, the back-seat passenger is here? He's dead?" David began to put all the pieces together.

"Yes, he's in the back room. You should see the expression on his face. When he coded in the trauma room, he looked around and then suddenly went 'straight line.' His heart just stopped beating. He looked like he saw something. His face has a horrible expression on it. Real creepy. You wanna see?" Christina said as she raised her eyebrows.

"Sure. Sounds like a great idea. I would love to see the guy responsible for all of this." He chuckled and returned the smirk. While they were walking toward the back room, David began to recall the white car and red-haired patient. His pace picked up when he realized what he had seen, and he blurted, "Oh Shit! I think I know who is in there!"

Christina pushed the door open as David rushed in the room. He stopped abruptly when he saw Robert and the deep bruises that were forming to stain the naked shell of the once powerful man. David drew a deep breath and prepared to find a way to his friend's side. Robert's death had freed Jonathan, now David's only concern was that Jonathan survived.

Debra arrived at Tampa General by ambulance and was quickly evaluated by the emergency department doctor who cleared her for admission to a labor and delivery bed. She had no injuries from the ambulance wreck, and the pain from her delivery had completely resolved. Once she arrived in her room, she was alone for the first time since this morning. Gradually, she began to recall all that had happened today. It seemed more like a dream, then more like a nightmare, and now just impossibly hard to accept. This morning, she thought about killing herself, then the ambulance wreck and she could have died. Her mind spun in circles, and the birth of the baby seemed more surreal than reality.

A large happy black nurse came in. Her eyes twinkled with delight, when in her strong Jamaican accent, she said, "Well, hello Ms. Debra. Your parents will be here in a minute, they got caught in traffic, they called while you were still down in the ER. But, they will be here soon." She grinned at her young patient, "So, you are the miracle mother! Congratulations!"

Debra was shocked by her smile. "I am no miracle. I'm nothing but bad luck. Anyone who gets around me just dies." then she turned away from the nurse and began to cry again.

The nurse's pleasant joy was not dissuaded, "Now, little lady, don't say that. You are a gift. A gift from God. Don't you ever forget that, do you hear me?"

Debra was bewildered by this joy. "But, I caused an ambulance to crash. I'm real bad luck. Everybody around me dies!"

Pearline, the nurse, came and sat on the edge of the bed. "Sweetie, you are a blessing. Why just today you delivered a miracle baby. I'd say that's pretty good luck to me. God is taking care of you."

"My baby," Debra looked into the warm dark eyes of this seasoned nurse, and breathed deeply trying to understand, "My baby is alive? How can that be? He was so small. I saw him. There is nothing to him. He must be dead, just like everybody else."

"Everything is fine with him. He is alive. I'm tellin' you the truth." Pearline rubbed the arm of this child-mother. "He is alive. He only weighs two pounds. But Girl," she paused, and a great big grin covered her face, "but girl, that's enough. He is doing just fine."

Debra wiped away her tears with her hospital gown. "Can I see him? Can I go to him?"

"Sure sweetie, why do ya think I came in here? Let's go see God's miracle baby." Her grin touched Debra, who then genuinely returned a smile as she eased into the wheelchair. She was ready to see her miracle.

"What ya going to call it, Miss Debra?" Pearline's voice was filled with joy and expectation.

Debra thought about it and joy reached her heart as she said, "I know what I'm going to call him. His name is Thomas Darien."

"Oh, that's a nice one. He'll grow up to love that one. You wait and see." Pearline pushed the girl a little faster to see her son. "Girl, don't you ever forget God brings the greatest miracles in the face of the greatest battles. It's just His way. Thomas is going to be a great man, you wait and see. God loves miracles. And, your son is a real one. "

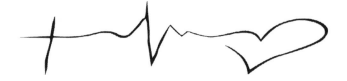

Joey awoke to find a large seven-foot tall man standing next to him. His face was shining with a glow that Joey had never seen on a man before, and the angel said, "My name is Michael. I've come to take you home."

"Take me home? Where am I?"

"You're in the hospital. You have suffered much, and your body is broken and dying. That is why I have come." His eyes held such kindness that Joey was sure that they could not be masking a lie. Yet, Joey didn't understand.

The stranger understood this young one's confusion. "Joseph. You are dying. I am here to take you to God. He sent me to walk with you so that you will not have to go to heaven alone. You will never have to be alone again." The angel's voice filled with awe, "Joseph, you are greatly loved by God. He is your father."

Joey's eyes filled with tears. "It can't be true. I remember now. I was being beaten. They put me in the car to take me to the boat. They were going to kill me. You must have made a mistake. God wouldn't want me. I'm responsible for the death of the other kids. No, I might die, but, I'm sure God would not send an angel for me. No good God would want me."

The angel held out his hand. "Joseph, you are loved. Did you ask Him to forgive you? He has completely, if you asked."

Joey's mind filled with the memory of the two days in the barn. He remembered his tears of sorrow and of repentance. He looked up at this one who he knew was a friend and whispered, "Really, facing what I had done wrong, and my cry to God is all that I had to do for Him to forgive me?"

The angel smiled and said, "Yes, you see, God's Son paid the price for all who have sinned. It is God's gift to forgive all that come to him and ask for his forgiveness. It is a free gift. Forgiveness is given to all who ask, because of the perfection of the work of His Son, Jesus. It's time to go and meet your Father. Your sins are no longer remembered against you. You are accepted and eagerly awaited. Come, it's time to go home. "

Joey took the hand of this large angel and felt a love he had never known before, "OK. I'm ready."

Slowly, Joey rose from his bed and followed him into the hallway. The nurses walked by without noticing them. Joey stood in the hallway for a moment watching the people who were rushing in and out of hospital rooms. Here was the simple proof that all of this was real. He was at peace. The cacophony of his own tormenting needs had been replaced with quietness and rest. As the freedom of this peace filled him, he found that he was no longer in the hospital. A warm, bright light instantly covered him, and he was gone.

Joey found himself standing on a long road in a large country meadow. He could see the green fields filled with small multicolored flowers and roads stretching out as far as his eyes could see. Michael walked beside him and pointed ahead. Joey began to walk down the road as he started on his journey home. Every step changed him. Slowly, he began to forget the hurts of his earthly father's rejection. Another step, he began to forgive himself for the things he had done wrong. Another step, he felt safe and secure. He paused and looked again at this countryside.

What was changing him? He knew he was about to discover real love and would find someone at the end of the path; this heavenly Father that Michael had spoken of. He walked with eager anticipation.

From a long way off, Joey could see someone running up to him. As soon as Joey was within grasp, He took Joey in his arms and hugged him. Tears flowed from the eyes of the One Joey knew to be his Heavenly Father, and with great joy declared, "My son has come home."

Joey cried, "I don't deserve to be your son. Please just let me be your servant. I have done much that is evil, and I'm ashamed."

Through tears, the Father said, "You are my son." And, He called for His servants to bring royal clothes for the boy and a ring of authority for his hand. With joy, He declared, "My son who was lost is now found. He was dead but is now alive."

At those words, every word of rejection and loneliness fled from Joey's memory. Love replaced every hurt, every fear, and failure. The boy fell on the neck of God and cried. He had come home.

A Careflight helicopter landed at Tampa General. Immediately, it was on its way back to St. Joseph's after a bandaged paramedic jumped out of the passenger side door and waved to the pilot as it lifted off. David raced into the ER and found Dr. Mintz. They knew each other well.

"How is Jonathan?"

"David, how did you get here so fast? I heard you went to St. Joseph's. How is your arm?"

David held up his right arm. "Look, I'm OK. This splint is fine, I'm in no pain. But, I have to know, how is Jonathan?"

Dr. Mintz led David to the physician's private room where they could speak alone. "He is still in surgery. They found a fractured spleen. They are removing it now. When they isolated it, he was able to retain some of the blood we were pouring into him. His back and neck look fine. We found no broken bones. The cerebral swelling is within a normal range considering the large hematoma on his forehead. We don't think that is the reason for his unconsciousness. It probably is a result of the gross blood loss. He has good neurological responses in all extremities."

David exhaled. "How long was he coded? I know I started on him immediately after impact."

"That's what I heard. I bet it was tough working a code on a friend. How are you doing?"

"I'll do better when I know my friend is OK."

Over the intercom, they heard, "Dr. Mintz, you have a call from OR."

Dr. Mintz smiled at David as he picked up the phone, "So, he's in recovery. OK, I'll get the word out." Dr. Mintz turned around just in time to see the ER door swing shut and David was out of sight.

David ran to the recovery waiting room. The nurses refused to let David into the room with Jonathan. "Wait, until his blood pressure stabilizes, then we will let you in. We promise." The nurse's words held a deeper meaning. David knew that Jonathan's life was still in the balance.

David waited in the staff lounge and cried as he kept reliving the last conversation he had with Jonathan in the unit when he said, "I know I'm not ready. I know I'm not ready to face God." And now Jonathan was dying. He didn't care who saw him cry as the reality of Jonathan's probable death hit him hard. David had always worked to fight death, but, it was way out there. He didn't know the people that had died in his care. Jonathan was his friend, and he sat there waiting, knowing he could not do anything to help him. Nurses would stop by to sit with him from time to time, and their hearts broke as they shared in his sorrow.

David looked at his hands and saw some remaining blood under his fingernails. He looked with detachment thinking, Whose blood is this? Is it Debra's, the baby's, Joshua's, Robert's or … Jonathan's? Blood had become so common to him. The sight of it didn't nauseate him like he knew it did others. He stared at the dark crimson stain on his fingers. The presence of enough blood within Jonathan would mean Jonathan could live. The absence, and Jonathan would die soon. Blood, that which was so common, now was so sacred. David rose to go to the restroom. He needed to cleanse himself of this blood. The door shut behind him. He was alone. He turned the water on, and it ran over his hand. The comfort of the warm water settled him. He took a deep breath and relaxed. Suddenly a great light appeared behind David, and he turned from the mirror and looked into the face of Light.

Light spoke, "David, do not be afraid. The Father has chosen you. You have been called to be a warrior, to fight and bring down mighty strongholds, and bring every thought that exalts itself against the knowledge of God into captivity. There is a Spiritual war within the minds of men; there are battles of choices that determine life and death, faith and fear, grace and law. Every human is given the right to choose, but the consequences are by eternal design. That which is invisible creates what is visible. The kingdom of God has come and is within your grasp."

"But how? What will I fight with? I know so little." David was overwhelmed by the vision before him, but that very vision gave him strength beyond his own.

"You have been given two weapons, by these you shall overcome. One is the perfect blood of the Lamb. It is the key to the promises of the Contract. It is the strength that heals. By it, you will always have access to God. The second weapon is your mouth. Life and Death are in the power of your tongue. Only the wise learn of this weapon. Most people use it against themselves. But, the wise bridle its great strength. By it, you have access to all good things! Only speak of the things of the kingdom of God that you personally have seen or heard. This is your testimony. And I'll confirm my word in you, with signs that all men might see your good works and glorify your Heavenly Father. The choice is yours. Will you stand in His authority?"

David bowed his head before the one that stood in linen and whose face was filled with Light, and his mind settled in clarity of thought, and the supernatural peace confirmed the reality of this One before him. David looked up in amazement and said, "Yes, I will."

The angel pulled from his breast a red coal the size of a fist. The fire danced within the red-hot embers. His eyes filled with that same fire as he slowly reached forward and touched David's lips with the coal. A soft gasp escaped David's lips as the air in his lungs pressed out the breath of his old life, and as he breathed in, tasting the heat and coal, he knew he was breathing in the beginning of his new life. The cleansing fire touched David's body, mind, and spirit. The pain in David's body from the accident slowly flowed into the force within the coal. The heat released the tension of fears and cleansed his heart of all the pain of the past. David closed his eyes as the warmth began to touch his mind and opened it up to a flood of knowledge and wisdom that was flowing from this Being of Light.

Suddenly, David was again alone with only his image in the mirror. He glanced around for any evidence of the Being that had touched him. Slowly, he looked again. His face glowed, his eyes were no longer swollen and red. He could see them sparkle with new life. He turned off the water and walked out of the restroom, knowing he had never felt or been so clean.

He walked past the waiting area toward the recovery room. The sensation that the angel was somehow still with him did not surprise him, nor did the knowledge of Jonathan's condition. Just as he reached the door, it swung open with an urgency. "David, David, I have something to tell you." She grabbed his arm and pulled him into the recovery room, leaving the door to bounce back and forth behind them.

David followed her into Jonathan's room. Just before they entered, she stopped and faced him, her voice was calm to hide her surprise. "Jonathan woke up. He woke up for a second, then went back to sleep. He wanted me to tell you something." She stopped speaking and looked down at the ground, then looked up into David's eyes. She drew strength from him and then continued, "The interesting thing is that as soon as he went back to sleep, his heart rate slowed and his blood pressure rose." Again, she hesitated, "His vital signs are stable."

David leaned in. "What did he say?"

"I hope you understand. He said, 'Tell David, I am ready. I am ready for battle. It's time to take a stand.'" She looked into this paramedic's eyes for an answer. "Do you know what he means?"

David took her hand. "Yes, I do. He's going to be fine." David entered the room of his friend and began to laugh. His laughter carried down the walkway. Those in the waiting room heard and knew that only life could bring that joy. They hugged each other, and an earnest laugh rose from them as they shared in this victorious celebration. Watchers, full of strength, raised their voices in unison with their human warrior and their laughter rolled down the halls of the hospital. Joy strengthened Health, Peace strengthened Hope as Life walked through these halls bringing healing as His reward. Throughout the hospital, Fear and Sickness ran in horror at the sounds of Life triumphant, and Faith restored.

David bent forward and took the hand of his partner and friend and said, "Jonathan, wake up."

Jonathan's eyes opened and focused, responding immediately to the light. "I am clean. I saw Him. He said He accepted me. . . Just as I am! Just as he created me to be. He said we were called to war, to bring life, and hope, and light into the darkness. He said..." Jonathan's eyes filled with tears of joy. "He said, 'Welcome Home, Son.'"

The nurse walked over to her patient and asked, "What happened to you?" Then she softly whispered in awe, "What did you see?"

David watched as his friend spoke of the vision he had seen. His mind filled with the memory of being in the ambulance with his patient, Terri, when she had told him of her vision. He remembered the simple prayer that changed his life. Suddenly, his mind focused on the conversation of his partner with this nurse. He recognized the prayer.

Jonathan took the hand of the nurse, and said, "We'll pray this prayer together. You can repeat these words after me, Dear Father ... I know I am a sinner ... Please forgive me..."

Salvation and Life overcame Death again.

Just as I am

by Charlotte Elliott, 1835

Just as I am, without one plea,
But that Thy blood was shed for me,
And that Thou bidst me come to Thee,
O Lamb of God, I come, I come.

Just as I am, and waiting not
To rid my soul of one dark blot,
To Thee whose blood can cleanse each spot,
O Lamb of God, I come, I come.

Just as I am, though tossed about
With many a conflict, many a doubt,
Fightings and fears within, without,
O Lamb of God, I come, I come.

Just as I am, poor, wretched, blind;
Sight, riches, healing of the mind,
Yea, all I need in Thee to find,
O Lamb of God, I come, I come.

Just as I am, Thou wilt receive,
Wilt welcome, pardon, cleanse, relieve;
Because Thy promise I believe,
O Lamb of God, I come, I come.

Just as I am, Thy love unknown
Hath broken every barrier down;
Now, to be Thine, yea, Thine alone,
O Lamb of God, I come, I come.

ABOUT THE AUTHOR:

Faye Hamilton was a paramedic for almost 20 years working in the Tampa Florida region. 25 years ago, while working as a paramedic assigned at the Gibsonton fire station, she wrote the novel, Rescue 12 Responding.

Once she left the fire department, she returned to school, finished her bachelor's degree with a major in Religion and then graduate school. For the last 12+ years, she has worked as a Physician Assistant in an emergency department in Phoenix Arizona.

Faye has been a conference speaker for many years, sharing the life lessons that she has learned from the raw, real-life stories of those she has cared for. She has served in many capacities within local Christian ministries.

She is the mother of two awesome children, Tiffany and Matthew and one grandchild, Darien. A little over a year ago, she became a widow and, in that loss, began to explore what really matters. Matthew told her, shortly after her husband's death that it was time for the world to see who Faye Hamilton really is. And, in that reveal, came the knowledge that the time had come to dust off the book written so long ago and publish it. And, in its release, the process to write the next in the series can begin.

May I ask you a favor?

If you have enjoyed this book, would you mind going online to Amazon.com and writing a review (even a short one)? Many people determine from book reviews whether a story is worth their time. Your review will mean A LOT to me and may help someone else make the decision to read this story.

I also invite you to come to my website: Rescue12responding.com There will be a link to my Blog and places where you can share your thoughts or questions about the story. I look forward to sharing with you and hearing your feedback.

Made in the USA
San Bernardino, CA
19 June 2019